REX STOUT

25879-6 ★ IN U.S. $4.99 (IN CANADA $5.99) ★ A BANTAM CRIME LINE BOOK

THE MOUNTAIN CAT MURDERS

INTRODUCTION BY KAREN KIJEWSKI

THE REX STOUT LIBRARY

Available from Bantam Books

ISBN 0-553-25879-6

9 780553 258790

50499>

Rex Stout

REX STOUT, the creator of Nero Wolfe, was born in Noblesville, Indiana, in 1886, the sixth of nine children of John and Lucetta Todhunter Stout, both Quakers. Shortly after his birth the family moved to Wakarusa, Kansas. He was educated in a country school, but by the age of nine he was recognized throughout the state as a prodigy in arithmetic. Mr. Stout briefly attended the University of Kansas, but he left to enlist in the Navy and spent the next two years as a warrant officer on board President Theodore Roosevelt's yacht. When he left the Navy in 1908, Rex Stout began to write freelance articles and worked as a sightseeing guide and an itinerant bookkeeper. Later he devised and implemented a school banking system which was installed in four hundred cities and towns throughout the country. In 1927 Mr. Stout retired from the world of finance and, with the proceeds of his banking scheme, left for Paris to write serious fiction. He wrote three novels that received favorable reviews before turning to detective fiction. His first Nero Wolfe novel, *Fer-de-Lance*, appeared in 1934. It was followed by many others, among them, *Too Many Cooks, The Silent Speaker, If Death Ever Slept, The Doorbell Rang,* and *Please Pass the Guilt,* which established Nero Wolfe as a leading character on a par with Erle Stanley Gardner's famous protagonist, Perry Mason. During World War II Rex Stout waged a personal campaign against Nazism as chairman of the War Writers' Board, master of ceremonies of the radio program "Speaking of Liberty," and member of several national committees. After the war he turned his attention to mobilizing public opinion against the wartime use of thermonuclear devices, was an active leader in the Authors' Guild, and resumed writing his Nero Wolfe novels. Rex Stout died in 1975 at the age of eighty-eight. A month before his death he published his seventy-second Nero Wolfe mystery, *A Family Affair.* Ten years later, a seventy-third Nero Wolfe mystery was discovered and published in *Death Times Three.*

The Rex Stout Library

REX STOUT

The Mountain Cat Murders

*Introduction
by Karen Kijewski*

BANTAM BOOKS

NEW YORK · TORONTO · LONDON · SYDNEY · AUCKLAND

This book is fiction. No resemblance is intended
between any character herein and any person,
living or dead; any such resemblance is
purely coincidental.

THE MOUNTAIN CAT MURDERS

A Bantam Crime Line Book / published by arrangement
with the estate of the author

PUBLISHING HISTORY
Bantam edition / July 1982
Bantam reissue edition / December 1993

ISBN 0-553-25879-6

Published simultaneously in the United States and Canada

Bantam Books are published by Bantam Books, a division of Bantam Double-
day Dell Publishing Group, Inc. Its trademark, consisting of the words "Bantam Books" and the portrayal of a rooster, is Registered in U.S. Patent and
Trademark Office and in other countries. Marca Registrada. Bantam Books,
1540 Broadway, New York, New York 10036.

PRINTED IN THE UNITED STATES OF AMERICA

OPM   0 9 8 7 6 5 4 3 2

Introduction

Rex Stout is as American as Cheerios, Wonder Woman, and Norman Rockwell. It is possible to grow up and not notice, not read Nancy Drew and the Hardy Boys. But not read, not notice Rex Stout, not love Nero Wolfe and Archie Goodwin? Not possible. That's like not noticing that Elvis brought a new dimension to kinetic pelvic motion.

To reflect on Rex Stout is to think of Nero Wolfe, and rightly so. Like others before him—Sherlock Holmes and his Watson, Miss Marple, Hercule Poirot, Sam Spade—he is instantly recognizable, lovable in a curmudgeonly fashion, and unforgettable.

He is also an old-fashioned good guy. Forget bad guys made to look good: mafiosi eulogized for their strong family values and loyalty and never mind all those busted knuckles, blown-out knees, machine guns in violin cases, and widows and orphans. Forget vigilante justice and the private investigator who anoints himself judge, jury, and executioner. Forget rogue cops hollering, "Make my day, scumball!" and blasting away with a .345 Magnum in each hand and hitting and killing the bad guys, who just happen to outnumber the good guys by 37 to 1.

No, Nero Wolfe is a different kind of good guy, a man of intelligence, finesse, method, and high moral standards. A man who wears yellow silk pajamas and expensive tailored suits, with matching elegance galore, and who weighs in at a seventh of a ton. A man with a hothouse of orchids that would dazzle and daze a bevy of debutantes, a gourmet palate, and an ear for the finer points of English language and literature. A man who works within the system and with the police and the district attorney's office, albeit often grudgingly and always in his own way and time. Not a knight in shining armor, not *that* old-fashioned, but, well, close.

And Archie Goodwin? He is equally unforgettable, equally delightful. Quick-witted, quick on his feet, ever-handy with notepad and typewriter, he is business partner, personal companion, perfect secretary. Add a dash of wit, a splash of irreverence and cockiness, a slight unpredictability and his winning way with the ladies, and who could resist?

Nero Wolfe and Archie, as indispensable, appealing, and delectable as toast (homemade bread from Fritz's oven) and jam (imported marmalade, no doubt).

Stout gives us these familiar and delightful characters in an equally familiar setting. There is a charm and comfort to this, as easy and relaxed as a summer afternoon, swimming, volleyball, and cold beer. But that's California, that's what I know, and to think of Nero Wolfe is to think of New York, of Manhattan, and that I don't know. I go there quite a bit, but I don't *know* it. I don't see, feel, *understand* the *real* New York. I know this because New Yorkers tell me so with a sad, sometimes patronizing, look in their eyes. But Nero Wolfe's New York? That I do know and understand. I need only open a book and there it is. The brownstone on West Thirty-fifth, the cabs, the restaurants and nightclubs, the particularly and peculiarly New York establishments and ways and weather.

The wonderful thing about mystery in general and Rex Stout in particular is the satisfaction of a good, well-crafted, well-plotted story. Once this was common, once we could take it for granted, even be blasé about it; but not now, not so. I am reminded of this often as I browse through current titles at the bookstore. Good stories, gripping plots that actually make sense, a book with a beginning, middle, and end: Is this passé? Is this too much to ask? No. And it is there in Stout. The final satisfaction, the element as familiar, comfortable, and comforting as the characters and setting, as the story? The ending. The good guys figure it out, they (and we) win; the bad guys get nabbed; good triumphs over evil. Consider, in Dickensian fashion, Archie's name: Goodwin. I rest my case.

To pick up a Rex Stout novel is to find standards, codes, an eminently civilized man living in an eminently civilized manner. Stout comes down squarely on the side of civilization, of justice and decency and the proprieties, large and small, of life. He shares all this with us, and in the process we, too, are a bit refined and improved. To pick up a Rex Stout novel is to enjoy the comfort of an old, dear, honest, and exacting friend.

The strength of Stout's work is not in any one book but in the body of work and, most particularly, in the Nero Wolfe novels. *The Mountain Cat Murders* breaks with several of the things we, or I at least, too readily assumed. It is not a Nero Wolfe novel, nor does it take place in New York. The central characters are young, even naive, winsome and fresh rather than seasoned, experienced, mildly eccentric. And it is a love story. What a contrast this is to the opinionated Nero Wolfe, who abjures the company of women in his personal life, whose colleague-secretary, cook-housekeeper, and outside investigators are all male, and who does not disagree when Archie comments that he, Wolfe, is allergic to women.

But *The Mountain Cat Murders* is the exception, not the rule, a novel written in a period when Stout was particularly prolific: five novels in a single year. I have found no other references to Delia Brand and Ty (move over Matt) Dillon, the main characters here, nor am I aware of any other work with a western setting. Romantic themes, too, are an anomaly.

The book takes place in Cody, Wyoming, and though I am a native of California and not Wyoming, it is a state I know and love. It is evident that Stout's knowledge was more limited. His characters strike me as Easterners gone west but not western, not native; transplants, not local stock. Corruption hinted at is decidedly big city stuff, not small western town; there is confusion about the roles of sheriff and police chief and a policeman walking a beat, virtually unheard of in a small western town. There are brick buildings one is unlikely to see in Cody, or indeed in most parts of the West, and equally questionable clothes. References to corrals, bridles, broncos, pronghorns, and such are liberally used, often misused. Colorful but unlikely expressions—"Tickle my horse and watch him laugh!"—are introduced. All the cowboys I've ever known are more likely to eat their horse than talk like that. A boy refers to a gun as a gat. In Cody? Oh sure.

Still, these are small things, ones that merely point to Stout's strength in eastern rather than western settings, to his deeper understanding of the eastern rather than the western character. In context, this book becomes a fascinating piece of the whole, giving a sense of the dimension and breadth of Rex Stout's work.

Cheerios, Wonder Woman, apple pie, Norman Rockwell, the Fourth of July, Rex Stout: great American traditions all!

—Karen Kijewski

The Mountain Cat Murders

Chapter 1

There were no customers at that moment on that Tuesday morning in June, and the clerk behind the counter at MacGregor's Sporting Goods Store stood with his back propped against shelves of fishing tackle, his eyes half closed, half dreaming. It was an old and hackneyed dream and could have done with some new twists, but he wasn't bothering to invent any on so hot a day. It had to do with the entry of a customer, up to then never seen, young, female, blonde and beautiful. Having asked to look at tennis rackets and purchased one, she would observe with a shy smile that she guessed she would have to play with a jack rabbit, since she was a complete stranger to Cody and had met no one but her lawyer; and he would tell her his name, which was Marvin Hopple, and declare humorously that now she had met him and he was no jack rabbit . . . and then swift developments . . . and the separation settlement by her wealthy husband, whom he would never see or want to see, would be a lump sum, avoiding the recurrent annoyance of alimony payments. . . .

He killed a yawn and straightened up with a jerk. The customer was actually entering—young, female, apparently beautiful though not especially blonde, and with a swinging grace in her walk. He arranged his face for the all-important first impression it would make; and then, as she approached the counter, relaxed in disappointment.

Nuts. This was no eastern princess. Delia Brand had been in the class below his at high school, right there in Cody. Still he looked at her and greeted her with some interest, since he had not happened to see her, to speak to, since the recent tragedy in her family, made more remarkable and conspicuous by the one which had preceded it some two years before. He was a little shocked, seeing her face close; it looked dead, all but her brown eyes, and what burned in them made him uncomfortable and turned his greeting into an unfinished stammer.

She nodded and said hello, put her leather handbag on the counter and opened it, extracted a revolver, took it by the barrel and poked the butt at him, and asked, "Have you got cartridges for that?"

"Sure." He released the catch and swung the cylinder out and in again, and squinted into the muzzle. "What do you want, hard or soft?"

"I don't know. Which is best?"

"Depends. What do you want to use it for?"

"I'm going to shoot a man with it."

He looked at her eyes again. He felt embarrassed and even a little irritated, because although jokes about shooting people were sometimes mildly funny, it seemed to him in bad taste, next door to indecent, for Delia Brand to crack one in view of the happenings in her family. He had a strong sense of propriety and didn't enjoy having it outraged. He turned without a word, went to the case and selected a box of cartridges, wrapped it and put a rubber band around it, and handed it to her.

As she put the cartridges and revolver in her bag and closed it, he told her sarcastically:

"Don't try for his head unless you're a good shot. Give it to him around here." He circled his abdomen with his finger. "Anywhere around the middle."

"Thank you very much," she said as she turned to go.

He watched her go through the door into the blazing sunlight of the sidewalk, with a frown, then sighed and went to the rear of the store where his employer was marking prices on some newly arrived boxes.

"Delia Brand was just in and got a box of .38 cartridges."

Mr. MacGregor didn't look up. He finished a cryptic inscription with his pencil and inquired, "Which one's that? I always get the names of those two sisters mixed."

"The young one."

"Well, I suppose they'll still pay their bills. They've both got jobs."

"She didn't charge it. She paid. She had the cannon with her, an old .38 Hecker. What I thought I ought to mention, I asked her what she wanted to use it for and she said she's going to shoot a man."

MacGregor cackled. "You asked for it and you got it. What did you want to ask her for? Wyoming may be more west than wild nowadays, but there's still a lot of folks around that like to pip at gophers and jack rabbits and tin cans, and as far as I'm concerned the more the merrier. We sell ammunition, son."

"I know we do. I sold it. But you should have heard her say it. You wouldn't think she'd be cracking jokes about shooting people."

"You asked for it, didn't you?"

Marvin Hopple insisted. "You should have seen her eyes when she said it. And before she said it and after she said it."

MacGregor let out a growl. "I'm busy. Get out of here and quit bothering me."

"It wouldn't hurt just to phone the police and tell them, would it?"

"Oh, for God's sake!" MacGregor flung out a hand. "Beat it! Tickle my horse and watch him laugh! I hear a customer out there. If he wants golf balls, be sure to ask him what for."

Marvin Hopple marched to the front, and sure enough it was old Judge Merriam for golf balls.

In the coruscation of the dazzling sunshine, Delia Brand walked a hundred yards before she reached the spot where she had parked the old open car which had been a part of the miscellany left behind by her father at the time of his death two years previously. Arrived there, she stretched a hand toward the door of the car, then withdrew it, stood for a moment considering, and turned and walked on in the direction she had been going. Cody residents, even in that hot sun, frequently preferred a ten-minute walk to a search for another parking space in the midtown section; but evidently there was a supplementary reason for her change of mind, for a block down the street she left the sidewalk to enter a drugstore. As she passed toward the far end of the long fountain bar, she halted momentarily to glance at a large and ferocious beast with glistening bared teeth and bright hungry eyes, which was about to leap upon her from the table where it was perched. Propped against its right foreleg was a card with the legend neatly printed: *Mounted by Quinby Pellett— For Sale.*

She exchanged a nod with the young man behind the bar, climbed onto a stool, and demanded, "A Park Special with two cherries."

The soda jerker took a large container and filled it to the brim by spooning into it from two vats, spouting from two spigots, and dipping from three jars. As he set it before her and picked up her money he remarked, "You'd better tell your uncle to drop in and take a look at that coyote. The hair's starting to slip on the right shoulder."

She nodded absently. "I noticed it." Her eyes went through him, and he got a cloth and began wiping the bar.

Back on the sidewalk, she went to the next corner, turned right, continued nearly to the end of the third block and stopped in front of the newest and largest structure in the city, the Sammis Building, on Mountain Street. Inside she took an elevator, left it at the fifth floor and halfway down the corridor turned the knob of a door, on the glass panel of which was lettered: *Escott, Brody and Dillon—Counselors-at-Law—Entrance.*

There was no one in the anteroom, either in the space to which callers were restricted by the railing or behind that, where a switchboard and two stenographers' desks were situated. Delia started for the gate in the railing, then stopped and stood irresolute; and then suddenly she became rigid. The voices she heard were followed in an instant by the appearance, through an inner door which stood open, of two people, side by side. The man was young, short of thirty, not chunky enough for a halfback but of good height and wiry, with the wide mouth of an orator and quick gray eyes. The woman, about the same age, was remarkable. She seemed to fill the room as soon as she entered, but that must have been an effect of electronic dispersion, for she was actually of medium size and height and quite compact. She seemed to be beautiful, but people who had never seen her, on looking at a picture of her in the Sunday Illustrated Section, would mutter that it was a good thing she had lots of money since she had no looks. Her skin was smooth and glowing, with no make-up. The startling effect she produced was partially accounted for when you got close enough to see that her irises were a dusky chrome orange and her contracted pupils lost their roundness and became slightly elliptical. That had been found either fascinating or fantastic by numberless persons in many different places.

At sight of Delia the young man broke off a laughing remark and stepped hastily forward.

"Del! Hello there!" He opened the gate. "I believe you have met Mrs. Cowles, haven't you?"

Delia remained rigid. It would have made her furious if anyone had suggested that any detail of her form —the head slightly tilted to slant her gaze, the shoulders drawn in for shrinking, the lower lip faintly back —had been copied from the technique of movie stars, for she professed contempt for movie acting and it was not on a Hollywood set that she had expected to fulfill her destiny. Nevertheless, any observant movie fan would have spotted it.

She said, in a cool tone meant for offense, with her gaze slanted at the man, "I met her when she was Mrs. Durocher. Or, as she might prefer, the Mountain Cat."

"Oh!" exclaimed Mrs. Cowles, amused, coming forward and looking at her. That was one of the times when, close enough, it could be seen that her pupils tended toward slits. "Maybe you can tell me—but I'm sorry, what's your name?"

"Delia Brand," the man put in.

"I'm sorry—but it's a waste of energy to remember women's names, they change so often nowadays. Maybe you can tell me, Miss Brand, who it was who first called me that? I mean Mountain Cat. I've been trying to find out, because I'd like to send him a silver bridle or a bottle of wine or something. Would you believe that that name has followed me to New York and Palm Beach, and even to France? I like it. Do you know who invented it?"

"Yes." Delia had shifted her gaze, but not her tone. "I did."

"Really? How lucky. Do you ride? Could you use the bridle, or would you prefer the wine?"

"Neither." Delia whirled, filled her voice with biting scorn to demand, "From you?" and then turned again and passed through the gate in the railing, continued to the inner hall, meeting one of the stenographers on the way, and entered the fourth door on the left, which was standing open. She closed it behind her, and was in a good-sized room with two windows, a case of law books, a desk, and chairs. She had been sitting in one of the chairs barely two minutes when the door opened to admit the young man. He stood in the middle of the room and looked at her for a moment, then passed around the desk and seated himself in the swivel chair.

He pressed his lips together, then suddenly released them to say with some force, "You ought to go to San Francisco. Or you ought to go to New York. You ought to go alone, and work or fight or something. You ought to do something. You always were stretched tight and now, naturally, you're tighter than ever. Why the dickens did you tell Wynne Cowles that you invented that name Mountain Cat? You know darned well you didn't."

Delia's eyes burned at him. "What does it matter?"

"It doesn't. It wouldn't matter either if I all of a sudden stood on my head and repeated the Gettysburg Address, but if I did so you'd be justified in asking me why. And why all the display of animosity and abhorrence to her? Was that just nerves? It only confirms—"

"I haven't got nerves. Not what you mean . . . well, I have a certain intensity. You know I have. I came here to see you. I came to ask you . . ." Delia raised her hand and pressed it to her forehead, then let it fall to her lap again. It fell relaxed, with a loose wrist. "I came, and I found you gay and laughing with that thing. If I didn't make an effort to stifle my emotions—"

"Piffle!" It was explosive. "What emotions? Personal? Jealousy? Or social? Moral revulsion? In either case—"

"I don't mind if you call it jealousy. I am perfectly capable of jealousy."

"You may be capable of it, but you're not entitled to it." He glared at her. "But let's say you are and dispose of that. I mean let's dispose of Wynne Cowles. Who am I? I'm Tyler Dillon, a Cody lawyer, in the best firm in town. Who is Wynne Cowles? A millionaire playgirl, known from Honolulu to Cairo. She came here two years ago to wait for a divorce settlement and now she's back, ready to repeat the order. The first time, she left over fifty thousand dollars in this state, and she probably will again. It's up to me to send her away a satisfied customer."

"Satisfied?" Delia was scornful. "It's notorious, what it is that satisfies her. You would be one? Would you?"

"I might." He picked up a pencil from the desk and flung it down again. "Why the devil shouldn't I? As far as that's concerned, I might even marry her. Why not? She makes a generous financial settlement at the pay off—"

"Ty!"

"Well?"

"Tyler Dillon!"

He gazed at her. After a minute he got up, passed around the desk, and stood looking down at her with his hands thrust into his pockets.

Finally he said, in a new and quiet tone, "Look, Del. I'm not trying to make a fool of you, though God knows you made one of me. You, a kid. Just a high school kid. That's all you were two years ago. That's all you are now, really, even if you are twenty. But maybe that's all Helen of Troy was at your age. Anyhow, your pretending to be jealous of Wynne Cowles is plain silly. You know what I think, I've told you once before. I don't think you're capable of any genuine emotion at all. I don't think—"

She started to get up.

He put a hand on her shoulder. "Please," he implored. "Please don't do that. Don't pull a haughty exit on me. Did you see me at your mother's funeral?"

"I don't know. I don't think I saw anybody."

He took his hand from her shoulder. "I was aware you didn't. I should note the exceptions. I know you've had enough trouble and grief to throw any ordinary girl off balance for good, and your feelings about that were genuine enough, I don't doubt that for a minute. That day at the funeral I bit a hole in my own lip from watching you biting yours, holding yourself in."

"I didn't see you, Ty."

"I know you didn't. You didn't see anyone. But

aside from your feelings about your father and then your mother, which I'm willing to admit were as deep and genuine as feelings can be, I say you're a pure unadulterated fake. Now you sit still. I've been chewing my cud a lot. I've been doing that because I can't help it, because I can't get you out of my system. And I—"

"Not even with Wynne Durocher to help you? I mean Wynne Cowles? I mean the Mountain Cat?"

"Rot. You're faking now. And you were faking when you pretended you were fond of me but you wouldn't marry me because it would gum up your career. You were no more fond of me than you were of one of your uncle's stuffed jack rabbits. Do you remember how you would fasten your eyes on me and talk down in your throat about Duse and Bernhardt?"

He stopped, staring gloomily down at her, then shook his head and returned to his swivel chair and sat down.

"I should have been wise to you then," he went on after a moment. "But I wasn't, because I was over my head in love with you. I still am, but I've had a chance to stand off and take a look. I actually thought you were going to be a great actress just because you said so. I didn't tumble that all you were doing with me was practice. I even went to that thing you were in at the high school and sent you a bunch of flowers and had a lump in my throat because I thought you were wonderful. Now I realize you weren't wonderful at all. The fact is you were lousy."

Instead of exploding with rage, which would have been one way to handle it, Delia merely smiled faintly. "I don't deny it," she said calmly. "It takes years of work and sacrifice to develop—"

"Bah! Excuse *me*, but I tell you I've been thinking

about it. You have to have something to work on, to start with. You no more have the makings of a great actress than I have. You've merely got the same ailment as a million other girls your age, you're stage-struck. That's all right, it's as normal and common as measles, but I just want to let you know that I know it and that you had no right to use me for a practice dummy! By God, you hadn't! And I'll say this, no matter how brutal it is; I'll say that I thought there was a chance that this—I mean your mother—coming on top of what happened to your father—I thought maybe it would give you a jolt that would bring you out of it—but here you are, coming here and striking a pose and pretending to be jealous of Wynne Cowles when the fact is that you don't care enough about me to feel jealous if you found me occupying a harem with literally thousands of wives and concubines and houris—" He broke off and breathed.

Then he put a fist on the desk again and said fervently, "I wish to God you would go away! I wish you would go to the coast or New York and start the work and sacrifice! But you won't, you never will! Deep down in your heart you're as wise to yourself as I am!"

The same faint smile moved her lips again. "Perhaps I am," she agreed. "Only in a different way. You are quite correct when you say I won't go away to work and sacrifice. Whatever sacrifice I make— Anyhow, I have abandoned the idea of a career."

He stared. He asked in a weak voice. "What? What's that?"

"I shall have no career."

A swift eagerness that had flashed into his eyes as swiftly disappeared. He demanded suspiciously, "What's the idea? Why not?"

She shook her head. "You'd say I was faking," she

declared without resentment. "I hope, Ty, that it won't make you miserable some day to remember what you've said to me this morning. I hope only that. And I hope if you do marry Wynne Cowles—" She stopped to swallow, and her hand fluttered. "Anyhow, I didn't come here to exhibit jealousy, fake or otherwise. I came to consult you. To ask you a question because you're a lawyer."

"It is possible," said Dillon, looking straight at her as if he hoped so, "that I am a damned fool."

She shook her head. "It's a legal question."

"But you say you've abandoned— All right. Consult me first. What's the question?"

"I must put it carefully." She hesitated. "It's what you call a hypothetical question. I've written it down." She opened the leather handbag and rummaged among its contents, but the revolver was in the way, so she took it out and laid it across her knees. Then her fingers found the paper she wanted, and she took it out and unfolded it and read it in a monotone:

" '*Question for Tyler Dillon:* If a person decides to commit murder, for reasons which she considers legitimate and justifiable, and if she does not intend to conceal the act but, on the contrary, intends to declare it and intends to plead the circumstances as a defense, would it help if she made an affidavit, or something like that, in advance and left it with a lawyer, telling about the circumstances, or would it be preferable for her to proceed with the act and tell her lawyer about the circumstances after the act was committed and she was arrested?' "

She folded the paper and returned it and the revolver to the bag, lifted her eyes to the lawyer, and said, "That's it."

He was staring at her. In a moment he said, "Give me that paper, Del."

She shook her head. "I only want an answer."

He continued to stare. "Where did you get the gun?"

"It was my father's."

"Is it loaded?"

"Not yet. I bought a box of cartridges this morning."

"Let me see it."

She shook her head.

"Who are you going to shoot?"

She shook her head.

Dillon got up, walked around the desk, and stood looking down at her. "I would give my right eye," he said slowly, "to know whether things that have happened really have got you unbalanced, or whether you are just practicing again. I have good reason to know that whether you have any ability as an actress or not, you have unlimited talent for dressing up a scene. I would give my right arm, too."

Delia had her head tilted back to look up at him. "You told me once," she said, "that a way for a client to refer a problem to a lawyer without committing or compromising either of them was to put it in the form of a hypothetical question. So that's what I'm doing."

Dillon groaned.

"Well, didn't you?"

He stretched out a hand. "Give me that paper. And the gun."

"Don't get dramatic, Ty." She had all her fingers on the handbag and her tone sang. "I won't take any spurs, you know very well I won't."

He gazed at her with his lips pressed together, breathing, in spite of her command, dramatically. After a minute he backed to the desk without turning, sat on its edge with his feet still on the floor, and said professionally, "Okay. I'm your lawyer and you've put a hypothetical question. In such a case my advice would be that all circumstances should be written down and submitted to a lawyer for him to put in the form of an affidavit. There should be nothing in it about an intention to commit murder, merely a recital of the circumstances. A lawyer is bound by his oath to reveal any knowledge that may come into his possession regarding an intention to commit a crime."

Delia stood up. "Reveal?"

"Right. Pass it on."

"To whom?"

"The proper authorities."

"Then it's a good thing I made it a hypothetical question. Thank you very much." She started off.

He let her get within a yard of the door and then sprang after her and caught her arm. "Delia! Del! For God's sake—"

She jerked free. Her tone was withering. "Didn't I tell you not to get dramatic?" She went.

It appeared that Ty Dillon was going to make another grab for her, but he didn't. Then it appeared that he was going to pursue her down the hall, but he didn't do that either. Instead, he waited until the door leading to the anteroom had closed behind her, and then headed in the other direction, stopping at the last door at the end. He had his knuckles raised to rap on it when it suddenly opened away from him and he was confronted by a bulky man in his shirt sleeves, with red suspenders.

There was a grunt. "You want me, Ty?"

But the sight of Phil Escott's shrewd and cynical old face made Ty realize that he had better try his own shrewdness first. So he said, "Nothing urgent. I just wanted to report that Mrs. Cowles seems to be all set. She was just in talking to me."

"Good. Excuse me. I have to play a tune." The senior partner tramped off.

The junior partner returned to his room and sat at his desk. He sat there motionless for a full quarter of an hour and then muttered half aloud, "She's an actress. Or she's a little stage-struck fool. Or she's a hundred percent fake. Or she's hyperpituitary or something like that. Or she's the girl I love, unbalanced by grief and getting herself in a jam."

He swung his chair, reached for the telephone book, flipped the pages and ran his eye down a column until it stopped at the entry: *Cole's Detective Agency 109 Vrgna St. . . . 3656.* He pursed his lips at it, considering, then finally tossed the book aside and shook his head for a decided negative.

"No good," he muttered. "If it's baloney I'd be a jackass, and if it's real it would be dangerous." He groaned. "But what the hell? I say what the hell!"

Five minutes later he reached for the phone book again, turned to a page, inspected it, scowled, muttered something and spoke into the phone. "Miss Vine, please ask Information for the number of Quinby Pellett over on Fresno Street. It doesn't seem to be listed."

He hung up, fiddled and fidgeted, and when the buzzer sounded got the receiver to his ear again. "What? He hasn't got a phone? I'll be darned. Much obliged." He shoved the phone back, grabbed his hat, and departed.

Chapter 2

Delia did a little shopping on her way back to where she had parked the car, then got in and swung into the traffic. Shortly after twelve o'clock she turned in at the driveway of the Brand home, a block away from the river, on Vulcan Street. It was an unpretentious house with a large yard which had been bought by her father at a time when she was eating with a bib on. As she circled the path she frowned at a border of scraggly calendulas, and she dragged the end of a hose there and set a sprinkler going before she entered the house. At the door she inserted her key, twisted it and found it wouldn't turn in the ordained direction, turned the knob and discovered that the door wasn't locked, and backed up a step, stiffening. She held the pose for a moment, then opened the handbag and took out the revolver. Gripping it in her right hand, she pushed the door open with her left and entered the hall. It was empty, but, hearing a noise, she called loudly, "Who are you?" Then, as the voice that answered was the most familiar voice in the world to her, she hastily returned the gun to the handbag and went by way of the dining room to the kitchen.

Standing at the electric range, frying eggs, was a tall good-looking young woman some three or four years beyond Delia's twenty.

"What's the idea?" Delia demanded.

Clara Brand flipped an egg and announced, "Home cooking is *so* much better than anything you can get—"

"Sure, I know." Delia discarded her hat and bag. "How'd you get here?"

"Walked. It's only ten or twelve minutes."

"What's the idea, really?"

Clara shrugged. "Nothing startling, only I don't like bum food and the lunches I am accustomed to at Mischne's cost over a dollar, and two eggs and half a cantaloupe here will come to about twenty-five, and since I will be out of a job beginning Saturday at noon —but on the other hand I may not, after all. I have a date at four o'clock for a talk with Atterson Brothers, and Jackson has generously allowed me to take whatever time I want this week to look for another place."

"*Very* generous," said Delia with bitter sarcasm, taking a pound of butter from her package and putting it in the refrigerator.

Clara smiled at her. "What the heck, he has paid me handsomely for over a year."

"He wouldn't have had anything to pay you with if it hadn't been for Dad. Here, I'll use the same pan. You won't get any princely salary at Atterson's."

"No, I imagine it will be a lot less. If I land it."

"And your savings are gone. You'll have to give up your trip to the coast."

Clara set her plate of eggs on the table in the breakfast nook and then turned to the other with exasperation. "Damn it, sis, can't you see I'm being cheerful and brave? Certainly my savings are gone, and the bank says the house wouldn't bring a dime above the mortgage, and Uncle Quin is a darling and a brick but you can't get blood out of a brick, and mother was our dearest mother but she did raise cain with the family finances, trying to get revenge that wouldn't have done anyone any good—"

"It wasn't revenge!" Delia, gripping the egg turner, faced her sister with flaming eyes. "Or what if it was? There are worse things than revenge, I can tell you!"

"All right, there are." Clara gave the younger one a pat on the shoulder as she crossed for the salt. "Take it easy, Del. I'm not kicking. Cheerful and brave." She sat at the table. "I still think it was foolish of mother to spend thousands of dollars, all she had, and mortgage the house, to pay a bunch of detectives to find out who killed Dad—especially since they didn't find out anyway, though that wasn't her fault. But it was her money and her house, and I don't know why the devil I mentioned it again. This month since she . . . she died . . . it's been enough . . ."

Delia let the egg turner fall onto the range and flew across and gathered her sister's head into her arms and crushed it against her breast.

After ten seconds Clara said quietly, "Okay, sis. Let's behave ourselves. Don't let your eggs burn, and before you sit down get out a jar of the grape jelly. We're not going to leave it there forever. That wouldn't do anyone any good either."

The next spoken remark was some minutes later, and was a purely practical suggestion from Delia to the effect that she could drop her sister at the Jackson & Sammis office on her way to school.

The Pendleton School, accommodating grades one to six, was a long-suffering brick building placed in the middle of a spacious graveled yard. It was 1:20 that afternoon when Delia Brand got out of her car and entered the schoolhouse. She exchanged nods with a teacher she met in the wide hall and proceeded to a room on the ground floor—a large room with no benches or desks, with no furniture at all except a table, a cabinet phonograph and a couple of chairs at one end. After depositing her hat and handbag on a shelf in a narrow cloakroom which was partitioned off, Delia returned to the main room, opened the cover of the phonograph, selected a record from a full rack on the table, placed it on the machine in readiness to play, and changed the needle.

The door opened and admitted a bedlam of scuffling feet. In they came, four or five dozen of them, brats, angels, kids, urchins, cubs, hoydens, lambkins, tendrils —it all depends. There was a good deal of variation as to height, weight and cleanliness, but they all appeared to be around nine or ten years of age. They cluttered in. There appeared in the doorway a large woman with sweat on her brow, who nodded at Delia and then vanished. A gong sounded somewhere and Delia commanded, "Places! All of you! Places!"

They began to arrange themselves in rows and files, with a surprising efficiency. The size of the room permitted a spacing of about four feet. When they were all in place, with the help of a few specific admonitions from Delia, and were standing quietly, she said in a throaty voice, "Good afternoon, children."

They chorused, "Good afternoon, Miss Brand."

She moved to the phonograph. "This afternoon, as you know, we will practice for the Closing Day Exercises. First I'll play the piece and go through it myself, then I'll play it over and you can try it. We must do much better than we did last week. Much better. Watch me closely."

She started the music going, moved to front center, raised her arms and began Rhythmic Movement. Sixty pairs of eyes were fastened on her, some studiously, some understandingly, some desperately, a few scornfully.

But the ultimate in scorn for Rhythmic Movement was not being displayed in the main room at all, but in the narrow cloakroom behind the partition. To slip in there unseen as the army trooped in was not difficult for agile feet, with quick eyes to seize on the moment, and apparently that was what had been done by the two boys who squatted in the corner, the one with big ears looking sternly at the one with red hair, with his finger pressed tight to his lips. But as soon as the noise of the music was heard, the former let his hand fall and whispered hoarsely to his companion, "They've started! Can't you just see 'em? They have started!"

The other shook his head and whispered back, hissing. "She does it first!"

"I can see 'em anyway! Standing there! Standing there waiting! They soon will! Oh, boy, they soon will!"

The red-haired boy nodded and hissed, "It's horrible."

For a while they were content to squat and whisper, but when their legs began to cramp they stood up. The big-eared one even tiptoed cautiously the length of the little room to the window, but drew back at sight of movement in the grounds outside. When, after a little, he returned to the corner, he had something in his hand.

"What you got there?"

"Miss Brand's bag. Boy, is it heavy!"

"Where'd you find it?"

"There on the shelf."

"What's in it?"

To answer that required action, not words, and they proceeded to act. Squatting again, with the handbag on the floor, they opened it.

"Jeeee-*sus!* She lugs a gat!"

The red-haired boy took it and aimed it at the window, and his whisper was deadly and sinister: "Ping! Ping! Ping!"

"Quit that!" the other commanded. "It may be loaded. You'd better wipe off your fingerprints. Hey! Lookit this! Do you know what's in that?"

"No. Neither do you."

"Oh, I don't, don't I? Feel the weight. It's catriches!"

The red-haired boy, grabbing for it but missing, said, "Take off the paper and see."

"I don't have to. Of course it's catriches. What good's a gat without catriches?"

"Is they any money?"

"I don't know and I don't want to know. There's places to take money and places not to take money."

"Aw, just a dime or maybe a quarter?"

"No, sir. Hey, lay off! But lissen. These catriches. We can use 'em. Put that in your pocket and give it to me after school."

"What can we use 'em for?"

"I'll show you when I get ready. Take it."

"Why don't you take it?"

"Because your pockets are better for the weight."

"If we can take catriches why can't we take money?"

"Because we can't. One is negotiable and one isn't. I'm telling you to take it!"

The red-haired boy, frowning, took the package and stuffed it into his hip pocket. The other nodded and said, "Now we've got to wipe everything. Here, we can use this. And put the bag back just where it was. And lissen. You keep your hands off that doorknob. I'll open it myself. It's got to be timed right."

The red-haired boy, feeling of his hip pocket, nodded morosely.

Four days of the week Delia had three schools to cover each afternoon, but on Tuesdays Pendleton was the only one. When she had finished there she got in the car again and headed for Main Street. Turning left, she continued until she had crossed the railroad tracks. After a right turn onto Fresno Street and another block, she pulled up in front of a two-storied frame building which could have used a coat of paint and various other attentions as well, though it was not precisely dilapidated. The ground floor front sported a large plate-glass window, elevated above the sidewalk, and the entire length of the window, inside, was occupied by an enormous brown bear who was licking a cub. Delia had not even the tribute of a glance for it as she mounted four steps and pushed open the wooden door and entered, clutching the handbag under her arm.

The room was about half as large as the one in the school which had been consecrated to Rhythmic Movement and was equally devoid of furniture, but it was by no means empty. On two wide wooden shelves which ran the length of one wall were more than a score of jack rabbits, representing practically every posture in the repertory of those leaping, long-eared crop destroyers. On similar shelves on two other walls were owls, grouse, wild geese, gophers, golden chipmunks, eagles, beaver, and other contemporaries. In one corner, with head up and haughty nostrils dilated, stood a black-tailed deer, a seven-point buck, and across from him was a yearling elk. Suspended from the ceiling by wires was a forked tree limb, and on it crouched a full-grown lynx with its teeth showing. There were black bear, pelicans, coyotes. On a raised platform in the center of the room stood a cougar, fully five feet long, its tail curled against its flank, the sides of its jaws flecked with blood or a simulation of it, and its left forepaw resting on the carcass of a fawn.

Delia, after glancing around, stood beside the cougar and called, "Hello!"

There was no reply. Stepping through a door to a smaller room behind, which had a large workbench and displayed a miscellany of tools, bales and boxes, and work in progress, and finding it uninhabited, she returned to the front and crossed to a stairway which led to living quarters overhead. Her foot was lifted to the first step when she heard a noise at the door, the knob turning. Quick as a flash she made a dive and concealed herself behind a moosehide which hung over the stair rail. One entering could not see her except by going to the stairway, but with an eye applied to a slit between the moose's side and his hind leg, she had a good view of the room.

She saw a man enter—a middle-aged man, slightly stoop-shouldered, in shirt sleeves and lightweight overalls and no hat, with a tanned face shining with sweat, and dusty graying hair. Three paces from the door he looked sharply around with gray squinting eyes, then, passing his palm over the rump of the yearling elk as he passed, he went to the platform and knelt to inspect the belly of the cougar. Then he leaped as if shot, a leap that would have been a creditable performance for the cougar itself, as an ear-splitting howl rent the air.

He landed flat on his feet, stared for a second, and said in a voice that had a suspicion of a tremble in it,

"Good Godamighty. Darn you anyway. Come out of that!"

Delia emerged, approached and stretched on her toes to kiss his cheek. "It's been over two years since I've done that," she said. "I don't know why I did it, only I heard you at the door and I was there by the stairs. It's something to know I can still do a coyote howl. The door was unlocked."

He nodded. "I stepped down to the corner to phone." He pulled a handkerchief from his overalls and mopped his face. "I guess I'd better get a phone put in —I would if I could afford it—or lock the door. My gizzard's not as tough as it used to be. I darn near busted a gut that time." He mopped his face again.

"I'm sorry, Uncle Quin. I shouldn't have done it. I'm old enough to know better. What's the matter with Noel Coward? Is his hair slipping? By the way, you ought to take a look at that coyote down at Kilbourn's drugstore. The right shoulder."

Quinby glanced at the cougar. "No, his hair's all right. I was just looking at a patch. You say the one at Kilbourn's? I'll stop in." His squinting gray eyes inspected her. "Did you come over here just to scare the daylights out of me?"

"No, I came to ask you something."

"Want to go upstairs?"

"It's cooler down here." She went and sat on the edge of the platform which held the cougar, took off her hat and propped it and her handbag against the carcass of the fawn, and frowned at her toes.

Quinby Pellett seated himself beside her and began slowly wiping his face some more.

After a moment Delia said, "It's still hell about Mother."

"It sure is."

"I go to the cemetery every day. I go in the morning."

"I know you do. You ought to quit it."

"You go, don't you?"

"Sure I do." He glanced at her and away again. "I'm nearly fifty years old and it's a natural thing for me to fasten onto the past. She was my only sister and I didn't have any brothers. But you're just a youngster. Besides, I'm a grouch and that's a good place for a grouch, a cemetery. But you ought to cut it out. You were strung too tight to begin with."

"Maybe I was. Maybe Mother was too, the way she was affected by what happened to Dad. But the way it ended with her was worse than the way it ended with him. Did you ever try to put yourself in the place of someone feeling so terrible she wants to kill herself and does it? Did you ever try to feel it? And it was my mother, my own mother!"

Pellett said harshly, "She was my own sister, wasn't she?"

Delia only looked at him. He looked at her and their eyes met, and then separated. After a little she said, "I have a sister, too. She's being cheerful and brave. She has lost her job. Jackson fired her."

"The hell he did. When?"

"Yesterday. Ending Saturday noon. It's unspeakable. All the money they ever made, they made grubstaking, and Dad made that for them. Didn't he?"

"I guess so. I guess he mostly handled it. What'd he fire her for?"

"He said something about it's being as much for her good as his because there's no future for her. It's an alibi. I'm going to see him and find out. She has an appointment at Atterson's office at four o'clock and I'm going while she's away. That's what I came for, anyhow one thing, to ask you to go with me."

"To see Jackson?"

"Yes."

"What are we going to say to him?"

"We're going to remind him of the facts and tell him he can't fire Clara."

Pellett shook his head. "He knows the facts, and one of them is that he can fire Clara. He and Lem Sammis own the shebang, don't they?"

Delia flared. "They shouldn't! He has no right to!"

"Legal right, yes. Moral right, maybe not. But that kind of an argument won't get you anywhere with Dan Jackson if he's made up his mind. It wouldn't help any for me to go there with you. I have an appointment to see him on another matter and I'll have to go at him myself. By the way, it's not Jackson you're getting ready to shoot, is it?"

Delia's head jerked around at him. "Who told you?"

Her uncle regarded her sourly. "That young partner Phil Escott's got. Dillon. He came around to see me and ask me to help head you off. He thinks you mean it. He don't know you as well as I do. Still got the gun in your bag?"

"Yes."

"Dillon said you said it's your father's."

"Yes."

"And you're still wearing the paint and feathers?"

"Yes." Delia was gazing at him, her eyes burning as they had burned at Marvin Hopple across the counter. She said, "You think you know me, Uncle Quin."

"I know darned well I know you. Haven't I seen a lot of the exhibitions you've put on? Dillon wanted to know if I thought there was any chance you were faking and I told him no. I never knew you to fake. What you do, you work yourself into a fix like a prospector crawling an old tunnel he's never tried before. But his fix may end by his starving to death, while yours is only in your mind. You're just like a man that's been hypnotized, only you hypnotize yourself. But a man that's been hypnotized can't be persuaded to do anything really violent or dangerous, and neither can you. You may persuade yourself to go around toting a gun and buying cartridges and scaring young lawyers, but when it comes right down to it you'll get a cramp in your trigger finger. See if you don't."

"I'll see," Delia said calmly, with only a suggestion of steel in her voice.

Her uncle nodded. "That's one reason you fool people, you don't go raving and yelling around, you just make quiet statements. Mostly. You use your eyes more than your tongue. I'll give a little proof that I know you as well as I say I do. I know who you're getting ready to shoot."

"You said Jackson."

"Oh, no, that was just palaver. It's the Reverend Rufus Toale."

She stared an instant, then sprang to her feet, and confronted him, rigid. "You . . ." she gasped. "You told . . . you told—"

"Now take it easy. Sit down."

"You told Ty Dillon . . ." She gasped again.

"I told you and nobody else. Our family troubles have been on the front page enough without me trying to put them there again."

"How did you know?"

"That it was Toale?" Pellett lifted his rounded shoulders and let them drop. "Who else would it be? Didn't I see what was going on the last two months of your mother's life as well as you did? Maybe not as much as you, but I saw enough. I saw what was in your head, too, and I saw you put your foot down and refuse to let him preach the funeral sermon, and I knew you were working yourself into a fix. Though I had no idea you would go so far as to buy cartridges and so on. But when Dillon came here today and told me what you were up to, naturally I knew."

Delia was still rigid. "You didn't tell him."

"No. All I said to him was that I would have a talk with you as soon as I could."

"Well, you've had it." Delia took three quick paces, stooped and got her hat and bag, and set out for the door.

Her uncle, without getting up, called after her in exasperated alarm, "Godamighty, Delia, now! Hey now, I only said—"

But she was gone. For a full minute he sat looking at the door which she had closed behind her, slowly shaking his head, then he lifted his handkerchief to his face and began mopping again.

Chapter 3

The new Sammis Building, at 214 Mountain Street, was the imposing structure where Delia had gone that morning to call on Tyler Dillon. The old Sammis Building, bought by Lemuel Sammis many years before he had attained state-wide eminence both economically and politically, and much less imposing, was over on Halley Street. Its ground floor was occupied by The Haven, the biggest and most popular gambling room in the city. Walled off from The Haven, making a separate entrance, were the narrow hall and equally narrow stairs which led to the second floor, where an even narrower hall, so dark in the daytime that strangers almost had to grope, afforded only two doors. The one in the front bore on its glass panel an old dingy inscription: *Evelina Mining Co.*—left there as a matter of sentiment by old man Sammis because it had been named in the distant days after his wife Evelina, who had once been a beanslinger at a lunch counter in Cheyenne. The door at the rear had a much fresher label: *Sammis & Jackson*, with no designation of function. About midway of the hall stood an old wooden bin, half-filled with jagged chunks of ore, some smaller than an egg and some larger than a big man's fist; and an ancient discolored card tacked to the bin conveyed the invitation: *Solid silver—help yourself to a souvenir—Evelina Mining Co*. It had been probably close to two decades since the invitation had been accepted by anyone.

When Delia parked the car in the neighborhood of the old Sammis Building that afternoon, she chose a spot fifty yards away because she had a reason for not parking directly in front even if there had been a space. It still lacked twenty minutes till four o'clock when she arrived, and she didn't want to be seen by her sister Clara as she left for her appointment at Atterson's. Also she didn't want to enter the building until she was sure Clara had gone, so she sat in the car with her eyes glued to the entrance. Ten minutes passed before she saw Clara emerge and strike off in the other direction, mingling with the sidewalk crowd. She waited a minute or two and then climbed out.

She was at the head of the narrow stairs, in the dark upper hall, before she realized that she didn't have her handbag. She stopped, frowning. She knew very well her wits were wandering. She concentrated. Yes, she had taken it with her from Uncle Quin's place; she remembered it beside her in the car as she drove. Then she had left it on the seat. She turned to go back after it, then turned again. She was hot and the sun outside was hotter. She remembered distinctly now that the bag was at the end of the seat, against the door. No one could see it from the sidewalk, and no one was apt to snoop around that old car in search of valuables. She went to the door at the rear of the hall and stood there a moment before opening it, gazing at the inscription on the panel and thinking of the time when it had been *Brand & Jackson* instead of *Sammis & Jackson*. Then she became aware of voices within, a loud voice especially, raised in anger. So Jackson wasn't alone. But she knew Clara wasn't there, so she pushed the door open and entered.

The room she was in was small, with one window, and contained the desk with a typewriter where Clara would have been sitting. Now it was empty, but through the open door which led to the room beyond the words of the angry voice, a man's, were audible: ". . . and I'll run you right out of the State of Wyoming and see how you like that! If dirt won't do it, and there's plenty of dirt and you know it, I'll try something that will!"

"Now, Dan, be yourself—"

"And drop the Dan stuff! My name's Jackson! Mister Jackson to you! You keep your hands—"

Delia sang out, "Excuse me, I can hear you!"

"Who the hell are you?" the voice came, and the next instant a man appeared in the doorway. He was a bone-and-muscle man, tall, between forty and fifty, with a scar over his left eye that gave him a leer. "Oh, you," he said, seeing Delia, his voice down. "What do you want?"

"I'll wait."

"Okay, go wait outside. Or sit there and wait, I don't give a damn."

"She doesn't need to wait." A woman slipped past him, careless of brushing him, and was in the small room. It was Wynne Cowles, looking as surprisingly cool as her voice. "Oh, Miss Brand? How do you do? Have you changed your mind about the bridle?" She turned on Jackson. "That date I have tonight, I'm going to keep it. And I have never been run out of any place yet, except a hotel in Rome once, and that was done by setting the building on fire."

She moved, halted to give Delia a pat on the shoulder and to say, "Nice kid. I like you," pulled the door open and went.

Jackson stared at the door a second and then told it, "I'll cut her up, by God, and feed her to the pelicans."

"Not if I was a pelican, you wouldn't," Delia declared.

He transferred the stare to her. "She called you a nice kid. I guess you are. Come in and sit down."

He backed through the door and she followed. His room was larger and furnished with foresight, containing, besides a desk and half a dozen chairs and a row of shelves and files, a huge and massive safe and three spittoons. After they were seated, she across the desk from him, Delia looked him in the eye and said, "You're not going to fire Clara."

He looked startled, then he grinned. "Hell, my child," he protested, "I've already fired her."

"I know you have. Then you're going to hire her again and keep her hired."

"Who says so?"

"I do."

"Not enough. You're not even old enough to vote."

"I'll see Mr. Sammis about it."

He frowned. "I wouldn't advise you to."

"I will."

"Go ahead. I'm running this office. Did Clara send you here?"

"No." Delia took off her hat and held it dangling. "I came myself. I came because I'm going to do something . . . something vital and I want to do this first. Clara will have a job here as long as she wants it. She ought to have a good deal more than a job. You and Mr. Sammis have made thousands and thousands of dollars, I guess millions, out of grubstaking, and it was her father and my father who did it all. He was murdered doing it. Everybody says you're no good at all compared to him, you have no judgment and no head for it, and you can't hold the prospectors the way he could. The ones you do hold Clara does it for you. It was her father's job and she likes it and she's going to have it, even if she doesn't get paid half of what she earns."

"Well, by God!" Jackson's voice matched the leer the scar gave him. "You are a nice kid! You certainly are. Who are some of the everybody that says I'm no good?"

Delia brushed it aside. "I only mentioned that. But as far as that's concerned, you never were any good. I often heard my father tell my mother so when they didn't know I was listening."

"I don't doubt it. But that's not good testimony, you know. Not allowed. Your father's dead."

Delia's color went, and she gripped the brim of her sun hat until it was crushed. In a moment she said calmly, "I know he is. And maybe you ought to know this. Maybe you ought to know that on every list that mother made up of the people who might have killed him, and on every list that the detectives she hired made up, and on every list that I made up, there was your name."

"I don't doubt it."

She still gripped the hat. "Well?"

"Well what?" He grimaced. "See here, Delia. You may be a nice kid, but you're a funny one and you always have been. As for your mother, your father's death put a kink in her that never did get straightened out. No man in this state admired Charlie Brand more than I did. He didn't like me much, but I admired him and I even liked him. I had no more reason or desire to kill him than you did. When he was alive he bossed the grubstaking part of this business and that suited everybody, including me. But now I'm bossing it, with all my faults, and that's that. Clara does not handle the prospectors. If she tells you she does, she lies. She's only a stenographer and bookkeeper, and she and I don't get along very well. When your father was here he pulled his share out every year, and if he squandered nearly all of it that's not my fault; with all his virtues he had that weakness. I don't owe Clara anything nor you either, and anyway she's a clever girl and she can do just as well or better somewhere else after she makes a start. She leaves here Saturday noon."

Delia's color was back. She demanded, "You mean you don't even consider—"

"Clara leaves Saturday," said Jackson doggedly.

"Then I must see Mr. Sammis. I have to get this done today."

"Go ahead." Jackson frowned at her, and added, "But I wish you wouldn't see Sammis."

"Of course you do. You'll wish it still more when you hear from him. He's my godfather and Clara's, too."

"Oh, I have no fear of the consequences." Jackson was still frowning. "He may be your godfather, but he's my father-in-law. I was thinking more of the possible effect on Clara than anything else. What she needs and what she's really fitted for—" He broke off abruptly, cocking an ear. "What the devil was that?"

Delia heard it too, a noise from the hall as if a bag of potatoes had been rolled down the stairs.

Jackson arose. "Excuse me, nice kid, I think I'll take a look."

"I'm going anyway." Delia got up too, put her hat

on, and followed him, through the little room and the door to the hall. It was so dim there that they could see nothing for a moment. Jackson peered around, then went over to the head of the stair and stooped to pick up a small dark object from the floor. When Delia asked what it was he muttered, "Nothing. A piece of ore from that old bin. How the devil did it get there?"

Keeping it in his hand, he started down the stairs. Halfway down Delia, at his heels, heard his sudden ejaculation but couldn't see the cause of it, since he was obstructing her view. He quickened his step, and by the time she reached the bottom he was bending over the form of a man stretched on the floor of the lower hall. One of the man's legs was curled under him and the other extended with a foot resting on the lowest step of the stair. Delia, halted on the third step up, clutching the rail and setting her teeth on her lip, watched Jackson squat to find a heartbeat with his fingers. Then, as Jackson moved, muttering, "He's all right," and she caught a glimpse of the prostrate man's face with blood trickling around an ear, she gasped, "Uncle Quin!" and leaped over the extended leg and knelt on the dirty floor.

Jackson repeated, "He's all right. Get away and let me see." He squatted beside her to examine the head and, in a moment, grunted, "Looks like he was hit with that piece of ore. Where the devil is it?" He looked around, saw where he had tossed it and reached for it.

"All that blood! He's not dead?"

"Hell no. That's only a couple of spoonfuls. He's out, all right, but he's far from dead. You wait here a minute, and don't start shaking him in case he's got a fracture."

He opened the street door and disappeared. Delia, still kneeling, took a handkerchief from a pocket of her dress, hesitated a moment, and then started dabbing at the blood. It was matting the dusty gray hair back of the temple. There seemed to be several places where the jagged edges of the ore had broken the skin.

"Uncle Quin!" she said urgently. "Uncle! Uncle Quin!" Then she jerked her hand away as she saw his eyelids flutter. They closed again and then opened once more. He moved his head, moaned, moved his head again, and was staring at her.

"What . . . what in the name . . . what you trying to do?"

"You got hurt, Uncle Quin." She put a hand on his shoulder. "You stay still."

"How'd I get hurt?"

"I don't know. Now keep still. Mr. Jackson will be back in a minute . . . here he is now—"

The door opened. Jackson had a pitcher of water in his hand, and entering behind him was a well-fed short man with a deadpan for a face—a deadpan well known to the habitués of The Haven, since he was the assistant manager.

Quinby Pellett, struggling to sit up with one hand against the wall, demanded, "What is this? What the hell happened?"

"Oh, you woke up." Jackson looked at him sharply. "You'd better take it easy, Quin, you may have a cracked skull. I've sent for a doctor and a cop. They're phoning next door."

"Cop? Hey, what . . ." Pellett put his hand to his head, took it away, and looked at the blood on his fingers. "How bad am I hurt?"

"I don't know, but I don't think bad. You got conked and you fell downstairs."

"Who conked me, you?"

"No. I was in my office with Delia when it happened. What would I want to conk you for, practice?"

"I don't know." Pellett slowly moved his head and eyes. "Oh, Delia. You here. Didn't you say you were coming here? Sure you did."

"You should keep quiet till the doctor gets here, Uncle."

"Sure you did. So did I." He turned his head again. "Wasn't I coming to see you?"

Jackson nodded. "I guess you were. You were supposed to. How far did you get, the head of the stairs?"

"Yes. I did. I was going upstairs and I got nearly to the top—hey!"

"What's the matter?"

"That's where I got hit, at the top of the stairs!"

"So I suspected. Who hit you?"

"How the hell do I know?"

"Didn't you see anyone or hear anything?"

"He ought to be quiet until the doctor comes," Delia put in firmly.

The door popped open and a man in the uniform of a police sergeant entered, briskly. He nodded to Delia and the others and looked down at the man sitting on the floor with a grin.

"What's the matter, Quin?" he demanded. "Doing a little research on the law of gravity?"

Twenty minutes later, upstairs in Jackson's office, the police sergeant finished asking Delia a few questions, getting corroboration of Jackson's story. The doctor had disfigured her uncle's head with a bandage and stated that apparently there was no serious damage, and her uncle had insisted that he felt well enough to remain there for the business he had come to see Jackson about, so Delia departed.

She got into the car and made her way through the

traffic, heading south and continuing beyond the city limits into the valley. The attack on her uncle and the sight of him lying on the floor unconscious with blood on his head had started her nerves quivering and upset the order of her thoughts, so she was into the country before she remembered to look for her bag. She glanced at the seat beside her. The bag wasn't there.

The car swerved and nearly slid into the ditch. She jerked it back into the road, then slowed down, steered to a wide spot in the roadside and stopped. A search behind the seat, under it, between the seat and the door, on the floor, yielded nothing. The bag was gone!

She sat behind the steering wheel, with her teeth clenched, concentrating. She was absolutely sure that she had left the bag there when she parked the car to go to Jackson's office. Some passerby had snitched it. She was an incompetent little fool and always had been and always would be.

That gun was her father's. She had meant, had utterly and with all her heart meant, to use that gun for the retaliation of the Brand family to the evil malignity which had murdered her father and driven her mother to suicide. She had so intended. Her teeth clenched harder. She had, she had!

What Ty Dillon had said. What Uncle Quin had said. About her getting a cramp in her trigger finger. They were dead wrong.

But she had left that bag, with that gun in it, on the seat of the car parked in the street and hadn't gone back after it. Wasn't anyone who would do that either a brainless fool or a cheap fraud?

And now what? Her father's gun, her chosen weapon, was gone. Now what? It was to have been tonight. That had been irrevocably decided. Now what? Her jaw, aching from the clenching of her teeth, began to quiver. Now what? Her head fell forward to the steering wheel, her face against her crossed forearms, and she began to cry. She hadn't cried since her mother's death. She cried quietly, not convulsively, but every minute or so her shoulders heaved as her indignant lungs issued the ultimatum, oxygen or death. She might, in the despair and dolor of that moment there at the roadside, while passing cars decelerated for the prolongation of curious glances, have preferred death, but nature requires something stronger than a mere passing preference to enforce that decision.

When finally she straightened up, her face and forearms were wet. She disregarded them. She had not answered the question, now what, as to the ultimate retaliation she had designed, but she was going on, at least, with the immediate job. She released the brake and shifted the gear and the car shot forward.

Ten miles farther on she slowed down again and turned right into a graveled and well-kept drive. At the edge of the public domain it passed under an enormous stone arch across the top of which was chiseled: *Cockatoo Ranch.* The Cockatoo had been the name of the lunchroom in Cheyenne where Lemuel Sammis had found Evelina long ago and when, in his opulence, he had bought a thousand of the most desirable acres in this valley and built a mansion thereon, he had named it Cockatoo Ranch; some whispers said to remind his wife of her lowly origin, but that was not true. Lem Sammis was a man of enduring sentiment. It was true that he had shouldered aside many men on his march up the hill, had broken not a few and never put scruple on his payroll, but it was undeniable that he had sentiment.

Flowers were blooming, sprinklers were going, and the lawn was clipped and green. Delia left the car on the gravel a hundred feet from the mansion and started across. Three or four dogs came running at her. A woman with three chins who weighed two hundred pounds stopped trying to reach a lilac twig and yelled at the dogs. Delia went and shook hands with her.

It was Evelina. "I haven't seen you for a coon's age," she declared, looking Delia over. "What you been crying about?"

"Nothing. I came to see Mr. Sammis."

"First we'll have some tea. If you've been crying you need it. Come over on the veranda. Oh, come on. One of the few things I like in all this damn business of putting on dog is this idea of afternoon tea. We'll have some turkey sandwiches and potato salad." She yelled at the top of her voice, "Pete!" and a Chinese appeared.

Delia, to her own surprise, ate. The sandwiches and salad were excellent. Lemuel Sammis himself came out of the house and joined them, accompanied by a tired-looking man whom Delia recognized as the State Commissioner of Public Works. The fact that Mrs. Sammis did a lot of talking seemed not to interfere with her eating. It began to appear to Delia that tea threatened to have a collision with dinner.

At length Sammis finished his third highball and arose. "You want to see me, Dellie? Come on in the house."

Delia followed him. He was the only person who had ever called her Dellie besides her father. In a room with, among other things, an ornate desk, a wall lined with deluxe books, and four heads of bucks, mounted, as she knew, by her Uncle Quin, she sat and looked at him. He looked like Wyoming, with his lean old face, his tough oil-bereft skin, his watchful eyes withdrawn behind their wrinkled ramparts from the cruel and brilliant sun. He inserted a thumb and finger into the small pocket of his flannel trousers and pulled out a little cylinder, apparently of gold, which looked like a lipstick holder; removing the cap, he shook it over his palm and a quill toothpick fell out. As he used it, his teeth looked as white as a coyote's.

"Turkey gets in your teeth worse than chicken or beef," he stated. "Seems to shred or something." He flipped detritus from the point of the pick with a finger. "What's on your mind, Dellie? I've got some important business to finish with that specimen of a man out there."

"Clara."

"What's wrong with her? Sick?"

"She's lost her job. Jackson fired her."

The old man's hand halted in midair, brandishing the toothpick like a miniature dagger. "When?" he demanded.

"Yesterday. She is to leave Saturday."

"What for?"

"Jackson says they don't get along together and that she'll be better off somewhere else. I just saw him this afternoon and that's all he said. My own opinion is that there's somebody he wants there, I don't know who, and it's none of my business. But you know the whole country talks about his—the way he likes women."

Lem Sammis looked uncomfortable. "At your age, Dellie, I should think that kind of talk . . ."

Delia nearly smiled. "I know, Mr. Sammis, you're a prude and anyway I shouldn't have mentioned it. I suspected you didn't know about Clara's being fired, and when I threatened to come to you about it and Jackson said he wished I wouldn't, I was sure. He also said he was the boss and he was running that office, which struck me as funny, because I always thought you were the real owner of it and always had been, even when the name on the door was Brand & Jackson."

"So he's the boss. Huh?"

"That's what he said."

Sammis leaned back in his chair and took in air with his mouth open, then expelled it by the same route, with a noise like a valve held open on an inflated tire. The duration of the noise spoke well for the condition of his lungs. His eyes behind their barricades were still the old Sammis poker eyes.

"Dellie," he asked as if requesting a favor, "will you kindly tell me something? Will you kindly explain how my and my wife's daughter Amy ever happened to stake a claim to a patch of alkali dust like Dan Jackson?"

"I don't know, Mr. Sammis."

"Neither do I and I never will." The old man frowned at the toothpick, screwing up his lips.

After a moment Delia ventured, "And about Clara . . ."

"Sure, Clara. Him having the gall to fire Charlie Brand's daughter! The fact is, I've about decided to give up grubstaking. I'm nearly seventy years old, and it's no better than a dogfight with a bunch of pikers edging in, including that what's-her-name woman buying off my men. I hear she's just come back with another divorce. I can't keep an eye on it any more."

"You won't close up the office!" Delia exclaimed in dismay.

"No, I guess not. I'd hate to see that old office shut up for good. As a matter of fact, I'd put Clara in charge if I could think of anything else to do with Dan Jackson." He added bitterly, "I might put him to renting rowboats out on Pyramid Lake."

"Then Clara won't be fired?"

"She will not. No, ma'am. I'll see Dan maybe to-night, or more likely tomorrow." He got up. "It's going on six o'clock and I don't want that fellow staying for supper. Anything else on your mind, Dellie?"

"Yes. I'd like to have the satisfaction—I have a particular reason for wanting to get this done today, done and finished. Just a personal reason. Of course I know you'll see to it, since you say you will—but if you'd write a note, just a line, I'd like to take it to Jackson myself. I can write it on a typewriter if you want me to, and you can sign it . . ."

Sammis cackled down at her. "Why, you derned little long-legged heifer! Don't trust me, huh? Think Dan might talk me out of it?"

"No," she protested, "certainly not! It's just a personal reason!"

He glanced at her keenly. "You're not saying you have anything personal with Dan Jackson?"

"Oh, no, heavens no, not personal with him. Just personal."

He looked at her a moment, then sat at the desk and reached for a sheet of paper. "All right, I'll make it plain enough so he can understand it," he said, and began writing.

Chapter 4

Delia didn't get away from Cockatoo Ranch until nearly seven o'clock, and then with difficulty, on account of Evelina's determined insistence that she should stay for supper. As she steered the car into the highway, the note signed by Lemuel Sammis was beneath her dress, pinned to her underwear. She couldn't put it in her handbag because she had none, and didn't want to trust it to the dashboard compartment because she would be getting out of the car at the cemetery and there was no way of locking it.

It was beginning to cool off as the sun prepared to call it a day and take to the hills.

The question, now what, as regarded her ultimate design, was still waiting for an answer, and it was for that, half consciously, that she was going to the cemetery. She drove some twenty minutes and, a mile or so before she reached Cody, turned into a side road and skirted the city. When she arrived at the cemetery entrance she left the car there and entered on foot, since the gate for vehicles would be locked by the caretaker at sundown. Two cars that had been inside were leaving, and there was no one around.

Her father's and mother's graves, with modest

headstones, were side by side, and the plot was neat and creditable, with grass and flowers and four little evergreen shrubs. Delia read the inscriptions, as she always did on arriving, stood a while, and then sat on the turf at the edge of the plot and took off her hat.

She sat there nearly two hours.

Still no answer was forthcoming. Objectively considered, it might have appeared far-fetched, and even ridiculous, that one resolved on so supreme a retaliation as the taking of life could be completely disconcerted by having her handbag stolen from her car seat, but such seemed to be the case. Surely one could buy or borrow another gun, or use a knife to stab with, or devise from all the possibilities some workable method. But Delia could not, or did not, even get her mind focused on the question as a practical problem, though it was at that very spot, some days before, that her original determination had crystallized.

Her thoughts staggered around. She did not cling morbidly to misery and affliction and rancor, but shock and grief had overburdened her and her blood did not readily assimilate distress. She thought of the time two years ago when Lem Sammis had appeared at their home in the middle of the night and gone with her mother to the front room and her mother had collapsed, and the two girls had not learned until morning that their father had been murdered in a remote prospector's cabin in the Silverside hills. She thought of seeing him in his coffin and her mother collapsing again; and then those dreary months, inexpressibly dreary because for so long her mother would not forget or let them forget, or offer any welcome to time's desire to obliterate. But after nearly two years her mother had begun to seem reluctantly willing that a curtain should be drawn, and to permit the existence of today and the probability of tomorrow; she had one evening laughed aloud at some story Clara brought home; and then, three months ago, the new evil had come, insidious, lacking the brutal instantaneity of a bullet in the heart, but no less deadly. Delia had not ever pretended, and did not now, that she had actually comprehended that evil, but she had known it was there; and certainly she had seen with her own eyes its consequences, since it was she who had gone into the bedroom that morning a month ago, after Clara had left for the office, and found her mother dead, poisoned in the night by her own hand.

Delia closed her eyes and read the note her mother had left—read it seeing it, though the paper itself was in a box at home in her closet. She read every word, her throat constricting. But her mother's terror of the evil had been so great that she had made no attempt to attack it even in that farewell to her daughters; it had contained no mention, no reference at all, to the Reverend Rufus Toale. Nevertheless, Delia and Clara had known. Clara had admitted to Delia that it stared them in the face. And in spite of that, only two weeks ago, only a fortnight after their mother was buried, Clara had allowed Rufus Toale to enter their house and had talked with him! And again and again! And had put Delia off with evasions when she had expostulated.

Delia shivered in the coolness the evening had brought.

She opened her eyes. She heard the sound of footsteps at a distance on the path, but gave it only enough attention for a flitting assumption that it was the caretaker on his rounds. It was twilight, nearly dark, and she realized with a start that Clara might be worrying about her, and besides, she had something to do. She didn't want to leave. If there was an answer anywhere, it was here. She had always before come to the cemetery in the morning, but now that she had been here in the dusk of evening, she would come again. It was more . . . it was better, with no sun shining, with night falling, with the air chill and silent gloom preparing to blanket the graves. . . .

She became aware that the footsteps had approached quite close—and had stopped. As she started to turn her head a deep, musical voice sounded almost directly above her:

"Good evening, Miss Brand."

She leaped to her feet and was facing the Reverend Rufus Toale.

His ludicrous straw hat, which he wore winter and summer, was in his hand, strands of his dark hair, with no gray, straggled on his high broad forehead, and a faint compression and twisting of his lips, obviously habitual, might have been characterized, by an impious or hostile tongue, as an unctuous smirk.

"Praise God," he said.

Delia began to tremble from head to foot.

"I haven't seen you here before," he said, "since your mother was taken, though I know you have been coming. My services to the living, for His glory, take up my day and I can come only in the evening. You don't let me see you, my child, though I have a message for you. I can help you, we can be helped together, by His grace and power and goodness and wisdom. You come, I fear, to this resting place of that sorely tried woman, your dear mother, only to sorrow in her defeat, but I come for strength." He extended the hand that was not embarrassed by the hat. "I would like to lead you—"

"Get out of here." Delia thought she was screaming, though in fact her voice was low, a dull dead monotone. "You—you—get out of here . . ."

Then she gave up. She couldn't shoot him, because she had no gun. She couldn't touch him—she couldn't do anything. So suddenly she darted past him, to the path, leaving her hat there on the grass next to her mother's grave, and ran. Her heroic resolve on a supreme retaliation to evil had descended to the level of that trite grotesquerie: a headlong terrified flight through a cemetery at the fall of night. She stumbled once but caught herself and arrived at the gate breathless.

She sat in her car, trembling all over, for a while, until it occurred to her that he might come, and then she started the engine and got the car moving, headed for Cody.

The driving helped to steady her. She liked to drive. Her father had taught her and she was good at it. The dashboard clock said 9:50 as she entered the residential section. She considered telephoning home, or going by way of Vulcan Street to stop at the house, but the route there would take her within two blocks of the Jackson address—and besides, when she saw or spoke to Clara she wanted to be able to announce an accomplished fact. So when she got to Blacktail Avenue she turned left and in another minute rolled to a stop at the curb in front of number 342.

She unfastened three buttons of her dress, retrieved the note from where she had pinned it and buttoned up again. Then she switched off the lights, climbed out and started up the path toward the door of the house; but came to a stop as the rays of headlights swept across her and a car turned into the driveway, scrunching the gravel, and halting opposite her. She heard the car door opening and a voice called:

"Hello, that you, Jean?"

"No! It's me, Delia Brand!"

"Oh!" A dark blotch that was a wrap and a white spot that was a face approached across the lawn. "Surprise party?"

"I came to see your husband."

"Then I'm afraid the surprise is on you. He's not home. He's down at the office."

Delia glanced at the house.

"I know," said Amy Jackson, born Sammis. "The lights are on. I always leave them on when I go out after dark. I've only been gone a few minutes, ran downtown to get something."

"Are you sure he's at the office?" That was tactless, Delia knew as she said it, but it was out.

"Yes, I—yes, that's where he said he was going."

"Much obliged. I guess I'll drive down there. I just want to see him about something."

She returned to the car, clutching the note in her hand, got in, and drove to Halley Street.

There was as little space for parking in front of the old Sammis Building as there had been in the afternoon; even less, for Delia was forced to go nearly to the next corner. She walked back. The sidewalk there was well lit and well populated, for The Haven was one of the centers of the town's strange night life. Salesgirls and garage employees could and did bet a dime on the even at the roulette wheel, but Mortimer Cullen of Chicago had once dropped eighty thousand dollars at faro in five hours.

Delia had never been inside The Haven. She gave its bright windows only a passing glance as she went on to the door admitting to the stairway. The stairs themselves were quite dim, but, mounting, she found that the upper hall, with an electric bulb glowing, was better lit than in the daytime. On the door which said *Sammis & Jackson* the glass panel looked dark, with no light behind it, but she tried it anyway, found it unlocked and pushed it open. With the note in her hand she felt armed with authority, so she flipped the light switch. The door leading to Jackson's room was closed, and she went and knocked on it. Silence. She knocked again and called his name, but got no response, so she opened that door too. The room was dark, as the front one had been. She wasn't familiar with that light switch, but soon found it and turned it on. Then, after one glance, she jerked her head up and stiffened, and stood not breathing, and neither Ty Dillon nor anyone could have accused her of mimicry of movie stars as she held the pose.

A man was in the chair behind the desk, but not in any of the approved, or even disapproved, positions. It was as if he had bent far over to reach something on the floor, got hung on the arm, and whimsically stayed there.

Delia's nerves were already quivering, had been for some time, and her impulse, after the first shock into rigidity, was to turn and flee screaming down the stairs. Doubtless she would have done that had not the familiarity of an object on the desk demanded, and got, her attention as her eyes began their movement away from the man in the chair. It lay near the edge of the desk closest to her, and she stared at it in amazement.

It was her handbag.

She continued to stare, still rigid; then instinctively, without thinking, stepped forward to get it. She took it in her hand, saw that it was indeed and unbelievably hers, started to tuck it under her arm, and then rested it on the desk again and with fingers that trembled not at all opened it.

There was no gun in it.

She looked around, not at the man in the chair, but searching; and almost at once she saw it. It lay on the seat of a chair near the door. Three quick steps took her there, and she grabbed it up. Yes, it was the gun, her father's gun; there was the notch which she herself had playfully scratched in it one day with her father's knife when he had spattered a gopher. In the first instant when she had turned on the light and seen the man in the chair the blood had left her head, blanching her; but now it was rushing back as she began to realize, vaguely but overwhelmingly, the significance of the properties she was collecting on this sinister stage. With her teeth clenched and the gun in her hand, she started around the desk toward the chair on the other side, but halfway there was stopped in her tracks by a voice behind her.

"Better lay it down, ma'am."

She had heard no steps; apparently her ears hadn't been working. She wheeled. A man with a weathered face and nearly white hair stood towering a pace from the doorway, with his eyes no more than slits. Delia stared at him without moving or speaking. She knew him; it was Squint Hurley, the prospector who had been put on trial for murdering her father and had been acquitted. She stood and stared.

He came forward with a hand outstretched. "Give it to me. The gun."

She said idiotically, "It's my father's gun."

"Give it to me anyway. I'll keep it for him. Who's your father?" He peered down at her. "By all hell! It's Charlie Brand's girl. I don't want to twist that thing away from you, ma'am. Just hand it over."

She shook her head. His extended hand shot downward and he had her wrist. She made no struggle or protest as, with his other hand, he eased the gun from her fingers and rammed it into his pocket without looking at it. Then he strode to the chair on the other side of the desk and stooped to get a look at the face of the man who was still whimsically hanging there.

In a moment he straightened up, observing, "It appears that Dan Jackson won't do any more grubstaking." He faced Delia and demanded in a grieved tone, "What's the idea, anyway?"

Chapter 5

So the Brand family troubles made the front page again, in spite of Quinby Pellett's assertion that they had been there enough. This time the prominence and space given it, not only in Cody, but in distant cities, was considerably greater than on the two previous occasions, for the dish was a more highly seasoned one than a killing in a remote prospector's cabin or the suicide of a desolated wife. A girl had been found with a gun in her hand, in an office at night, approaching the body of a man with a bullet through his heart who had liked the ladies; and the girl was variously described as strikingly beautiful, glamorous, seductive, enigmatic, captivating, and on up and down.

Of all the people involved and active in the affair one way or another—relatives, friends, associates, officials, photographers, politicians, reporters—the only one who was in a state of indifference at ten o'clock Wednesday morning was the girl herself. She was sound asleep on a cot in a cell of the county jail, lying on a clean white sheet, with no cover, clad in soft, clean, yellow pajamas which her sister Clara had brought to the jail, along with other accessories, shortly after dawn. Seated on a chair in the corridor outside the cell door was Daisy Welch, wife of the deputy warden, slowly fanning herself with a palm leaf and from time to time sighing heavily. It was a self-imposed vigil. One day a few months ago, when little Annie Welch had tumbled downstairs at school and had bitten a hole in her tongue, Delia had driven her home in her car.

At that moment, in the principal's office of the Pendleton School, the large woman with sweat on her brow who had glanced in at the door during the assembly for Rhythmic Movement the preceding day, was seated at her desk regarding with grim disapproval a young man who stood before her with a notebook and pencil in his hand. She was saying:

". . . and you might as well get out of the building and stay out. It won't do you any good to snoop around anyhow, because I'm sending a memo around to the teachers that they are not to speak with you. I've told you that Delia Brand's work and character and personality have been completely satisfactory and that's all I have to say."

"But Miss Henckel, I tell you we want to give her a break! Comments by you and all the teachers, quoting them by name, would help to sway public opinion—"

"Of course you do," said the principal sarcastically. "You mean you want to break her. I read the *Times-Star* this morning, didn't I? I ask you once more to leave this building."

He soon accepted defeat and departed, hoping for better luck at one of the six other schools, since Delia had had a class in each of them. It was his own idea.

At the Brand home on Vulcan Street, Clara sat on the bench in the breakfast nook in the kitchen, her elbows on the table and her forehead resting on her palms with a plate of three greasy-looking fried eggs, untouched, in front of her. The floor began to shake from a ponderous tread and the form of Mrs. Lemuel Sammis came through the swinging door.

"That was someone like Vatter or Vitter on the phone," Evelina Sammis announced.

Clara said without looking up, "Mag Vawter."

"Mebbe. I told her I was here and you don't want any company. Also I called the ranch and told Pete to drive in and bring a turkey. We've always got a roast turkey or two. There's no use cooking anything because you won't eat it while it's hot, like those eggs, and with a turkey around, any time you're ready to swallow there it is. Pete can stay here today at least and answer the door and the phone. I'm not built for a canter any more."

"Thank you so much, Mrs. Sammis, but I'm perfectly able—"

"Forget it, girlie." She sat down. "I'm taking my shoes off." She did so and wiggled her toes. "On the ranch I can keep my shoes on all day, but these town shoes start turning on me. Now listen. Lem'll have her out of there before night, don't you worry. What's the use of his owning the state nearly, if he can't get a girl out of jail? As for her shooting Dan Jackson, that was only a question—"

"I tell you she didn't do it!"

"All *right*." Evelina looked annoyed. "Don't start an argument. Her shooting Dan Jackson was nothing more nor less than a blessing. I'm surprised Lem didn't do it himself years ago. My Amy is in a state fit to be tied, but she'll get over it. As soon as Pete gets here I'll put my shoes back on and go back over to Amy's and see if she's eating yet. She's going to be a different

woman. After all, she's half Sammis and half Freyvogel
— There's that damn bell again." She got up with a
grunt.

"I don't want to see anyone, please," said Clara as
Evelina made off in her stocking feet.

But it became evident in less than a minute that
Evelina had met her match at the front door. Her
raised voice was heard, and other footsteps approaching down the hall, and when Clara lifted her head a
young man was standing there.

"Oh." She nodded.

As the man opened his mouth to speak Evelina appeared. "He shoved past," she declared indignantly. "I
grabbed for him, but he tore loose—"

"It's all right, Mrs. Sammis," said Clara. "This is
Mr. Dillon. Tyler Dillon."

"Oh, Phil Escott's fellow from the coast?" She put
out a hand and they shook. "Looks like a smart colt. If
he's staying I guess I'll be getting back over to Amy's.
Would you mind handing me those shoes?"

Dillon stooped for them, gallantly offered to put
them on and did so, using the handle of a teaspoon. She
thanked him, stamped with each foot, grimacing, told
Clara not to worry and that she would phone in case
she heard anything from Lem, and departed. Dillon
went to open the front door for her. When he returned
he moved the kitchen chair around and sat on it and
said, "That was Mrs. Lemuel Sammis?"

Clara nodded.

"I hear she's clever."

"I guess she is."

"What did she want?"

"She's my godmother. Delia's too. She wanted to
cheer me up and make me eat."

Dillon frowned. He looked as if he needed fully as

much cheering up as Clara did. "I tried to get you on the phone three or four times."

"I haven't been going to the phone. Mr. Sammis told me not to."

"When did you see him?"

"Down at the sheriff's office about seven o'clock. They had me there asking me questions, and when he came he made them stop." Clara shifted on the bench to look straight at him. "He advised me not to see anyone, too. I don't mind seeing you, but I suppose I shouldn't be answering questions. Have you seen her?"

"No. Sammis has frozen me out. Harvey Anson has been retained as her lawyer. They won't let me see her. I didn't learn about it until breakfast time, when I looked at the paper. It damn near laid me out, after—" He stopped.

"After what?"

"Nothing. I've been trying to get to her for over two hours. Welch, the deputy warden, told me a little while ago she was asleep and his wife was with her. Have you seen her?"

"Yes." Clara swallowed. "They let me be with her nearly half an hour, after Mr. Sammis came."

"What did she say?"

"She said—she told me where she went and what she did last evening, and of course she said she didn't shoot Jackson, but any fool would know that."

Dillon stared. "Do you mean to say you think she didn't do it?"

Clara stared back and said with quiet bitterness, "My God."

"My God what?"

"Do *you* think Delia would murder a man?"

"No. I didn't think so. But maybe I know things

about it you don't know. Have you seen your uncle? Quinby Pellett?"

"Yes, I saw him at the jail. What about him?"

"Didn't he tell you anything?"

"He told me he knew Delia didn't shoot Jackson. Naturally, since he has a decent share of brains. What else could he tell me?"

"Nothing if he didn't want to. Do you know where Delia's handbag is? Did she have it with her and did they take it?"

Clara's mouth opened and then closed again. She regarded him with narrowed eyes. "What do you know about her handbag?"

"I know there was a paper in it that would help to convict her, with my name on it."

"How do you know that?"

"In my office yesterday morning she took it from the handbag and read it to me and put it back again."

"A paper that would help . . . to convict her?"

"Yes."

Clara shoved the untouched plate away, so suddenly that one of the eggs skidded onto the table. Throughout her childhood and girlhood it had been a truism in the Brand family that Clara had no nerves, but she too had tragically lost a father and a mother . . . and now this . . . Disregarding the egg, she slid off the end of the bench, stood up, and said quietly, "I think you had better go. If you're a big enough fool to think she did it, or a big enough something—I don't know what. Go and look for that paper you want that will help to convict her."

Dillon stayed on the chair and said with equal quietness, "I'm not a fool. I love her."

"You certainly sound like it. You'd better go."

He shook his head. "I can't go. I've got to do something and I can't do it without you. You know I love her and you know she turned me down, and I love her so much I think I always am going to love her, and I think by God I'm going to marry her some day. If that makes me a fool, okay. She came to my office yesterday and said she was going to shoot a man. Kill him. She wanted legal advice. She said she had just bought a box of cartridges. She had a gun in her handbag, she took it out and I saw it. She said it was her father's gun. I accused her of being dramatic. You know? And she walked out on me with her shoulders up. You know how she can walk with her shoulders up?"

"But she couldn't . . . she couldn't . . ." Clara sank onto the end of the bench. "She couldn't possibly have meant it."

"That's what I thought. Though I did go to your uncle and put it to him. I should have followed her or taken her to you or done something! How do you think I felt when I saw that headline in the paper?"

"I don't believe it. She never did it. And anyway, if she had intended—if she had hated anyone that much, it wouldn't have been Jackson."

"Why not? Who would it have been?"

"I don't—I don't know. But it couldn't have been—"

"You do know. You know something. Who?"

She slowly shook her head.

He exploded. "Damn it, Clara, I tell you I love her and I tell you she's in terrible danger! I tell you I've got to do something! If it's her secret, or yours, I'll keep it. You've left her to Sammis just because he's your godfather. How do you know you can trust him? Jackson was his partner, and he's as ruthless as a mountain cat when he wants to be. I've got to know all there is to know. If Delia wanted to kill somebody and it wasn't Jackson, who was it?"

"She never told me she wanted to kill him."

"She told me. Who was it?"

"Rufus Toale."

He gaped in astonishment. "Toale?" He stared. "The preacher?"

"Yes."

"Good lord, why?"

"Because she thought he drove my mother to suicide. So did I."

"Drove her how?"

"By talking to her." Clara pressed her teeth to her lip and was silent. In a little she continued in a controlled voice, "I don't want—you have no idea—how excessively painful it is to talk about it."

"Oh, yes. I have. I've learned a few things about pain myself. What did he talk to her about?"

"I don't know. Mother had always been a member of his church, but with no special—nothing special. She just went there to church and had him to dinner once or twice a year. Then about three months ago, when mother had begun to get more—well, healthier—about father's death, Toale began coming to see her. They had long confidential talks, day after day. From the time it started she began to look like—I don't know how to say it—there was doom and death in her eyes. She wouldn't tell Delia and me about it, not a word. We tried to eavesdrop, to sneak where we could hear, but they were too careful. We never found out."

"What did you think it was?"

"Delia thought it was some kind of hold he had got on mother, she couldn't guess what, and he was deliberately torturing her. I thought he was torturing her too, I could see he was, but on account of her long effort, all the time and energy and money she spent, trying to find out who had killed father. He preached a sermon on the wickedness of revenge soon after he started coming to see mother. He's a fanatic, you know. It got worse and worse with mother, it got so she would hardly talk to us about anything or hardly eat. Then one morning Delia went in her room and found her. Of course Delia's reaction was different from mine, because we are different, but I think another reason was that it was Delia who took a cup of coffee to her room and found her dead."

"So you think—when she told me she intended to shoot a man—she meant Toale."

"I'm sure she did." Clara locked her fingers together. "Another thing, I'm afraid I made it worse, just recently. One evening two weeks ago he came here to see me. Delia didn't want me to let him in, but I did, and I let him talk to me then and two or three times since, because I thought maybe he would let it out about mother. I asked him pointblank what he had talked so often with mother about and he said her secrets rested with her in the grave. He said he wanted to labor with me to return me to God. I hadn't been going to church since he had started coming to see mother. I couldn't stand it to sit and look at him and listen to him."

"How did that make it worse?"

"Because . . . I got a notion that Delia thought Rufus Toale was beginning to do to me what he had done to mother. I told her I was sort of stringing him along, or trying to, but I should have realized, the condition she was in about Rufus Toale, that that wouldn't reassure her. Mother had evaded our questions about him for two months."

Dillon gazed at her, frowning deeply, considering.

"But," he offered finally, "while she may have hated Toale enough to want to kill him, what if she hated Jackson that much too?"

"Why should she?"

"Well, what if . . . what if she . . . ?" He couldn't get it out. He demanded savagely, "Did you read the paper? Did you get all the hints? Do you know what the whole damned town is saying? About Jackson and women?"

"What has that got to do with Delia?"

Dillon blurted, "Is she a woman?"

"Oh, you mean . . . Oh." Clara compressed her lips, then opened them to say, "You're a swell lover, you are. You're a hot one. First you accuse her of murder and now you accuse her of being one of Dan Jackson's women—"

"I don't accuse her of anything!" The misery in his eyes was in fact anything but accusatory. "But good God, what am I going to think? What am I going to believe? What do you suppose I came here for? What in the name of heaven was she doing in Jackson's office at night with a gun in her hand?"

"The gun was there on a chair and she picked it up."

"What was she doing there?"

"She went to give Jackson a note, signed by Mr. Sammis, instructing him to keep me employed there. Jackson had fired me."

"Who told you that?"

"She did and Mr. Sammis did."

"Did you see the note?"

"No, I think the sheriff has it. But anybody who thinks Delia had anything to do with Jackson—that's utter nonsense. Or me either. I got those dirty hints in the paper, but I thought they were aimed at me. Neither Delia or I would have let Dan Jackson touch us with a ten-foot pole—what's the idea?"

He had jumped to his feet and pounced at her. "Shake!" He seized her hand and crunched the bones. "Put it there! What the hell! Dear sweet darling beautiful Clara! I'm going to set that—"

"I'm not your darling and you broke my knuckles."

"Okay. Excuse me." He grabbed her hand again, planted a kiss on the back of it and sat down on the bench opposite her. "There. Now I can fight with my heart in it. If I can make my brain work. What was it— Oh, yes! You say the gun was there on a chair. How did it get from her handbag onto the chair?"

"Her handbag was there too, lying on the desk."

"All right, who took the gun out?"

"She doesn't know. Nobody knows. The handbag with the gun and cartridges in it had been stolen from the car in the afternoon while it was parked on Halley Street."

"Who says so?"

"She does."

"How did she get it back?"

"She didn't get it back. The first she saw it again, when she went to Jackson's office to give him that note, he was there dead and the handbag was on the desk and the gun was on a chair."

Dillon stared with bulging eyes. "She didn't take the handbag to the office at all?"

"Certainly not, how could she? She didn't have it. It had been stolen."

"And it was there when she . . . and the gun . . . good God." Dillon's mouth worked. "Then look here. It's worse even . . . so that's what it's like! And you've turned her over to the mercy of Lem Sammis."

"You said something like that before," Clara protested. "He wouldn't do anything to hurt Delia. I'm sure he wouldn't."

"Maybe not. You may be sure, but I'm not. That kind of man feels about people the way a general feels about soldiers. He loves them and he's proud of them, and he's especially proud of them when they die for the side he's leading. That's natural; it's part of the make-up of a good general. Jackson was Sammis's partner and son-in-law. There's no telling what politics or what kind of plot is behind this. I said we've got to do something, and I say it now louder than ever. The chief thing I came here for—I got more than I expected and thank God I did—the chief thing was that I want to be Delia's counsel."

"You mean her lawyer?"

"That's it."

"But Mr. Sammis has already engaged Harvey Anson."

"I know he has, but listen. In the first place, no matter what you think, you can't be sure of Sammis, especially with that planting of her handbag. I tell you she's in terrible danger. In the second place, that paper I spoke of that she read to me yesterday—my name was on it and it was a long question about the consequences of committing murder. If I'm her counsel I can't be asked about it and I think I could keep it out of evidence, and if I don't it would convince any jury that she did actually premeditate murder. Of course you could go on the stand and testify that it was really Rufus Toale she thought she wanted to kill and give the reasons why . . ."

Clara closed her eyes and shuddered.

"Sure, I know," Dillon said. "But what else could you do? And the chances are the jury wouldn't believe you anyway. It's a pretty queer story if you don't know

Delia and all the circumstances. It would be a big advantage if we could keep that paper and her visit to me out of it. Maybe you think I'm too inexperienced to trust her life to, but the firm would be counsel of record—Escott, Brody and Dillon and old Escott is as good as Harvey Anson any day. You're her nearest relative and you can designate the firm—shall I answer that?"

It was the phone ringing in the front room. Clara nodded and said, "Yes, please."

While he was gone she sat twisting her fingers in and out, gazing at the egg on the table. She knew she should have been thinking, preparing an intelligent decision for the problem he had put, but she couldn't manage her brain. It felt tired and battered. There was that egg. Less than twenty-four hours ago she and Delia had been there eating eggs together, and while they hadn't been precisely gay, still they had been together and healthy and free. . . .

Dillon returned through the swinging door and she looked up at his face. There was strained urgency in his eyes.

He said, "When I was down at the jail trying to see Delia, the sheriff said he wanted to talk with me and told me to wait there. I was sure he wanted to ask me about that paper and whether Delia had asked me the question on it. I sneaked out and came here. He's been phoning around and that was him, and he's sore. I told him I'd be there in five minutes and I've got to go. Can I tell him I'm Delia's counsel?"

Clara untwisted her fingers and clenched them into fists. "Do I have to decide?"

"You're her sister."

"Would it mean—would I have to tell Mr. Sammis she is changing lawyers?"

"Yes. Or if you don't want to offend him, you might persuade him to tell Anson to take me on as associate. Which of course Anson would hate to do."

Clara sat with her fists clenched, slowly shaking her head, trying to think about it.

Dillon waited. Finally he said, "All right. Come on down with me. If you can't decide on the way, maybe you can see Delia and put it up to her the way I've explained it. You trust me, don't you, Clara?"

"The way you talk," she said miserably, "I can't trust anybody." She moved. "Come on. I'll go."

Chapter 6

At the time that Evelina Sammis was taking off her shoes in the Brand kitchen, her husband was seated at his mahogany desk in his private office on the top floor of the new Sammis Building at 214 Mountain Street, obviously in bad humor, though not displaying the sidewise set of the jaw which foretold the imminent approach of one of his famous fits of temper. Two other men were with him. The one in the armchair, above middle age, who hadn't shaved that morning, with shrewd cold eyes and a thin-lipped mouth, was Harvey Anson, generally regarded as the ablest lawyer in the state. The other was Frank Phelan, the Cody Chief of Police. He sat with his ankles crossed, displaying bright green socks, looking as hot and harassed as a dog chasing a dragonfly.

"I wouldn't say that," he muttered protestingly.

"I would," Lem Sammis declared with irate conviction. "I made Bill Tuttle sheriff of this county, and I made Ed Baker county attorney, and now they start playing with that damn bronco that thinks he can cut my cinch. They figure I'm seventy years old and about ready to turn up my toes, and when that happens that squarehead will take it over and they want to be already in his corral. But he figures it wrong himself. The way to do it is to start throwing the bridle while I'm still alive. Believe me. I've still got a little say-so in this state and this county and this town. Have I, Frank, or haven't I?"

"Sure you have." The chief of police scratched his elbow. "You're the boss and with me that goes one hundred percent. But this isn't just a matter of say-so. It's murder. You can't expect Ed or Bill either to turn that girl loose when she was caught flat-footed like that. There'd be more whizzing around their heads than they could ever duck."

"The girl's innocent. Dellie Brand never did it."

"Oh, my God, Lem. Have a heart."

"Did she do it, Harvey?"

Anson smiled thinly and said, "I'm her attorney."

"And you say she'll have to stand trial?"

"She will if Ed Baker indicts her and it looks like he's going to."

Sammis's jaw started a slow sidewise movement. The chief of police saw it and put in hastily, "Now for God's sake, Lem, take it easy. You know I'm for you like I'm for three meals a day. Maybe you're right about Ed and Bill playing a little mumblety-peg with the squarehead, but whether they are or not, they couldn't act any different in this case and stay in Wyoming. Look here."

Frank Phelan drew his feet in, leaned forward with his elbows resting on his thighs, and put the tip of his right index finger on the little one of his other hand. "One. She was found there by Squint Hurley with the gun in her hand, still warm, and it was her gun and she was acting dazed but with no fight in her, the way a girl would be after shooting a man. Two. Her handbag was on the desk, not under her arm, and why would she have put it down if she had just entered the room? Three. Since you had given her your word that her sister wouldn't be fired, why did she have to go there in such a hurry at night to give Jackson that note? Four. There was a paper in her handbag with a question in her handwriting, addressed to a lawyer, asking how to escape the penalty for committing murder. Five. She was sore at Jackson and had had a scrap with him in the afternoon."

He shifted hands. "Six. She bought a box of cartridges at MacGregor's yesterday morning and told the clerk that she was going to shoot a man. Maybe you haven't heard about that. That's what she did. The clerk, a kid named Marvin Hopple, phoned us on his lunch hour yesterday and told us about it, but the boys just laughed it off and didn't even bother to report it to me. I've talked to Hopple, and that's what she did. Now I admit here's a funny thing. She denies she had any intention of shooting Jackson or any reason to shoot him. She admits she wrote that question on the paper and she told Hopple she was going to shoot a man, but she won't say who it was she had it in for. She only denies it was Jackson. Well, if it was Jackson, and she announced it in advance and didn't intend to conceal it, but was going to plead justification, why did she change her mind and take the line she didn't do it? I admit that's funny. Maybe she just lost her nerve. . . . Anyway, seven. We don't have—"

"Excuse me." It was Harvey Anson's tight deceptively mild voice, parsimonious of breath. "She doesn't admit she wrote that question on the paper or that she had any intention of shooting anyone."

"She did before you got hold of her and sealed her up."

"So you say."

"Certainly so I say." Phelan looked more harassed than ever. "Hell, I'm not on the witness stand, am I? I'm the chief of police, and here I sit spilling my guts to the defense attorney, don't I? Is this a friendly talk or what is it?"

The lawyer nodded faintly and repeated in the same voice. "Excuse me."

"All right." Phelan still held his fingers on the count. "Seven. We don't have to assume that Jackson's firing her sister was her motive, which I admit sounds weak, especially since her sister wasn't being fired after all. Everybody in this town knows Jackson's reputation, whether we like it or not. Investigation will show whether Delia Brand was one of the females—"

"You can keep that in your throat!" Lem Sammis's jaw finished the movement this time. "None of that from you or anybody else! And not only about Dellie Brand! Get this, Frank, and by God, keep it: whether it's connected with Dellie Brand or no matter who, there'll be no investigation of my son-in-law's dealings with women and no court testimony, and no publicity! My daughter married that polecat and she's had enough trouble from it!"

The chief of police lifted his broad shoulders and dropped them. "If you can stop Bill and Ed and the whole shebang. There was that piece in the *Times-Star* already this morning—"

"And the fellow that wrote it is already out on his neck!"

A shade of awe appeared in Phelan's eyes. "You made 'em tie a can to Art Gleason?"

"I did!"

"Okay. You win that round, Lem."

"And you sitting there counting your fingers! Take what you say about the handbag! She didn't have the handbag! It had been stolen from her and it had the gun in it!"

"Who says so?"

"She does, damn it!"

"Now, Lem, be reasonable." Phelan upturned a pleading palm. "We're not holding court, we're just having a talk. What would you expect her to say? She had to say something or nothing, didn't she? Of course it would have been better for her if she had made it nothing, even before Anson got there. That story about the bag being snitched from her car simply stinks and you know darned well it docs. Picture how it will sound to a jury if she gets on the stand and tells it, without any corroboration, and she'll have to tell it because no one else can, and if she's put on the stand picture how she's going to answer—"

"She won't get on the stand! She won't go to court! I say she won't!"

"All right, Lem." Phelan slowly shook his head. "I've seen you do everything to this town except hang it on the line to dry, and I've wore out three hats taking them off to you, but if you keep that Brand girl out of a courtroom I'll just go bareheaded!"

Bill Tuttle, Sheriff of Park County, sat in his office in the courthouse, which was on the basement floor, at the near end of the corridor leading to the warden's office and the jail at the rear. In appearance he was not a frontier-style western sheriff, but neither was he streamlined. His visible apparel, from across the desk, consisted of a pink shirt, a purple tie and a black alpaca coat; and the most striking fact about his face was that someone had at some time or other hurled a boulder at his nose and hit it square. Hardly less would have accounted for its being so grotesque a slab.

He was wishing he was somewhere else. There would be no profit and no glory from the Dan Jackson murder case; quite the contrary. The Brand girl had been caught flat-footed and there was nothing to it; but it was dynamite. He knew Art Gleason had been fired by the owners of the *Times-Star* and he knew why. Art Gleason booted into the alley! When Tuttle had made a long distance call, around dawn, to Senator Carlson (called, by some, the squarehead) in Washington, he knew what Carlson meant when he said that all good citizens would demand that justice be done without fear or favor; he meant that this might possibly be the long-awaited opportunity to put old Lem Sammis on the ropes; and though Carlson was unquestionably the coming man, it was too early to say that Sammis was even going, let alone gone.

In the meantime, in conjunction with the county attorney and the chief of police, he was proceeding with his duty, the collection of evidence, already overwhelming. He didn't know that at that moment the chief of police was in friendly conference with Lem Sammis and the defense attorney, but he wouldn't have been surprised if he had.

The phone buzzed and he picked up the instrument and asked it testily, "Well?"

"Dr. Rufus Toale again. Wants to speak to you."

"Put him on."

He made a face at a corner of the desk, which with his nose was scarcely necessary, and in a moment said with great amiability, "Yes, Dr. Toale? This is Sheriff Tuttle."

"God bless you and keep you, Brother Tuttle. I am anxious about Delia—Miss Brand. Is she still asleep?"

"Yes, she is. She was ten minutes ago."

"Praise God. The precious child. The precious soul. You won't forget to let me know when she awakens?"

"I'll notify you at once, Dr. Toale."

"God bless you. And tell her, please, that I am coming to see her. As I warned you, she will say no, but we must trust to His grace and goodness and I must see her."

"I understand. I'll tell her. Er—Mrs. Welch will tell her."

"That fine woman! She's a fine woman, Brother Tuttle!"

"She sure is. Thank you for calling." The sheriff hung up and shoved the phone from him as if it with its own tongue had Brother Tuttled him. Not that he was irreligious, but he was then feeling that no man was his brother. After glaring at the phone a little he pulled it back and spoke into it. "Is that reporter out there, the one that flew from San Francisco? Send him in here."

That interview lasted half an hour, partly because it was interrupted four or five times by phone calls. The door was closing behind the reporter when the phone rang again to say that Tyler Dillon was outside, accompanied by Clara Brand. They were ushered in and they both took chairs.

Tuttle glanced at Clara's strained face, at her hands twisted in her lap. "Is there something I can do for you, Miss Brand? I told Mr. Sammis I wouldn't need you any more, at least for the present. Didn't he tell you?"

"She's with me," Dillon put in.

"I don't need her with you. I'd like to see you alone. What's the idea, anyway? Didn't you say you'd wait outside till I could see you?"

"I got tired waiting. I had an appointment with

Miss Brand and I wanted to keep it. For a consultation in the interest of my client."

"Who's your client?"

"Her sister, Delia Brand."

"*Your* client?"

"Yes. She was my client even before this ridiculous charge was brought against her. On another matter, of course."

"She was?"

"Yes. She called at my office yesterday morning to consult me."

"She did? You admit that?"

"Admit it? I state it as a fact."

"Was it on that occasion that she asked you a certain question which she had written down on a piece of paper?"

"Now, Sheriff. Really! Surely you know that you can't question counsel about interviews with his client."

"No?"

"Certainly not. That's elementary."

Tuttle frowned. "I can't ask you about a piece of paper with your name on it and a question about how to do a murder?"

"Not if it has any connection, or is supposed to have any connection, with my client."

"You refuse to answer?"

"Under the circumstances, of course."

The sheriff's frown deepened. He stood up abruptly, said, "Wait here a minute," and left the room.

There was a silence. They looked at each other and Clara said, "This may be a terrible mistake. I should have talked to Mr. Sammis first. I . . . I'm scared."

"Buck up, Clara." He tried to smile encouragingly.

"I haven't involved you yet, anyhow. I'll push ahead as far as I can without you, but you stick. Huh?"

She nodded wretchedly.

Ten minutes passed before the sheriff returned, and when he came he was accompanied by a plump competent-looking man in a natty tropical worsted suit with a cornflower in the lapel. He exchanged greetings with Dillon and crossed to shake hands with Clara, replying to a question from Tuttle:

"Sure I know Miss Brand, we're old Cody folks. I knew her when she wore a braid down her back, before I ever thought I'd be county attorney. I hope you realize, Clara . . ." He stopped, gave that up, and turned to the young lawyer. "What's this the sheriff tells me, Dillon? About Delia Brand being your client?"

"That's right. She is. And I want to see her."

"She hasn't made any mention of it."

"Maybe she hasn't had a chance, with a stampede rushing her."

Ed Baker, Park County Attorney, smiled tolerantly. "She's had plenty of chance to say anything she wants to. You're not her counsel of record. Harvey Anson is."

"I'm her counsel."

"On this case? This murder charge?"

"I'm her counsel. She came to my office just yesterday morning to consult me."

"So I understand. Was that when she asked you a question she had written on a piece of paper?"

Dillon shook his head. "Privileged communication, Mr. Baker."

The county attorney shrugged. It might have ended there, with nothing more violent than a shrug, but for the interruption that suddenly interposed. The door was flung open and Lem Sammis entered on the charge. Behind him was Frank Phelan, chief of police, panting a little, and bringing up the rear was Harvey Anson, somehow keeping up with no appearance of precipitancy.

Sammis got to the center of the room, glared around, and picked on Ed Baker. His lower jaw was set a full half inch to the left. "What the hell do you mean phoning Anson to ask by what authority he is representing Delia Brand?"

The county attorney met the glare manfully, but he stuttered a little. "I t-t-told Anson on the phone. There seems to be a little mix-up. Young Dillon here says he is Delia Brand's counsel."

"Bah!" Sammis whirled. "I don't know you. Who are you?"

"I'm a lawyer. Tyler Dillon. I came from the coast two years ago and I'm with Escott, Brody and Dillon."

"What are you doing here? Cough it up! What is it, Phil Escott trying to horn in or Ed Baker here trying some trick riding?"

"Neither one. I'm Miss Brand's counsel, that's all."

"Who says so?"

"I do."

Sammis snorted contemptuously. "I knew a man once that said he was a grizzly bear with cubs. Get out of here! Get out of this courthouse and stay out! Vamoose!"

"This courthouse," said Dillon firmly, "belongs to the people of the County of Park and you're only one of them. I'm aware that I may be required to furnish confirmation of my statement that I am Delia Brand's counsel. I suggest that you ask her sister here."

His eyes, turned to Clara, were appealing, even desperate. But it was too much to expect of her. Lem Sammis's eyes were on her too, gleaming from behind their ramparts, and all her twenty-four years had been lived in the domain of which he was the uncrowned monarch. He growled, "You gone crazy or something, Clara?"

"No—I . . ." She swallowed. "I don't know anything about it. I only know what he told me this morning. I know he's a friend of Delia's—"

"Friend hell!" Sammis wheeled. "Get out before I kick you out, and I can still do it!"

Dillon's face was pale, but with his feet planted he said resolutely, "I demand to see Delia Brand! I demand—"

Sammis started for him. Others moved too, but not eagerly, for the complications of trying to stop Lem Sammis on the warpath had been demonstrated on various occasions. There was a general expression of relief when it was seen that a figure had got squarely between the old man and the young one. It was Harvey Anson, himself close to Sammis's age. With his hand raised, not belligerently, to the level of Sammis's advancing chest, he allowed his thin lips to emit words:

"Wait, Lem. No use of all this. This young fellow looks like a good honest boy, even if his name is on Phil Escott's door." Having halted Sammis, he turned around. "So your name's Tyler Dillon. I understand the sheriff and county attorney asked you some questions that had to do with Delia Brand and you refused to answer. That right?"

"It is."

Anson nodded with a minimum of effort. "This morning Delia told me that she went to see you yesterday for legal advice. Naturally that made you her counsel."

"That's what I say, I'm her counsel."

"Of course you are. But do you say that she specifically engaged you to defend her on this murder charge?"

"How could she?" Dillon was truculent. "There hadn't been any murder—"

"Did she?"

"No."

"Has anyone?"

"Not yet."

Anson smiled the ghost of a smile. "Then it's quite simple. There's no occasion for any fuss. You're not defending her on the murder charge and you're not going to. I am. But you are her counsel, you know in what connection, I don't." He turned to confront the county attorney and his voice, though it remained scanty as to volume, was suddenly full of bite. "Ed, have you ever tried reading any law? And would you like to see a list of the Bar Association members of the committee that deals with infractions of ethics like trying to coerce information from a counselor regarding a privileged communication? And would you like to get Washington on long distance, as you did at twenty minutes past four this morning, and ask Carlson what job he has to suggest for you in case you happen to lose the one you've got now?"

Baker opened his mouth and shut it again.

Tyler Dillon demanded of the room and all in it, "I want to see Delia Brand! I have a right to see her!"

"Not now, my boy," said Harvey Anson. "I'm sorry, but not just at present. Why don't you drop in at my office this afternoon? Maybe we ought to have a little talk."

Dillon looked around at the faces and saw it was hopeless. There was no one there susceptible to any appeal or pressure within his power. Sammis was still choleric, Phelan was impotent, Tuttle was hostile,

Baker was speechless and Anson was impervious. There was nothing he could do. He wanted most of all to see her; he had a feeling that if only he could see her, for a brief moment even, he would then be able to think of things and do them—startling and efficient and conclusive things. He had gone about it wrong, he saw that now, but he must and would see her. . . .

He turned on his heel and left the room.

Halfway down the gloomy basement corridor he heard quick light footsteps behind him and then was stopped by a hand on his arm.

It was Clara.

"I'm sorry, Ty," she said, looking up at him. "I mean that I didn't make good on what I said. But I didn't know Mr. Sammis would be there and I just couldn't. Anyway, it's all right now, since they can't question you about that paper."

"I hope to heaven it is," he said morosely. "But I've got to see her. I've got to find out . . . and what are they going to do? What are they doing? Someone has to do something!"

"They are. Surely they are."

"I wish I thought so. I'm going to the office and see Escott and put it up to him. He's friendly with Baker and maybe he can arrange for me to see her. Do you want to come along?"

"I guess I'll go back home."

They were outside in the shaded areaway and were about to emerge into the sunshine. Two men and a woman stood at the foot of the stone steps, talking. There was an exchange of glances, and the men and Dillon lifted their hats. The woman left them and approached. The electronic dispersion seemed to work as well outdoors as within walls; it competed successfully even with the sunshine.

"How do you do," said Dillon as she got to them. "Have you met—"

"Sure," Wynne Cowles said brusquely. She passed him up for Clara. "You poor thing. Lord, what a mess! I was out at the ranch and slept late and didn't hear about it until eleven o'clock. I couldn't get you on the phone, so I drove in, and you weren't home so I came here. They told me you were inside and I've been waiting. You poor kid!" Her strange eyes probably made a display of compassion impractical, but it was in her voice. "What can I do?"

"Nothing," said Clara. "There's nothing you can do."

"But there must be. I've never seen a situation yet where money couldn't do something. And while I know you don't want any charity, I would supply almost any amount, and call it a contribution to the public welfare, to keep that child from paying any price whatever for the removal of Dan Jackson."

"She didn't remove him. She didn't do it."

"No? Just as you say." Wynne Cowles apparently allowed it as not worth arguing about. "But I mean it, Clara. Aren't we partners? I'll get a real lawyer from the coast, or the east, instead of one of these renovators—excuse it, Ty, my love, said only to offend—or I'll buy a jury, I'll buy the whole county which is nothing but volcano leavings anyhow, or I'll round up a bunch of witnesses. I mean it. Anything."

"Thanks, Mrs. Cowles, but—"

"Make it Wynne. We're partners, aren't we? Or M.C., that's what they call me at the ranch. Short for Mountain Cat."

"All right. But about being partners . . . I'm not sure—"

"Why not? You were yesterday."

"Well—anyhow, it would have to wait."

"Wait for what?"

"For this to be—my sister. I couldn't discuss anything now—or start anything—"

"You're a softie, Clara. It will do you good to be doing something. Don't worry about your sister, we'll take care of her. She's a nice kid. Saw her yesterday. You ought to snap out of it; you look and talk as if someone had blackjacked you. Let's go over to my suite at the Fowler and have a cocktail and some lunch and get your mind started working. Or out to the ranch—it only takes forty minutes—"

"I don't want to go anywhere. Not today. I'm going home. Later I'm coming back here and see Delia."

"Then I'll go home with you. Let me go home with you?"

When they had settled for that, Dillon accompanied them to where Wynne Cowles's long low convertible was parked before he headed for his office on Mountain Street. He hadn't known that those two were acquainted and certainly not that they were partners.

Chapter 7

At The Haven gambling parlors in the old Sammis Building on Halley Street, which, in a half-hearted sort of way, opened for business before noon, the awning was left down until the sun's angle had passed beyond the perpendicular of the building line. Around three o'clock an employee in shirt sleeves emerged from the door with a crank in his hand. Before applying the crank and winding up the awning, he directed a look of appraisal at a man who stood near the door, in a niche between two stone pilasters. There was nothing extraordinary about the man—middle-aged, shoulders a little stooped—though he differed from the normal by having two strips of adhesive tape extending down his right cheekbone from under the brim of his hat, and by possessing a mustache of a quite unusual color, almost a fawn. The employee, having finished his task, glanced sharply at the man again and then disappeared inside.

In a few minutes the door opened again and the assistant manager of The Haven stepped out. With his habitual deadpan for a face, he went directly to the man in the niche and inquired, "You taking a census, brother?"

The man grunted and said, "I'm looking for a friend."

"You must be pretty short on friends, with all the looking you've done. You were here when I came, nearly four hours ago, and you're still here. Why don't you try some other spot a while?"

"I'm doing no harm. The sidewalk is public property."

"So it is. What does your friend look like?"

The man with the mustache shook his head. The assistant manager eyed him a moment, then turned and strolled down the sidewalk some thirty paces until he met a policeman in uniform. They exchanged nods and the assistant manager asked, "Have you seen that bird with the handlebars taking root in front of my place?"

"Sure I've seen him. All day. He says he's looking for a friend."

"How about advising him to go look somewhere else?"

"I suppose I could." The cop grinned. "What's the matter, you afraid he's a G-man with a line on that two bits somebody lost?"

The deadpan didn't respond to the grin. "I just don't like it how patient he is. With Jackson murdered upstairs last night, the place has had enough of the wrong kind of advertising. One reason I asked, I thought maybe he was a gumshoe working on the murder."

The cop shook his head. "Not a member of this club. He don't look ferocious. I'll keep an eye on him."

The assistant manager, accepting that assurance, retraced his steps, re-entered The Haven and resumed his duties in the service of society. The cop sauntered after him, keeping close to the buildings for shade, approached the man in the niche and inquired casually, "Your friend show up yet?"

"Not yet. Thanks."

The cop sauntered on.

Thirty minutes later, when the little disturbance occurred, the cop was across the street listening to a man cussing at a flat tire and therefore missed the preamble of the brief climax to the man's long vigil. It was all over in no time at all. The man with the mustache suddenly and abruptly left his niche, moving to intercept a husky-looking young man, rather shabbily dressed, who, coming along the sidewalk from the north, had altered his course with the evident intention of entering The Haven.

The man with the mustache, blocking the young man's path, said urgently, "I want a talk with you, young fellow. There'll be a reward in it. Now don't start—"

The young man shied back, ready, it appeared, to bolt. The man with the mustache sprang and seized his arm, getting a good grip. The young man's right fist swung and landed square on the other's jaw. The man with the mustache dropped to the concrete, rolling, and his assailant leaped back, wheeled and scooted like a deer down the sidewalk, nearly knocking a woman over, swerving to disappear into a narrow alley forty feet away.

Passersby collected and one of them stooped to give the fallen man a hand. Disregarding it, he scrambled to his feet, looked around with glassy eyes, and demanded, "Where is he? Which way did he go?"

A dozen voices answered him at once. The cop, having trotted across the street, took him by the elbow and observed sarcastically, "A swell friend that was you were looking for. Come along with me."

"He got away! I've got to catch him!"

"We'll catch one at a time, starting with you. Come along."

"You damned fool!" The man grimaced, worked his jaw, and grimaced again. "You know me! I'm Quinby Pellett!"

"Yeah? Where'd you get the lip grass?"

"Oh, for God's sake." The man took hold of his mustache and gave it a jerk, and it was gone. "Which way did he go, damn it? I have to find him!"

"He's out in the sagebrush by now." The cop had released the elbow, but he looked neither sympathetic nor amused. "What's the idea of the handmade tassel? —Hey, wait a minute, where you going?"

"None of your business! Turn loose of me! I'm going to see Frank Phelan."

"Okay. Come on, folks, let us by, open up there! I think I'd better go along, Mr. Pellett. If you happened to run across any more friends of yours on the way, you might not make it."

Quinby Pellett offered no objection as the policeman climbed in beside him on the seat of his dilapidated coupé, parked around the corner on Garfield Street. He got into the channel of the traffic stream and drove with the apparent assumption that he was an ambulance.

"You know, I could give you a ticket anyway, sitting right here," the cop observed.

Pellett stopped working his jaw long enough to grunt.

They went to the police station, and were informed that the chief was out and might be at the courthouse. Upon Pellett's refusal to converse with the lieutenant in charge, a phone call to the courthouse got the information that Phelan was there in the sheriff's office, so they returned to the coupé and drove to the court-house, missing fenders by inches on the way. They tramped down the dim basement corridor. The man in the anteroom told them the chief and the sheriff were busy and they would have to wait; then, obviously impressed by Pellett's violent reaction, used the phone, nodded toward the rear, and told them to go on in.

Bill Tuttle was seated at his desk. Two men who looked like detectives, which was what they were, stood at the opposite side of the desk. Phelan, in a chair not far from Tuttle, frowning at the newcomers as they entered, spoke:

"Hello, Quin. What's on your mind?"

The cop put in, "First I think I ought to tell you, Chief. He's been standing all day in front of The Haven, wearing a phony mustache, looking for a friend, he said—"

"Go on and chew the rag while he digs himself a hole," Pellett said bitterly.

"Spill it, Quin, we're busy. Who's digging a hole?"

"A man I tried to collar. By this time he's to hell and gone for the hills."

"Not him," said the cop scornfully. "That bum wouldn't get more than a mile from a pavement—"

"What bum?"

"The one that socked you. Al Rowley, his name is."

Pellett gaped. "Do you mean to say you know him?"

"Sure I know him. He's one of those—"

"Then find him! Get him!"

"That wouldn't be—"

"Get him, damn it!"

"Keep your shirt on, Quin." Phelan sounded impatient. "If the boys know him they can get him. Then what do they do with him?"

Pellett went to a chair and sat. "Listen, Frank. I'll

tell you about it. But first tell them to get that man. Have you ever known me to take a fool hen for a grouse? Tell them to get him."

Phelan turned. "Who is he, Tom?"

"His name's Al Rowley," said the cop. "He came in with that carnival last year, the one that busted, and he's been hanging around ever since, mostly at one of the joints on Bucket Street. Every once in a while he gets ahold of a buck, I don't know how, and makes a deposit at The Haven."

"Do the boys all know him by sight?"

"Sure, he's one of our most prominent citizens."

Phelan requested Tuttle's phone, got it, called the station and asked for the lieutenant in charge. After a few concise but thorough instructions, he hung up and shoved the phone back and turned to Pellett.

"All right, Quin, they'll get him. Now spill it. What's he done besides sock you?"

"He stole my niece's bag from her car yesterday afternoon."

Bill Tuttle jerked into a stare. Everybody stared. The cop said involuntarily, "Ouch!" Phelan demanded, "This bum—stole her bag? Delia Brand's bag?"

"Yes."

"The one with the gun and the cartridges in it?"

"Yes."

The sheriff broke in, snapping, "How do you know he did?"

"I saw him."

"You saw him take it?"

"Yes."

"You saw him take it and you didn't mention anything about it here this morning?"

"Nobody here seemed to give a damn about anything I might say this morning. You were all so sure of what you had you didn't want anything more from anybody. Besides, all I could do was describe him, I didn't know who he was, and what good is a description?"

"So instead of telling us you went and planted yourself—"

"Wait a minute, Bill." Phelan reached for the phone again, and called the station. In a moment he spoke: "Mac? Frank. That order I just gave you about a bum named Al Rowley. Make it hot. Put every man you can get on it. I want him and no mistake, and quick. And take him good. It may be murder."

As Phelan hung up, the sheriff barked at Pellett, "Is that the idea? That this bum stole the bag with the gun in it and murdered Jackson?"

"No. He couldn't have, because I took the bag away from him."

"You did *what*?"

"I caught him stealing the bag from her car and I took it."

"What did you do with it?—Wait a minute." The sheriff included the two detectives and the cop in a look. "You fellows go out front and wait there. The three of you. And keep your traps shut. Understand?"

They said they did, with evident reluctance, and marched out. The sheriff leaned back and sighed heavily.

Phelan said, "Maybe we ought to get this the way it happened. In order. This is quite a—quite a surprise."

"It's all of that." Tuttle fastened his eyes on Pellett and demanded, "What did you do with the bag?"

Pellett shook his head. "I think Frank's right. You ought to have it in the order it happened. In the first place, my niece came to see me yesterday afternoon—"

"What for?"

"It doesn't matter what for. It had nothing to do

with killing Dan Jackson, you can be damn sure of that.
The fact is, she wanted me to go with her to persuade
Jackson not to fire Clara—my other niece. I told her it
would be better if we didn't go together, and that I had
an appointment to call on him that afternoon on another matter and would speak to him about it then.
Not long after she left my place, I left, to keep my
appointment with Jackson. He had phoned that he
wanted to consult me about some information he had
got hold of regarding the death of my brother-in-law
two years ago. While I was looking for a parking space
on Halley Street I saw Delia's car there. I had to park
up ahead, and as I walked back I saw a man closing the
door of Delia's car with her bag in his hand. He didn't
look like a man she might have sent for it, so I confronted him and asked him if it was his bag. He said,
'It's not yours, is it?' and I said, 'No, it belongs to my
niece, and so does that car.' He said, 'Then do me a
favor and take it to her,' and shoved it into my hand
and walked off. He was so damn cool about it I just
stared at his back."

"You didn't call a cop?"

"With the bag in my hand, what was there to tell a
cop?"

"Did anybody see all that? Anyone stop to look at
you?"

"Not that I know of." Pellett was frowning.

"Okay. You're standing there on the sidewalk holding the bag. Then what?"

"I started for Jackson's office. I had intended to
wait there by my niece's car until she came out, because I didn't want to interrupt her talk with Jackson,
and I went to the corner and had a glass of beer. That
took five minutes, maybe a little more. When I went
back her car was still there, and it occurred to me she

might have got through with Jackson and gone somewhere else nearby, so I went to the entrance there
alongside The Haven, and went in and climbed the
stairs. When I got nearly up, about two or three steps
from the top, something hit me on the side of the head.
I must have rolled all the way down. When I came to I
was there at the bottom landing, and my niece and
Jackson were standing there—"

"Company halt!" said Tuttle savagely. "I'll stop you
if I've heard it! And the bag was gone? Sure the bag
was gone? Sure the bag was gone! And the ones who
found you there unconscious were your niece, who is in
a cell, and Jackson, who is dead!"

"That's right." Pellett raised his hand and rubbed
the left side of his jaw, slowly and tenderly. "Look,
Sheriff. Don't figure on getting me sore. I knew what
your attitude would be, and that's why I went there
and laid for that man in case he might show up. But
while it was my niece and Jackson that found me, because they were in his office and heard me rolling
downstairs, Jackson went to The Haven right away, to
telephone, and someone from there came back with
him. I think he's the manager or the bouncer, because
it was him that came out and spoke to me today. And
before they helped me upstairs to Jackson's office a
police sergeant came, Gil Moffett, and a doctor. They
decided I had been hit with a piece of ore out of that
old bin up there; Jackson found it on the floor near the
head of the stairs. I suppose Gil Moffett reported it;
anyway, you can ask him. I had a little natural curiosity about who had tried to crack my skull open, and I
phoned Gil at his house last night and he said they
hadn't found any tracks."

Tuttle asked with a scowl, "Was it your theory that

someone trailed you up and beaned you when you got to the top?"

"I didn't have any theory. But he couldn't have trailed me up and then got a piece of ore from that bin. He must have been already up there."

"Yeah, I was expecting that. It was somebody already up there and so it was Jackson. Huh?"

"It couldn't have been. My niece was in his office with him at the time I was hit."

"That's too bad. And the minute you came to, you looked around for the bag and it was gone."

"No, I didn't. I was groggy. After they got me up to Jackson's office Gil Moffett helped me go through my pockets to see if anything was gone, but all I had that amounted to anything was my wallet with about sixty dollars in it and my driver's license, and that was there, so I told Gil nothing had been taken. I was still dazed. Then a little later, when I was talking with Jackson, I remembered about the bag, and Jackson and I went to look for it, and it wasn't there. We looked upstairs and down. It was gone."

"Had Moffett and the doctor left before you missed the bag?"

"Yes, and my niece too. We were alone."

"Did you see anybody or hear anything before you got hit?"

"Not a damn thing. It's dark up there in that hall."

The sheriff leaned back and gazed at him a while. Then he turned to the chief of police, still scowling. "How do you like it, Frank? Got any suggestions?"

Phelan slowly and reflectively shook his head. "I don't know, Bill. We might go into details a little more."

"Go ahead."

Phelan did so. He wasn't aggressively skeptical, as the sheriff had been, but he wanted to know; that was his tone as he questioned Quinby Pellett. He was painstaking; he covered, thoroughly, everything that happened up to the time that Pellett and Jackson had searched for the bag, but he found no discrepancy, and the only new fact he got was that Pellett thought it possible that the murder of Jackson was connected with the murder two years previously of Charlie Brand. Pellett could support that surmise only by saying that Jackson had summoned him to the office for the purpose of discussing a new angle on the Charlie Brand murder, and had shown him a piece of paper alleged to have been found in the cabin in the Silverside Hills where Brand had been killed; and since Jackson had been killed a few hours later, it seemed likely that there might be a connection. Asked what was on the piece of paper, Pellett couldn't say; his head had been so befuddled from the blow he had got that they had postponed the rest of the discussion until the next day and, after the futile search for the bag, he had gone home. It was while they were on that that the phone rang, and Tuttle, after answering it, handed it across to Phelan.

The chief took it. "Yes, Mac? No! Good work! Where? Remind me to buy you a drink. No, let that go. Send them on over here with him and step on it."

He hung up, looking pleased with himself. "Pretty good gang I've got, Bill. They've picked up Al Rowley."

"Ha, they've got him!"

"They have, you know, Quin. Over on Bucket Street. They ought to be here in five minutes."

"I'll handle him," Tuttle announced.

"You will like hell. My boys got him."

"This is my office, Frank."

"And a damn smelly office it is, Bill. This is my meat."

"I'll handle him. I'll take him first."

"Not if my voice holds out you won't. And if you start trying, I'll march him right back out and over to the station. It was me Pellett came to in the first place, wasn't it? Didn't he come here only because I was here?"

That argument, with ramifications, was still in progress when the arrival of the disputed booty was announced and Tuttle ordered that it be ushered in, including escort.

Quinby Pellett stood up and Phelan told him roughly, "Sit down, Quin. Your knees are shaky. And behave yourself."

The escort, entering, proved to be two plain-clothes men and two in uniform. The booty, flanked on both sides, was, unmistakably, the friend Pellett had been looking for. He looked surly, somewhat scared, and a little bellicose.

"Sit him down," Phelan ordered, and he was instructed into a chair. "Is that the man, Quin?"

"That's him," Pellett declared, without removing his eyes from the booty.

The sheriff barked, "Is your name Al Rowley?"

The chief of police jumped up and started for the door, calling, "Bring him along, boys, back to the station!"

The escort looked bewildered. The sheriff yelled, "Hey, you damn fool! All right, all right!"

Phelan turned on his heel, went and stood in front of the booty, glared down at him and stated a series of facts. "Your name is Al Rowley, you're a vagrant and a bum. I can lock you up or toss you out on your ear or whatever I damn please, and about an hour ago Mr. Pellett here stopped you on the sidewalk in front of The Haven and you socked him in the jaw. Right?"

"I'm not a vag—"

"Oh, shut up! Did you hit Mr. Pellett?"

"Maybe, but I didn't—"

"I said shut up! What did you hit him for?"

"He had no right stopping me like that—"

"How did he stop you?"

"He just got in front of me and stopped me."

"Did he do you any violence?"

"No, he said something, I don't know what, and when I stepped back he made a grab at me, and just on the impulse I lammed him."

"And ran like hell. What were you scared of?"

"I wasn't scared, it was just an impulse—"

"Some day you'll get impulsed once too often. Take a look at Mr. Pellett. I said look at him! When you saw him today he was wearing a mustache, but the time before that he wasn't. Did you recognize him today in spite of the mustache?"

"I didn't recognize him at all. I never saw him before."

"What about yesterday?"

"Yesterday? Whereabouts yesterday? Not that I remember."

Phelan looked disgusted. "Oh, come off it, Rowley. We've got you. Three different people saw you take that bag from that car and then hand it to Pellett when he stopped you."

"That's a lie, chief. A damn lie. They're all dirty liars."

A low growl came from Quinby Pellett, and Phelan shook his head at him and then resumed, "Do you deny they saw you on that street?"

"I don't know if they saw me, but nobody saw me take any bag from any car. If I was on the street and they saw me then they saw me. What street was it?"

"Shut up. Where were you yesterday?"

"Well, yesterday." Rowley considered. "Let's see. In the morning I managed to earn four bits—"

"How'd you earn it?"

"Oh, just working around—"

"Skip it. Where were you in the afternoon?"

"Well, in the afternoon I was tired and I took a little rest, and then I went for a walk and stopped in at The Haven and dropped the four bits, and then I came out and walked around some more and went back to my boarding house—"

"When you came out of The Haven what did you do first?"

"I walked."

"Yeah. You walked to a car and saw a handbag there and lifted it, and Pellett stopped you and you handed it over—"

"Listen, Chief." Rowley leaned forward and waggled a finger for emphasis. "I may be a vagrant and a bum, if that's the terms you want to use. But I'm not a sneak thief. No, sir. Anybody that says they saw the kind of thing you described is a pure liar. I don't include Mr. Pellett in that. He don't look like a liar and I'll apologize that I hit him. I'm willing to call it a mistake in identity. If he made a mistake—"

"Shut up! The people that saw you aren't liars."

"They are if they say they saw me take anything out of a car yesterday afternoon. In full daylight like that, right on the street? I will never in God's world say anything except to say that they're liars."

That proved to be, in substance, all that could be coaxed or threatened out of him. After another twenty minutes of it Phelan offered him to the sheriff, but Tuttle said he was satisfied as it was. Quinby Pellett was permitted to do some questioning, but got nowhere.

Phelan had another try, but finally threw up his hands in disgust and told the escort, "Take him and throw him in the river!"

"My God," Pellett protested, "you're not going to turn him loose!"

"What can I hold him for? If we book him as a vag we just have to feed him."

"He knocked me down, didn't he? Didn't he assault me? For God's sake, don't let him go!"

"Do you want to charge him with assault?"

"I do."

Phelan nodded to the escort. "All right, boys. Take him over and assign him. Give him dried lizard for supper. Tell Mac, Pellett will sign a charge."

They trooped out, much less eager than when they had entered. The chief of police sat down, looking weary and fed up. The sheriff rubbed his nose.

Pellett looked from one to the other, got tired of waiting and demanded, "Well? What about my niece? How could she have killed Jackson if her bag was stolen?"

"She couldn't," Phelan said, and seemed to be through.

"Well then?"

Phelan aimed a thumb at the sheriff. Tuttle heaved a sigh. "I'll tell you, Pellett. That's a good story you've got. Now what about it? Officially I'll say this: we're much obliged and we'll investigate it thoroughly, all aspects of it, and form the best opinion we can. Unofficially, naturally you want to do everything you can to help your niece, and it's too bad you haven't got any corroboration at all for any of it that's connected with the bag, since even the man that helped you look for it on the stairs is the one that was murdered, and I imagine the jury will feel about the same way."

Pellett stood up, his teeth clenched. "You think I'm lying? You think I made it up?"

"I do," said Tuttle. "Unofficially."

"I don't know, Quin," said Phelan peevishly. "How the hell do I know?"

Pellett, his teeth still clenched, turned and left the room.

It was only a short walk to the new Sammis Building on Mountain Street and he went on foot. Arrived there, he took the elevator to the fourth floor, entered a door halfway down the corridor and told a young woman seated at a desk, "My name is Quinby Pellett. I'm Delia Brand's uncle. I want to see Mr. Anson."

She asked him to wait, and disappeared through another door. After a moment she came back and nodded to him. "Come this way, please."

The following morning the citizens of Cody found on the front page of the *Times-Star* a display box which read:

ADVERTISEMENT
ANYONE WHO HAS RESPECT FOR JUSTICE
AND SYMPATHY WITH UNDESERVED
MISFORTUNE, AND WHO HAS HAPPENED TO SEE
ON HALLEY STREET AROUND FOUR O'CLOCK
TUESDAY AFTERNOON, A MAN WHO STOOD
NEAR A PARKED CAR HANDING SOMETHING TO

ANOTHER MAN, WILL PLEASE, FOR
COMPASSION'S SAKE, COMMUNICATE WITH THE
CODY CHIEF OF POLICE AT ONCE.

THE PICTURE REPRODUCED BELOW IS OF
THE MAN TO WHOM THE OBJECT WAS HANDED.
DELIA BRAND.

It was a good likeness of Quinby Pellett.

Chapter 8

Tyler Dillon slept fitfully that night. He had not seen Delia. He had accomplished nothing. Phil Escott had listened to his recital and plea, and had said he would think it over but it looked like a bad one. So Dillon didn't sleep well. At six o'clock he got up and dressed because he couldn't lie still any longer. When the morning paper was delivered he read the display box on the front page three times, then, without waiting for breakfast, got his car and drove to Quinby Pellett's place, finding him in the living quarters above the taxidermy shop. He was there half an hour, and came away with a new hope and a new despair which approximately balanced each other. After getting some fruit and coffee at a lunchroom on Mountain Street, he went to his office. He wouldn't be able to see Escott, who would be in court all morning, but Wynne Cowles was expected at ten o'clock to sign some papers connected with her divorce suit. When she came he found occasion to remark that he hadn't known she was in a partnership with Clara Brand, but all he got in reply was a mind-your-business glance from her, with her pupils gone slightly elliptical.

As soon as Wynne Cowles had departed, he told his

stenographer he would be back after lunch and drove to Vulcan Street to see Clara. He found her more depressed and wretched even than she had been the day before. She had visited Delia at eight o'clock, but had been permitted to stay with her only ten minutes. She had seen the *Times-Star*, but even after Dillon told her all the details he had got from Pellett, her eyes took on no light.

"Do you think Pellett's lying?" Dillon demanded.

"I don't know," she said miserably. "Of course if he had to he would do worse than lie for Del's sake. He's crazy about her. He always has liked her better than me. But whether he's lying or not, you say the sheriff thinks he is."

Dillon let that go and went on to the chief purpose of his call. "I'm hunting for a straw to grab at," he declared, "and a thing Pellett said struck me. He thinks there may be some connection between the murder of Jackson and what happened to your father two years ago. That was just about the time I came to Cody and I don't know much about it. Your father was Jackson's partner in the grubstaking game, wasn't he?"

Clara nodded. "He was really Mr. Sammis's partner, but Jackson was let in on it when he married Amy Sammis. Sammis furnished the money in the first place and Dad did most of the work. In those days nearly everybody in Wyoming who had any cash tried their luck at grubstaking and quite a few did it on a big scale, but Dad was more successful than anyone else because he really worked at it. He didn't just pick up any loafer that came along, or sit and wait for the prospectors who were down and out to come to him; he went out and got the good ones. At one time they had nearly three hundred grubbers scattered all over the state. That meant an investment of over two hundred thousand dollars and Sammis furnished the money. They made big profits—it was one of their men that found the Sheephorn lode—but Dad didn't know how to hang onto money. It always fascinated me from the time I was a little girl, the idea of finding gold and silver and zinc and copper buried in the rocks, and sometimes Dad let me go on trips with him. That was another way he was different from other grubstakers; he visited his men no matter where they were, and advised and encouraged them and maybe got them out of trouble."

"And it was on one of those trips that he was murdered?"

She nodded again. "Down in the Silverside Hills. He was on a regular trip, but he had an unusually big sum of money with him—thirty-two thousand dollars —because he had got a tip that a wild duck had uncovered a big streak over east of Sheridan—"

"What's a wild duck?"

"A prospector on his own, that hasn't been staked. Dad was going to take a look at the streak and try to buy the claim if it looked good. He had several stops on the way and he hadn't got there yet when he was found dead in that old cabin on the rim of Ghost Canyon." Her lip quivered, and she stopped and got it firmed. "I had been to that old cabin with him just the year before. You couldn't get to it by car. We had to take horses at Sugarbowl and ride ten or twelve miles."

"Then whoever killed him had a horse."

"Maybe not. He could have walked from Sugarbowl or anywhere along the road there, or he might have been out in the hills already."

"Were there many around?"

"Almost no one. There are no sheep in those hills, nothing but sagebrush and greasewood and rocks, except a few piñon in a spot or two at the canyon. The only one known to be around was a prospector named Squint Hurley, one of Dad's men who was using the old cabin for headquarters. Dad had gone there to wait for Hurley to show up. It was Hurley that found him. Hurley was arrested and tried, but the bullet that killed Dad was from a different kind of a gun than Hurley's."

"And the money was gone."

"Yes."

"And none of it has ever turned up."

"Not that anybody knows of. Half of it was in tens and twenties, because that was the way Dad liked to have it for the men. Not even new bills. They don't like it new."

"But one thing." Dillon was frowning. "It must have been someone who knew he would be there and knew he would have all that money—shall I get that?"

"Please do."

He went to answer the doorbell. He opened the door and found himself confronted by a large woman with sweat on her brow, wearing no hat. Dillon, thinking he had seen her before but unable to place her, said good morning.

"Good morning." Her tone was businesslike. "I am Miss Effie Henckel, principal of the Pendleton School. I would like to see Miss Clara Brand."

Dillon did not know that the reason he stammered in replying was because of his subconscious memory of a similarly formidable principal in a school he had attended in San José. But he did stammer.

"M-Miss—er—M-Miss Brand is not seeing anyone. That is, I mean even her close friends. I'm Tyler Dillon, an attorney and a friend of hers. If it is something I can take care of—"

"I prefer to see Miss Clara Brand. It may be something very important."

"Of course. But under the circumstances—as I say, I'm an attorney. Won't I do?"

"You *might* do," Miss Henckel conceded, fixing him with an authoritarian eye. "So might the sheriff do, or Harvey Anson, who I understand is Delia Brand's lawyer. But I deal with men as little as possible because I much prefer to deal with women. I would like to see Miss Clara Brand."

Dillon acknowledged defeat without more ado, asked her to step inside and take a chair, and went to the kitchen and described to Clara the nature of the situation. With a weary sigh Clara arose and went to the front room, with him following her, greeted the caller, and sat. Miss Henckel, after an inspection of Clara's features, apparently to make certain of the identity, spoke tersely:

"I wish, Miss Brand, you would convey to your sister the sympathy and good wishes of myself and my staff at the Pendleton School. Tell her that even Miss Crocker joins us in that expression. Your sister and Miss Crocker don't get on very well. But though I am glad of this opportunity to send your sister that message, that isn't what I came for."

She opened her bag, a large hand-embroidered one, and took out something and handed it to Clara. Clara stared at it but took it. Dillon, leaning forward and perceiving what it was, looked startled and fastened his eyes on the principal, but kept his mouth shut.

"That," said Miss Henckel, in a tone that defied contradiction, "is a cartridge box and in it are thirty-five cartridges for a .38 revolver. This morning one of the patrons of my school, Mr. James Archer, came to my office with his son, James Junior, who is in the fourth grade, and told me that when he returned home from work yesterday he found that a structure had been erected in a corner of a shed adjoining his garage. The structure consisted of berry boxes held together with paper clips, tacks and rubber bands, and at intervals holes had been punched through the boxes with an ice pick or gimlet, and protruding from the holes on the outside were cartridges. He questioned his son and was told that the structure was a fort on the Yellow River in China. Then he dealt further with his son and learned that the cartridges had been stolen the day before, Tuesday afternoon, in the cloak vestibule of Room Nine in the Pendleton School, from Delia Brand's handbag."

Without stopping for a by-your-leave, Dillon snatched the box from Clara's fingers and pulled the lid off. He gazed at the contents in bitter disappointment. The box was no more than three-fourths full.

"To be sure." Miss Henckel lifted her brows at him and there was an edge of scornful condescension to her tone. "I said thirty-five cartridges, didn't I? I realized that it might possibly be of vital significance if the box was full. Mr. Archer states that he doesn't care to have loaded cartridges lying around his shed, and he searched with great thoroughness and is absolutely certain that he got every one. His son states that that is all there were. But I have been dealing with boys for nearly thirty years. I led him into details and, among them, he told of removing the wrapping paper from the box after he had taken it from the bag. The fact that there was still wrapping paper on it permits the assumption that the box had not been opened. I told the boy that, nearly an hour ago, but he sticks to his statement. It is a remarkable case of stubbornness, really remarkable. At that point I decided you should be notified, Miss Brand, so that you could take whatever—"

"Where's the boy now?" Dillon demanded.

"In my office with his father."

"I'll handle him! Come on—"

"I came here with information for Miss Brand. It is in her hands. If she thinks the police or Mr. Anson—"

"Clara, damn it all! Let me go! If we find the rest of those cartridges—Listen, you come too! We'll both go! All right, Miss Henckel?"

"Whatever Miss Brand decides. Though I can tell you, you're not going to choke it out of him. It will take finer handling than that."

"All right, Clara? Come on!"

Clara got up and started for the door.

Jimmie Archer said for the hundredth time, with tears in his eyes, "I tell you I'm not a squealer, doggone it! I tell you I'm not a rat! I tell you I won't squeal!"

They were beginning to believe him. Instead of showing signs of weakening in the last half hour, since they had tricked him into the admission that he had had a confederate in the robbery, the obduracy in his eyes, in spite of the tears, had grown more and more intense, and his jaw had stopped quivering entirely. He had confessed that there had been a division of the spoils and that he had kept thirty-five cartridges for himself, but there seemed to be no conceivable technique that would compel or entice him into the pronouncement of a name.

His father said, "No use licking him. I've tried that before. It tightens him up like a rusty nut. I used to pull his ears, I guess that's one reason they stick out, but I quit. It's no use."

Miss Henckel said, "We could check up on all the boys who were supposed to go to Miss Brand's class that day, but that would be an endless job. There was no roll call."

They were in Miss Henckel's outside office for a council of war, having left Dillon and Clara in the inner room with Jimmie. As the principal had said, it was a remarkable case of stubbornness, intensified to fanaticism when the issue had got down to the name of the accomplice. Clara's entreaties, Miss Henckel's appeal to reason, the father's threats, warnings and bribes, and Dillon's cross-examination, were all repulsed.

Dillon emerged from the inner room, closing the door behind him, and joined the council. "Look here," he said, "we're wasting our breath. He gets worse instead of better. There's not a chance in the world of our getting that name out of him. Are you sure his mother couldn't do it? It seems as though his mother—"

"Nothing doing." Mr. Archer was positive. "Usually him and the missis hit it off fine—the way she does it, she never goes against the grain. When he once gets that look in his eyes—of course, if she had two or three days for it—"

"She hasn't got two or three days! If you don't think she can do it, I've got an idea. It's complicated, but it will only take an hour or maybe less, and it may work. First I'll go in and tell him—"

Five minutes later Dillon left them there and returned alone to the inner room, where Clara sat gazing in hopeless exasperation at the criminal's obstinate tear-stained face.

"Look here, Jimmie," Dillon said sternly, "I'll give

you one more chance to tell me the name of your pal who has the rest of those cartridges. This is your last chance."

The boy shook his head, sullenly and inflexibly.

"Tell me." Dillon waited five seconds. "You won't? All right, then it's up to the law. We'll see if you can beat the law. You're in for it, Jimmie, I'm telling you straight. You can't fight the law by sitting there shaking your head. You will have to get a lawyer, and a mighty good one, and you'd better get him quick. Have you got a good lawyer?"

"I don't—" The boy's lip quivered. "I never really had a lawyer."

"Well, you'd better get one in a hurry. I've told your father what I'm going to do, and he's pretty scared about it, and I suppose he'll recommend a good lawyer to you if you care to consult him about it. That's all I have to say. It's up to the law now. I'll send your father in. Come on, Clara."

"But, Ty, we can't—"

"Come on!"

They left him there alone. In the outer room Dillon said to Mr. Archer, "All right. Let it soak into him for five minutes and then go in and try it. For heaven's sake be careful and do it right if you can. Don't take him over there until you hear from me."

He departed with Clara and drove as fast as the traffic would permit to Mountain Street, and in the new Sammis Building ascended to the offices of Escott, Brody & Dillon. There he had a stroke of luck. He had expected to have to haul his senior partner away from his lunch somewhere, but at the adjournment of court Escott had stopped in at his office and was there when the conspirators arrived. Dillon first telephoned the Pendleton School and then went to Escott's room and opened up on him. The veteran lawyer was at first annoyed because it bordered on interference in another firm's case; then he was amused and interested; and finally he agreed.

James Archer, Senior, must have encountered some resistance, for it was getting close to one o'clock when he entered with his son. There was no one in the anteroom but a young woman at a desk. Senior pushed Junior forward, and Junior looked at the young woman with glum eyes and mumbled at her, "I wanna see Mr. Escott."

"Name, please?"

"Jimmie Archer. Junior."

She went out. In a moment she came back, let him through the gate, led him down the hall and ushered him into a room. Old Phil Escott arose to shake hands with him, got him into a chair and, after the door had closed behind the young woman, addressed him man to man.

"Well, Jimmie Archer, what can I do for you? Something about the law?"

The boy sat with his shoulders hunched. "Yes, sir."

"What's the trouble? A lawsuit or something?"

"No, sir. They want me to squeal and I won't do it. I'll take the rap, but I won't squeal!"

"That's fine. I admire that. Shake!" Jimmie suspiciously and reluctantly stuck out his hand, and they shook again. "Who wants you to squeal?"

"Aw, it's a whole gang after me. There's my father, and Miss Henckel the principal, and a woman they call Clara that's got a sister in a jam, and a guy named Dillon, he's nothing but a big bully—"

"Ha! Dillon! I know that man Dillon. He's no good. What do they want you to squeal about?"

"About my pal that helped me take the catriches from Miss Brand's bag. I'm not a rat."

"Of course you're not. I can see that by looking at you. When did you take the cart—catriches?" As the boy was silent, Escott leaned back and pressed the tips of his fingers together. "Of course you realize, Jimmie, that if I am your lawyer I'll have to have all the details. Do you know what it means for me to be your lawyer?"

"Sure I do. It means you're my mouthpiece."

"That's right. That's it exactly." Escott's lip twitched a little, but he mastered it. "When did you and your pal take the catriches?"

"Aw, it was day before yesterday. At Rhythmic Movement. Him and me sneaked in the cloakroom because it makes us sick, and Miss Brand's bag was there, and we just thought we'd try and see if it would come open—"

"Wait a minute! And the catriches were in her bag!"

"Yes, sir."

"And they were in a box, wrapped up, and you took the whole thing!"

"Yes, sir."

Jimmie's brows were drawing together with renewed suspicion, but Escott swept on: "Why, my goodness, I know all about that case! In fact, I've been engaged by the man who sold the catriches to get them back! I'm his mouthpiece too! I'll be doggoned!" Escott opened a drawer of his desk and took out a cardboard box, and from it dumped onto the desk a pile of silver dollars. He stacked them, and fingered them like poker chips. "Look at that!"

"What's that for?"

"Why, that's the reward the man offered for whoever returned the catriches! Ten dollars! It's a mighty lucky thing you happened to come to me, Jimmie! I know that man Dillon; he was trying to get all the catriches so he could claim the reward! He's a slick one."

The suspicion on Jimmie's face disappeared to make room for another emotion which seemed likely to tap the tear ducts again. "But l-l-look here!" he faltered. "I ain't got the catriches any more! My father took 'em and now that c-c-crook Dillon's got 'em!"

"Oh, that's all right. Don't worry about that, Jimmie. You'll get the reward all right, because I'll pay it to you myself. Half will go to you and half to your pal. Of course the businesslike way to do it, to clean it all up at once, will be to get him here, and I'll give you five dollars and him five dollars—"

"Hey!" Jimmie's voice rang out and his face had changed again. "That ain't fair!"

"What ain't fair?"

"To give him half and me half! It ought to be the way we divvied up the catriches! I had thirty-five and he's only got fifteen!"

Escott, for a second, was speechless. He regarded James Archer, Junior, this time without affection or reservation, as man to man. "Well," he said finally, "that will have to be a matter for mutual agreement. He'll have to be here with you and me, and we'll have to settle it."

Jimmie had slid off the chair to his feet. "I'll settle it," he said grimly. "I'll go get him."

"It will be better if we send someone after him and you stay here. It'll be quicker that way. What's his name?"

"His name's Eric Snyder. He's red-headed. He lives at 319 Humboldt Street. He's in the fourth grade—"

Escott had pushed a button on his desk and the

door opened to admit a young woman. He told her: "Tell Mr. Tyler to get Eric Snyder, 319 Humboldt Street. That's right. He's red-headed and in the fourth grade."

When the young woman had gone Escott turned to his client again, "Well, we might as well figure this out and be ready for him. Let's see. If it's to be divided in the same proportion as the cartridges were, that will mean seven dollars for you and three for him. Right?"

"It don't sound right." Jimmie looked wary and suspicious again. "Three bucks for only fifteen catriches sounds like too much." He frowned deeply. "Gimme a pencil and a piece of paper."

Escott got them and handed them over.

Chapter 9

Kenneth Chambers, Sheriff of Silverside County, with only one eye on the spittoon eight feet away from his chair, squirted a beautiful stream of tobacco juice squarely into its middle.

"Yeah, I know," he drawled, "I know all about that. But take it from me, Squint Hurley had a hand in it."

Bill Tuttle, Sheriff of Park County, who was seated at his desk in his office, said in a voice made querulous by the heat, not to mention one or two other vexations, "You've got a grudge against Hurley, Ken."

"What if I have?" the other demanded. "Who wouldn't have? Didn't he murder Charlie Brand right square in the center of my county and then go scot free just because a couple of wisenheimers said the bullet wasn't from his gun? They call it science! Next thing they'll measure my hind end and tell me where I sat down last!" He spat again and nearly missed. "As far as that goes, couldn't he have faked up a catrich if he was a mind to? Couldn't he have used another gun?"

Tuttle sighed. "Well, Ken, I followed that trial pretty close. And I'll tell you. My candid opinion is that both you and that what's-his-name, the prosecutor, were as dumb as a pair of hee-haws. You didn't have a single damn thing on Hurley except that he was handy, still you went ahead and tried to bulldog him. If you'd found some of that money on him, or a place where he cached it, that would have been different."

"He was as guilty as a bear in a bees' nest."

"Maybe he was and maybe he wasn't, but you had no proof of it. And here you drive over here on a hot day just to add to my troubles as if I didn't have enough already! Didn't I tell you on the phone yesterday that Hurley had nothing to do with it except he went up there to ask Jackson for some money and found the girl right there with the gun in her hand?"

"I don't care what you told me," Chambers said obstinately. "I'm convinced Hurley was mixed up in it. How did he happen to be going to see Jackson at night? And how did he happen to be going to see Jackson at all? In the past year and a half, since that half-witted jury turned him loose, Jackson has refused to have anything to do with him and I understand he got a little nibble from Bert Doyle down at Laramie and since then he's been eating bunch grass. Where is he? I suppose you've let him slide along?"

"Certainly not. He'll be my star witness."

"He will like hell. He'll be one of the defendants." The sheriff of Silverside County spat. "I'm going to light a fire under him."

"Not in Park County you're not." Tuttle, from being querulous, became pugnacious. "Get my star witness sore just to nurse a grudge? Not on your life! There's not a bit of evidence that Squint Hurley was in it at all and no reason to suppose he was. You're all right for a neighbor, Ken, these counties being as big as they are, but I'm damned if you're going to start hazing my stock inside my fences. My God, as if this case wasn't bad enough already! Go on back home and flush a mutton-rustler or something! I'd like to trade places—Excuse me."

The phone had buzzed, and he pulled it across and spoke into it. After a moment he said, "Send him on in," and hung up.

Chambers, stirring, began, "I'll mosey along—"

"No, you won't. If you do I'll have you tailed. This is just a parson calling. You stay here till we get this thing settled."

The door opened and the Reverend Rufus Toale entered. His preposterous straw hat was in his hand, his black coat was buttoned up and a strand of his dark hair, pasted to his broad forehead by perspiration, curved to a point aimed at his left eyebrow. He came forward with his other hand outstretched, saying in his deep musical voice, "God bless you, Brother Tuttle.— Oh yes, yes indeed, I know Brother Chambers, or perhaps I should say I recognize him. I saw him, of course, during the trial of that poor man for the murder of Charles Brand. God rest his soul."

Ken Chambers, muttering something, resumed his seat. Tuttle got heartiness into his voice: "Sit down, Doctor, sit down. Anything I can do?"

"Praise God, there is." Rufus Toale, with his customary deliberation, hung the straw hat on the back of a chair and deposited himself on the seat, sitting straight, clasping his hands in front of him. "There is, Brother Tuttle. You can welcome the truth and let it serve you. God's truth is His alone and it alone is everlasting, but there is also worldly truth which, alas, is often chosen for a guide." His tone all at once became fierce and a fire gleamed in his eyes. "God's truth will prevail!" The fire receded and his tone calmed. "I have been three times to see Delia Brand and she will not see me. She refuses to let me speak to her."

"Yeah, I heard about that." The sheriff looked embarrassed. "I'm sorry, but the warden didn't see how he could—"

"I understand. Faith and grace cannot enter by force, and the servant of the Lord must wait for the door to open. That poor innocent child! God's blessing on her!"

Tuttle frowned. "You say innocent?"

"I do. I think she is innocent. I do not think she killed. But even if she is guilty by man's law, who are you to judge her? Only God can brand Cain. For my sins I answer not to man! By your insolent judgments and punishments you usurp His power and deny His mercy!"

"Of course," Tuttle agreed, "that's all right for preaching. But we've got to enforce the law. If they didn't want 'em enforced, why did they make 'em?"

Rufus Toale sighed. "I know. Practically, it's useless. That's why I am here. I, even I, must render unto Caesar the things that are Caesar's. So I came to tell you that the man whom Delia Brand desired to kill was myself."

The end of the sentence unfortunately caught Ken Chambers in the very act of spitting and he missed the spittoon by nearly a foot. Tuttle's mouth fell open and, staring, he neglected to close it. Then he demanded, "Huh?"

Rufus Toale nodded. "Let me explain. I was not aware that the poor child desired my death, though I knew that hatred for me had entered her heart. But when I read in the paper that when she bought the cartridges in the sporting goods store she declared her intention to shoot a man, I knew the man must be me. I am not at liberty to tell you what it was that caused her to conceive her hatred for me, but I assure you it existed. It is not an overstatement to say that she abhorred me. I have been trying to see her, it is true, to persuade her to trust in God's wisdom and mercy in this sore trial, but I also wanted to gain her permission to tell you of her hatred for me and, as far as it might be necessary, of the reason for it. She will not see me. So I can tell you nothing of the reason, but I can say that I know she hated me and it was me she desired to kill."

"Then she was a derned poor shot."

That came from Ken Chambers. Tuttle turned a glare on him; Rufus Toale ignored him. Tuttle said, "Well, Doctor, of course I'm pretty surprised. It sounds remarkable. It sounds close to incredible."

"It is true."

"Maybe so. You're not prepared to open up any about the reason?"

"I am not. The confidences of a shepherd with his flock are holy."

"Sure, I suppose they are. Did she ever threaten you or tell you she felt like shooting you?"

"No. But I saw her soul."

"Did she ever tell anybody that, that you know of?"

"No."

"Then what—you understand I'm not necessarily doubting it a bit—but what has this got to do with the fact that she was found standing in front of Dan Jackson with the gun in her hand he had just been killed with?"

"It has to do with it, Brother Tuttle, that it convinces me there has been a mistake and the poor child is innocent." Rufus Toale's voice lifted and became more sonorous. "And I will add, and I warn you, sir, to give it heed, that there is another quite different reason, which I cannot divulge, why I am certain that she did not shoot Jackson. God rest his soul."

"Certain's a strong word, Doctor."

"I am certain."

"Well . . ." Tuttle twisted in his chair and his voice changed. "See here. I suppose you know that the law doesn't recognize the right of any clergyman or even any priest to withhold knowledge of a serious crime, let alone murder. Now you spoke of confidences being holy and so on. That kind of talk won't be allowed to justify—"

"God will justify!" The fire showed in Rufus Toale's eyes again, a zealot's fire, and he spoke with a zealot's voice. "Do you imagine, Sheriff, that I respect your ordinances or bow to your compulsions through fear? God forbid! Do you suppose I would relinquish one small glance of favor from His blessed throne to earn any earthly justification you or anyone could bestow? A ghastly error not only in the sight of God, but in the sight of man!"

Tuttle gazed at him. He would sooner or later, presumably, have replied something or other, but the opportunity passed before he seized it. The phone buzzed. He took it and spoke into it, and gave instructions that someone was to be told to wait till he was free, but the instructions must have been either misunderstood or disregarded, for as he was shoving the phone back the door burst open and a man irrupted into the room. His momentum took him clear to the desk and he was talking when he got there.

"I said I was busy!" the sheriff yelled. "I said for you to wait!"

"I don't care how busy you are," Tyler Dillon declared. He was panting, more from emotion, it appeared, than from exertion. "Whatever it is, it can wait. I've got—"

"You can wait yourself! Who's your client this time?"

"I haven't got a client. I've got evidence that will clear Delia Brand!"

"The hell you have. Why don't you take it to her counsel?"

"Because there's no use delaying it. It's conclusive. Get a stenographer in here. I've got some witnesses. I want a record—get a stenographer—"

"Keep your shirt on." Tuttle reached for the phone. "You're not going to give me a ride on any more of your legal privileges." He told the phone, "Ask Ed Baker if he'll please step down here right away.—Hey, where are you going?"

"I'm going to bring in my witnesses."

"You are not. You stay right here and tell it to the county attorney."

"I can have—"

"You can have a chair, or a square foot to stand on, until he gets here."

Tuttle leaned back and glared, first at his brother sheriff, then at the Reverend Rufus Toale and, finally, at the young lawyer in search of a client. In a long experience he had never seen so much ruckus about one bullet in one man, from so many different quarters; and besides the ruckus, there were the correlative perils personal to himself and his job, which constituted, from his standpoint, by no means the least important feature of the case. He was around sixty and he was kind of tired, and he hadn't saved up much money. He was about deciding that he had better shoo the clergyman and the brother sheriff out of the room when the door opened to admit Ed Baker. He approached the desk, demanding, "Well, Bill, what is it?"

"This Dillon here again. Says he's got evidence."

Baker wheeled. "Oh, you. What kind of evidence?"

Ty Dillon faced him. "Evidence that will clear Delia Brand."

"Where's her attorney?"

"I don't know and I don't care. I'm taking it for granted that you have no ill will for Delia Brand and if you are given facts that create a strong presumption of her innocence, you'll turn her loose. I know you didn't believe Pellett's story about her bag, but you only had his word for it and he's her uncle. This is different. It's evidence."

"What is it?"

"Get a stenographer."

"Go on and tell me."

"Just as you say, I won't forget it. I've got witnesses, but I'll sketch it first. As you know, Delia bought a box of cartridges at MacGregor's Tuesday morning. The clerk who sold them to her took the gun she had and looked at it and it wasn't loaded; he said so in the interview he gave the *Times-Star*. Tuesday afternoon at the Pendleton School Delia left her handbag with her hat on a shelf in the cloakroom which is partitioned off from Room Nine. Two boys sneaked into the cloakroom and, while she was teaching the class, they stole the box of cartridges from her bag. That's all they took. They saw the gun there. They took the cartridges home with them and I've got them. Right here in my pocket. Fifty of them. All of them. Then where did she get a cartridge to shoot Jackson with? And the ones in the gun?"

Baker, eyeing him, grunted. "Somebody got a cartridge to shoot Jackson with."

"She didn't. Where?"

"Who says the cartridges you've got are the ones she bought?"

"Don't worry about that. That's sewed up. The boys are in the anteroom."

"She hasn't said anything about the cartridges being stolen. She says bag and all were stolen."

"That was later, from her car. She hadn't missed the cartridges. This thing is watertight. It's so tight that I didn't even have her sister see her before I came to you, to warn her not to say that she noticed the cartridges in her bag after she left the school. She couldn't say that, because they weren't there. This is open and shut."

The county attorney, still eyeing him, chewed at his lip. Finally he turned to the sheriff. "Get the boys in here, Bill."

In response to the sheriff's message, the population of the office was increased not by two, but by four. In front was Clara, her face a weary composite of hope and anxiety; next came Jimmie and Eric; in the rear was James Archer, Senior, carrying his coat over his arm. The young man from the anteroom stayed to help get chairs collected and occupied and then withdrew.

Names were supplied by Dillon to the county attorney, who opened up on Jimmie. "Were you at the Pendleton School Tuesday afternoon?"

"Yes, sir."

"What were you doing?"

"Doing my dooty."

"What were you doing while Delia Brand was teaching her class?"

"I was finding something because somebody had offered a reward."

"Oh, a reward? Did you get the reward?"

"Yes, sir."

"Who gave it to you?"

"Mr. Escott. My lawyer."

"I see. When he gave you the reward did he tell you what to say when you were brought here?"

"No, sir."

"Did anybody tell you want to say?"

"Yes, sir."

"What did they tell you to say?"

"The truth."

Dillon put in savagely, "Oh, cut it out, Baker. That's tommyrot. There's any amount of corroboration—the fathers and mothers and the school principal—"

"I'll handle it, thanks." Baker went on with Jimmie: "What was it you found?"

"A box of catriches."

"Where did you find it?"

"In Miss Brand's bag. I was there in the cloakroom with Eric, and I whispered to him, I said . . ."

Jimmie was off. It took over an hour. Ed Baker, first with one boy and then the other, exhausted every detail of the entire episode from beginning to end, and then started over again and repeated the performance. He questioned James Archer, Senior, with equal thoroughness and then went after Jimmie once more, regarding his visit to the offices of Escott, Brody & Dillon and his surrender to the bait of the silver dollars. He was working on that, and Dillon was pacing up and down in impatience, when he was interrupted by the sheriff, who had been speaking briefly on the phone.

"It's Frank Phelan," said the sheriff, covering the transmitter. "He says he's got something and he's bringing it over right away, and he wants you to be here."

"Well, I'm here!" Baker told him testily. "Tell him to bring it along!" He resumed with Jimmie. Five minutes later he had all he seemed likely to get. The questions stopped. He surveyed the boy a moment, then turned to face Dillon. "All right," he said grudgingly. "You said you have evidence. You have. Congratulations. But it seems to me you should have taken it to the defense attorney in the first place. You'd better take it there now."

Dillon stared. "Take it—why? What more do you want? Do you mean you've got the nerve to hold—" His voice was on the way, crescendo, to a shriek of indignation.

"Cool off, Dillon. Use your head a little. What's my nerve got to do with it? I admit you've dug up evidence, enough of it so that when Harvey Anson gets it he'll probably take a crack at a *habeas corpus* writ and then I'll have to decide whether to fight it or not. I've got to think it over. There's still a preponderance against her and if you were in my place you'd know it as well as I do."

"But damn you, what more do you want? This proves that she couldn't—"

"This proves only one thing, that if she shot Jackson she didn't do it with one of the cartridges she bought from MacGregor's clerk Tuesday morning. I admit that's something. I admit that it puts it up to me—now what?"

He wheeled. The door had been flung open and feet were tramping in. Everybody gazed at the new influx, which seemed to threaten, as it continued, to jam the office. First was Lem Sammis, followed by Quinby Pellett. Next in order, entered a uniformed policeman, a tall skinny young man in a polo shirt and seersucker slacks, with wavy blond hair, Chief of Police Phelan and another cop in uniform. At the tail end, as usual, progressing with a minimum of exertion, was Harvey Anson.

The Reverend Rufus Toale unobtrusively left his seat and went to stand by the wall. James Archer, Senior, chased the boys off of their chairs. But the newcomers appeared to be seeking not ease, but action. They stayed on their feet. Lem Sammis was saying to Ed Baker, "See how you like this one. So Quin Pellett's a liar, huh? When you go out of my gate, Ed, it shuts behind you!" Phelan was telling the sheriff he had better get some of the crowd out of there. But Harvey Anson had elbowed through to the county attorney and his thin voice, sparing of breath, took the attention:

"Uh, Baker. I can go up to Judge Hamilton. But maybe you'd like it better informally. As a favor to you. We have a witness you ought to hear."

Baker's lower lip was upthrust. "A witness to what? Who is he?"

Anson pointed a thumb at the young man with wavy blond hair. "Ask him. He'll tell you about it."

Baker's sharp glance took in the witness from head to foot. "We can take him upstairs to my office."

"Oh, no, that won't be necessary. He'll enjoy the audience. We all will."

The audience, for its part, was already engrossed. In the silence, the impact was plainly audible when the sheriff of Silverside County spat. One of the cops nudged the young man forward.

Baker faced him. "You've got something to say?"

"I have." The young man's voice was a little squeaky, but not with timidity or uncertainty. "Shall I go on and say it?"

"Just a minute. What's your name and who are you?"

"My name is Clement Ardyce Cooper and I'm a student at the university. I live at Comstock Hall."

Baker grunted. "Shoot."

"Tuesday afternoon about four o'clock I was standing at the curb on Halley Street, not far from The Haven, studying types—"

"Types of what?"

"People. Do you want me to explain everything carefully as I go along?"

"I want you to say what you were brought here to say."

"Then please don't interrupt me. I was standing at the curb and I saw a man pass by, among many others, and decided he was an extrovert, unstable, philotype B. He walked close to the curb and looked into several parked cars in a peculiar manner, taking precautions against observation, but I am accustomed to observing people without making them aware of it. I am a psychologist. I saw him open the door of a car and take something out—a leather handbag. He was about thirty feet from me. A moment later another man approached and accosted him. The first man said something in reply, thrust the handbag into the other man's hands and walked away. The other man stared after him a few seconds, then he walked off too, in the opposite direction, carrying the handbag. His name was Quinby Pellett."

"You mean you knew him?"

"Oh, no, not then. I had never seen him before. But this morning I saw his picture on the front page of the newspaper, in an advertisement. I read the advertisement and at two o'clock, after my classes were over, I went to the police station to reply to it. They sent for

Quinby Pellett and when he came naturally I recognized him."

"Naturally. From his picture in the paper."

"Oh, no. From having seen him on Tuesday." The young man looked amused. "You're so transparent, really. Almost infantile. I'd love to give you a test."

"Much obliged. If there's any testing, I'll do it myself." Baker was gazing at him resentfully, but the resentment was not for him. It was like Harvey Anson to spring a thing like that, informally he called it, before a bunch of rubbernecks, without any warning. . . .

"Anything else?" the psychologist inquired.

"Yes," Baker snapped. "Plenty. First about the man who took the bag from the car. Has he been described to you?"

"Described? By whom?"

"By anyone. Anyone who is now in this room, or out of it either. Or have you been shown a photograph of him?"

"Oh, I get you." The young man looked more amused than ever. "I'll tell you about that. I know I'm a little skinny, but I'm all right. I'm the second best in tennis up at the campus. If you'll have this room cleared, or if you'll come out in the alley with me, I'll beat some of that out of you."

Baker looked a little startled. "There's no occasion—"

"There's plenty of occasion." The student's voice got more of a squeak in it, but otherwise he maintained his calm. "I come here to tell you something I saw because I saw it and right away you start trying cheap insulting tricks. If you want to ask me if I'm lying and give me a chance to say no, I'm not, that's all right, but instead of that you start making cowardly insinuations. What's wrong with you is a fundamental lack of intelligence, to suppose that if I undertook, or had been persuaded, to invent a story, I wouldn't have sense enough to defend it against any attack you could possibly be capable of. I'm not surprised you're a lawyer. You probably couldn't make a living at much of anything else."

"I should have warned you, Baker." A cackle came from Harvey Anson's lips, which was a rare occurrence. "He's pretty hot. That's about the identical thing he said to me. Why don't you look into his connections? To see how we might have suborned him."

"Thanks, I will." Baker glared at the witness. "What does your father do?"

"He's a geodesist."

"A what?"

The youth smiled tolerantly. "A sectional director of the United States Geodetic Survey."

"Is he a friend of the chief of police? Or of Quinby Pellett or the Brand family? Or of Mr. Anson or Mr. Sammis?"

"No."

"Are you?"

"No. I wouldn't be. I have nothing but contempt for lawyers, financiers and politicians."

Another cackle came from Anson. Baker disregarded it. "Would you recognize that man if you saw him again? The one who took the bag from the car?"

"Certainly. Didn't I say I studied him?"

Frank Phelan broke in, "Why don't you try him on it, Ed? I'd like to see it myself. We can line Rowley up with a dozen or so—"

"Yeah, sure, I'll bet you'd like it, Frank." The county attorney appeared to be talking through his teeth. He eyed the psychologist. "You say the second man was Pellett and he walked off carrying the bag. What did he do with it?"

"I don't know. He went on down the sidewalk. A young woman came along, Mongoloid, with a typical—"

Quinby Pellett blurted, "I've told you what I did! First I went to the corner and had a beer—"

"I wasn't asking you. I know what you told me." To the witness: "Did anybody see *you* on Halley Street Tuesday afternoon? Did you see or speak to anyone you know?"

"Certainly. I spoke, intermittently, with my companion, Miss Griselda Ames, the daughter of a professor in the School of Mines."

Baker gawked. "You mean she was with you all the time?"

"She was."

"And she saw everything you saw?"

"She did."

Baker flung up his hands. "In the name of God, why didn't you say so?"

"I have said so." The witness was unperturbed. "As a matter of fact, it was only at Miss Ames's insistence that I replied to the advertisement. It seemed to me a bit quixotic. If you would like verification of my story, though it appears to me quite unnecessary, she would be glad to furnish it. Not that I regret having come." His head slowly pivoted for an interested survey of the throng. "The faces of excited people, under a strain of one sort or another, are unusually revealing."

Harvey Anson cackled again. The county attorney whirled on him and demanded, "Well?"

Anson shrugged. "Well, Baker, it looks as if the only question is whether you want me to go to the trouble of entering a writ. Fact is, I've got one in my pocket. I was going to argue it on the basis of Quin Pellett's testimony and then this came along."

"Yeah. And instead of letting me have this with decent professional courtesy, you have to grandstand it in front of a mass meeting!"

"That's right. Lem Sammis and I didn't much care for certain tendencies you seemed to be displaying. Shall I go on up to Judge Hamilton with the writ?"

"No," Baker snapped. He turned to the sheriff. "Bill, go and get Delia Brand and bring her in here. I'm going upstairs and move to dismiss and get an order. Keep her here till I get back; it'll only take a few minutes—you coming along, Anson?"

He strode out of the room, with Anson at his heels, and the sheriff bestirred himself and left by another door. Ken Chambers spat. A little involuntary cry came from Clara Brand's lips, and Ty Dillon moved to pat her on the shoulder. "Ty!" she said, "they're going to set her free! She's free!" He growled, "You're damn right she is," and left her to walk to the psychologist and grab his hand. The student politely tolerated it. The Reverend Rufus Toale left his spot by the wall to approach Clara Brand, beam down at her and exhort: "Praise God, my child! Praise Him for this timely and blessed interposition of His divine will!" Without awaiting, or apparently expecting, acquiescence, he moved back to the wall. Quinby Pellett came to replace him in front of Clara, bending to squeeze her elbow and demanding, "How's that for luck, Clara? Wonderful luck? That that fellow saw me getting the bag, that kind of a fellow, and the girl with him? How was that for luck?" With her eyes on the door instead of him, she agreed, "Wonderful, Uncle Quin, simply wonderful!" The door opened and her sister entered. The sheriff was right behind her.

Ty Dillon ran toward her three steps and then checked himself, looking foolish. Delia's face was composed and was certainly not pallid or haggard; indeed, if the psychologist wanted to study strained countenances, she was about his least likely prospect in the room. She took in the crowd with a glance, spotted Clara, trotted across to her and threw her arms around her and kissed her. "Sis!" she cried, "what's happened? Am I really—is it really all over?" They hugged each other. "What's happened? It is?—And Ty, you here? All right, kiss me on the cheek. Go ahead! Look at you, you're trembling all over—All right, Mr. Sammis, then you kiss me—you too, Uncle Quin, though I know you're not very demonstrative—"

They were all around her and all talking at once, having for spectators Frank Phelan and the two cops wearing broad grins, the psychologist smiling tolerantly, Mr. Archer and the two boys staring sympathetically, Ken Chambers pretending it was none of his business, and the Reverend Rufus Toale moving his lips as if in silent prayer. That was still the scene when the door from the anteroom opened to admit Harvey Anson and Ed Baker.

Baker went across to the sheriff, handed him a paper and said, "There's the order, Bill, give it to the warden." Then he turned and called sharply, "Miss Delia Brand! Please!"

They all faced him. He was crisp. "Miss Brand, you are released from custody. I am sorry if you have been temporarily charged with a crime you didn't commit; I offer no apology, because the charge was made in good faith, under the weight of circumstances which seemed all but conclusive. Your being released now does not prohibit a future renewal of the charge in case new evidence warrants it, though I admit that seems un-

likely; I merely want to make your position clear to
you." His eyes moved to include them all. "There have
been intimations that in holding Miss Brand I have
been moved by considerations other than a desire to
enforce the law. That is not true. If Miss Brand is innocent and I now believe she is, no one is happier than I
am to see her free. But let me tell you this: I am more
than ever determined to investigate fully the murder
of Dan Jackson and find the guilty man and punish him.
Or woman! I congratulate you, Mr. Anson, on ob-
taining the freedom of your client, but I remind you
and everyone that the question still remains and I'm
going to find the answer to it: who killed Dan Jackson?"

"Go to it, Ed." It was Lem Sammis. "Go right
ahead."

"I'm going to, Lem. I'm going to follow this investigation wherever it leads. I'm just letting you know.
And the first thing I want to do is ask some questions
of Delia Brand.—Now wait a minute, please. You are
aware, Anson, that I've had very little information
from Miss Brand. From the time you got hold of her
Tuesday night she has said nothing. But she was found
in that office with Jackson shortly after he was killed
and he was killed with a gun that had been in her possession, and that certainly makes her a material witness if there ever was one. It was perfectly proper for
you to keep her sealed up as long as she was charged
with murder, but not now. I want to ask her some
things and I'm going to, and if I don't get answers I'll
detain her as a material witness. I'm aware that I can't
force answers, but I can expect them and I do expect
them."

Anson said mildly, "You might let her have a
night's sleep in her own bed first."

"No. I will if she insists on it, but I want to start this investigation now and with her. What about it, Miss Brand?"

Eyes turned to Delia. She hesitated. "Will I have to answer everything you ask me?"

"You won't have to answer anything. But you will, if you're a law-abiding citizen—anything that has a bearing on the crime."

Anson said, "I want to be present. She is still my client."

"No," said Delia, "I am not."

"What's that? You're not?"

"No." She leveled unfriendly eyes at him. "You thought I was . . . you thought I had killed Jackson. Not only that, you thought I killed him because . . ." She flushed. "You know what you thought. So I don't want to be your client and I'm not."

"How about me?" Tyler Dillon demanded. He was flushing too, but he was eagerly seizing a chance. "You ought to have a lawyer, Del, and if you don't want Mr. Anson—"

"No. I don't want a lawyer." She sounded as if she meant it. "You're all right, Ty, but I don't think I'll ever do anything or say anything that will make me need a lawyer. I realized a lot of things up there in that cell, lying on that cot . . . when I opened my eyes I could see, through the bars, Mrs. Welch sitting out there, for no reason at all except to be human. I thought about things I never thought about before, and I—what I really mean is, I never thought at all before. At first I was scared and nothing else, but then I began to think. For the first time in my life I realized how silly it is, and it's even dangerous, for people to go along day after day taking it for granted that they're not fools. I'm never going to take that for granted again. And no one is in a position to say whether you're a fool or not except you yourself, because no one else knows enough about it." She looked at Ed Baker. "You can question me without my having a lawyer, can't you?"

"I can. I would prefer it that way."

Lem Sammis put in, "Maybe you're a fool now, Dellie. Anson got you out of jail, didn't he? What's the difference whether he thought this or that? It only shows he was a fool too."

But one result, apparently, of her mental exercises as she lay on the cot in the cell, was that she was through, at least temporarily, with lawyers. She was firm, and in spite of the protests of Anson and Lem Sammis and Clara and Ty and Uncle Quin, she went out with the county attorney, headed for his office upstairs.

Five minutes later the room was deserted, except for the two sheriffs. They sat in silence. Finally Tuttle sighed.

"Well," Ken Chambers demanded, "and how do you like it now? What did I tell you?" He flourished a packet of fine cut. "No, you said, don't go monkeying with Squint Hurley, because the Brand girl did it and he's my star witness. No, you said, speaking to me, you'll sit right here and if you try leaving before we get this thing settled I'll have you tailed—"

"Shut up," Tuttle told him bitterly. "Not that I didn't have all the sympathy in the world for Delia Brand, but look at it now! Did you hear what Ed Baker said? Follow the investigation wherever it leads. It's apt to lead him and me straight out of a job before it's over. You say it was Squint Hurley that did it. Maybe. What if it turned out to be Lem Sammis himself?"

The phone buzzed. Tuttle reached for it, spoke into

it briefly, mostly with grunts, shoved it back and got to his feet. "You seem to have company," he observed. "Anyhow, that was Ed Baker, and he wants me to haul in Squint Hurley and have him ready for a talk as soon as he gets through with the Brand girl."

The Sheriff of Silverside County stowed away the packet of fine cut, arose and stretched. "I guess I'll go along."

"If you do you'll keep your mouth shut."

They went out together.

Chapter 10

Wynne Cowles, with a heavy automatic pistol in her hand, sat on a rock, peering intently around the edge of an enormous boulder which was perched on the rim of a narrow canyon. The pistol, rock, boulder and canyon were all her property, all being within the confines of Broken Circle Ranch which she owned. It had been a dude ranch at the time of her first arrival at Cody two years ago and, taking a fancy to it, she had bought it. The energy, acumen, time and money Wynne Cowles had expended on whims might have built a railroad.

Impatience stirred within her. Leaving her ambush behind the boulder, she crept to the edge of the precipice to see if the sheep's carcass was in fact there; and saw it, unmistakably, a grayish blur at the bottom of the canyon. The bait was all right; why didn't they come? She returned to the ambush and resumed her vigil, glancing at her wrist watch and noting that it was nearly five o'clock. She would give them thirty minutes more. But not half that allowance had gone when her keen eyes detected a group of black dots moving far up against the blue sky. She watched them, releasing the safety on the pistol and hugging the boulder. The black dots descended moving in wide graceful circles, then narrowing into spirals of shorter radius, becoming not dots but things with wings—wings that did not flap but only banked and steered. They came lower, centering on a point in the canyon directly beneath her, and now they were huge and she could see the nakedness of their necks and almost the greediness of their sharp glittering eyes. Her own eyes gleamed with distaste; she disliked vultures because they disgusted her. She waited until they got almost to her level, circling into the canyon's mouth, then drew a deep breath, leveled the pistol with nerveless aim and fired. Nothing stopped the bullet. She fired again and one of the vultures, at least a hundred yards away, keeled over, seemed to hang suspended for an instant and then fluttered into the canyon like an enormous black leaf. The wings of the six or eight others were flapping now and they were moving off. She fired four more shots, but the distance was so great that only luck could have guided the pistol bullet to its moving mark. She stepped to the edge of the canyon and saw that one down there, not twenty feet from the carrion, flopping on the rocks like a decapitated chicken.

A voice sounded behind her. "That's too bad, boss. Honest it is. Them turkey buzzards keep a place clean."

She turned and saw a wiry little man with good-humored eyes. "I only got one, Joe. Did you see it go? Riding the air like an eagle and then suddenly losing it, turning loose of its grip on the air. I'm sick of popping gophers because I never miss any more. What are you doing out here?"

"Got a message. Do you know Ed Baker, the county attorney?"

"No. Should I? What about him?"

"He just phoned he wants to see you. At his office in the courthouse any time before midnight, or he says he could drive out here. He said to tell you he's interviewing everybody who talked with Dan Jackson the day he was killed. I told him I'd call him back."

"But I thought—" Wynne Cowles frowned. "Oh, hell. I don't like being interviewed." She returned the pistol to its holster on her belt. "At that, maybe I can get in a lick for that kid. That Brand girl."

"You were going into town for dinner anyway."

"I know it. Come on."

She found her horse in the shade of the towering brown rocks where she had left it. His was there too, and together they rode the mile to the ranch house, past corrals, outbuildings and irrigated fields. The house was low, painted white, had a patio and was surrounded by trees. A tiled veranda was shaded with a bright green awning, and a similar awning covered the entire expanse of a first-class tennis court, near which was a large enclosure containing a dozen pronghorns. On a low forked limb of a tree near the veranda, startlingly life-like, a cougar crouched in readiness to leap, seemingly onto a table below which held a stack of magazines, a bowl of fruit and a carved bishido cigarette box. Broken Circle Ranch was a picturesque and expensive layout, but it was also an efficient going concern; Joe Paltz was the best sheepman in northern Wyoming. Wynne Cowles turned her horse over to him on the path at the corner of the veranda, went to her suite overlooking the patio, removed her clothes and gave her body an approving glance in a Tronville mirror, and stepped into the shower cubicle.

Lem Sammis, at his mahogany desk in his office on the top floor of the new Sammis Building, was saying irritably, "I tell you, Harvey, that don't matter. Dellie Brand is out of it and no thanks to you either. What we've got to do is shut Ed Baker off!"

Harvey Anson offered mildly, "The governor said he'd see him this evening and Ollie Nevins—"

"Phut! Talk! More talk! Have you lost all the sense you ever had?" Sammis hit the desk with his fist. "Do you know what's going on or don't you? That squarehead Carlson has decided to use this for a showdown. Do you understand English? He has picked on this because he thinks he can force it and he knows I've got to fight at a disadvantage. He knows I can only handle it one way on account of Amy. The dirty coward, getting at me through my daughter! He knows me, all right. I won't permit it! I won't have it, right here in my own state, my daughter dragged into a public mess, maybe questioned in a courtroom, about her married life with that polecat! Good God, when I think what I've kept out of courts and newspapers, you tell me I can't keep this out?"

"This is murder, Lem."

"You talk like a Sunday School teacher!"

"No, I don't." Anson spread out his palms. "Now here. The fact that it's murder and the people want it gives Carlson a chance to put pressure on Baker to see that they get it. Everybody in this county has heard talk about Jackson and various women, and here is their chance to get the details, and they want them. His wife being your daughter doesn't make them any less eager, either. Baker can't possibly hush it up. Carlson could run him right out of the state. I stick to my advice: don't try to force Baker to a jump he can't take, or he'll grab the bit in his teeth. He'll have to.

Play with him. Give him all the help he wants in his investigation and tell Amy to do the same, with the understanding that he keeps everything under the lid that he doesn't have to use in court when he gets it lined up. That's another thing, he may never get it. It looks doubtful to me."

"You mean let him pry into my intimate family affairs? My daughter's?"

"I mean let him investigate whatever he wants to, with the understanding—"

"I won't do it! That little squirt that used to bellyache around for a hundred dollar fee!"

"Have it your way, Lem." Anson shrugged. "I know you're bullheaded, but I've seen you pull in your horns when you had to. I've seen you throw in many a bum hand. Why are you playing this one up against your chin? Maybe my advice is no good, but if so it's only because I don't know all the facts, and I'm beginning to suspect that's the case."

"You know all the facts I do. Somebody went to Dan's office at night and shot him and killed him. That's all I know."

"All right. But see here, Lem, maybe your judgment is bad because it touches Amy so close. Maybe your head isn't quite as cool as it ought to be, whereas mine is. I'm for you, you know that, but I can't give you good advice unless you give me good information. If you know some little fact that I don't, it would be a lot better if you'd tell me. Otherwise I don't quite understand why you don't see that the way I suggest is the best way to handle it."

"I don't know anything you don't know."

Anson shrugged again. "All right, Lem."

Delia Brand arose to her feet. Her face did show strain now, much more than it had two hours previously, when she had been conducted by the sheriff to his office, to find a crowd there to welcome her. The county attorney's questioning had been courteous enough, but it had been thorough. She asked, "Is that all?"

"Not quite."

"I—I'm pretty tired."

"I know you are." Baker screwed up his lips, regarding her. "You remember that I told you downstairs that your being released now doesn't prohibit a future charge against you in case new evidence warrants it. I want to be sure you understand your position clearly, especially since you submitted to this questioning freely, with no lawyer present."

"But there can't be any charge! There can't be any evidence—"

"Yes, there can. That's what I want to make clear to you. At this moment I don't believe you shot Jackson, but somebody did, and with a gun you had been carrying around in your bag. The gun had left your possession, I admit that as established, but it is possible that you had recovered it. Nothing is known—"

"But I couldn't! I've told you! I went straight from Jackson's office to the Cockatoo Ranch and didn't even miss the bag until I was far away, and from there I went to the cemetery, and then—"

"I know. But there is a peculiar fact about the bag being taken from Pellett, your uncle, when he was knocked down the stairs—the fact being that you are the only living person who was there when it happened. I don't say that I am accusing you of hitting him with that piece of ore—"

"You couldn't accuse me of it if you wanted to. I

was sitting in Jackson's office with him when we heard him fall."

"You say you were," Baker said drily. "Jackson is dead."

Delia stared at him with her mouth open.

"Don't misunderstand me," he went on. "I'm not accusing you of hitting your uncle on the head or recovering the bag or anything else, I'm just making your position clear to you. Pellett walked up those stairs carrying the bag with the gun in it, and from the moment he got knocked on the head I have no idea what happened to the bag or who got it. You might have got it as easily as anyone else—in fact easier, since you were there on the spot. Nor have you been entirely frank and open with me. You refused to explain your statement to the clerk at MacGregor's, and the question you had written down to ask Tyler Dillon, by telling me about Rufus Toale as you could have done, and I learned that, and could ask you about it, only because the sheriff phoned up to tell me about Toale's visit to him this afternoon. Not only that, but there is the matter of Amy Jackson driving into her yard Tuesday night just as you were going up the path."

"What do you mean?" Delia looked puzzled. "I told you about that."

"About her driving in, yes. But you didn't say anything about her father being in the car with her."

"But I—but he wasn't! He was out at Cockatoo Ranch!"

"What makes you so sure he wasn't? It was dark, wasn't it?"

"Of course it was." Delia frowned at him. "It seems to me like you're contradicting yourself. First you say I'm not being frank because I didn't tell you Mr. Sam-

mis was in her car with her and then you say I couldn't
tell whether he was there or not because it was dark.
Anyway, I *have* been frank. I've told you everything I
know that could be connected with Dan Jackson. I've
told you that I never liked him and I didn't know him
very well even when Dad was alive and they were
partners."

Baker leaned back in his chair, gazing at her. She
stood, waiting, and finally asked, "Is that all?"

"I guess it is. For now."

"Then I want—may I have my handbag, please?"

"No, you can't. It's locked up. It's evidence."

"I don't mean the gun. Just the bag."

He shook his head. "It was there on the desk and
you say you didn't take it there. It's important evidence."

Her lip quivered; she controlled it. "There's a picture of my mother and father in it. May I have that?"

"I'm sorry. The bag and its contents will be kept
intact. You'll get it back when—when the time comes."

"Thank you," she said, and turned and walked out
of the room.

She had already decided what she was going to do
next, but there was a little delay in her plans. Though
it was close to six o'clock, the anteroom of the county
attorney's office was far from empty. Four men, one in
the uniform of a state trooper, sat in a corner talking in
subdued tones. Another group of three men sat against
the wall: Bill Tuttle and Ken Chambers, and between
them the roughly dressed man with a weathered face
and nearly white hair whom Delia had last seen Tuesday night when, with a warm gun in her hand, she had
turned at the sound of a voice. Her glance had encom-
passed those two groups when she was attacked from
two directions. A pair came trotting at her, one with a

noisy vocal barrage and the other aiming a camera; and simultaneously, from the other side, her name was called and she saw Clara, Ty Dillon and her Uncle Quin. Dillon, on the run, swerved to intercept the reporters, with Pellett supporting, while Clara seized Delia's arm and hustled her to the door and through it.

"But Sis—why—you shouldn't have waited all this time—"

"There's a mob out front, Del—it's awful—come this way—"

They made it to the back stairs and clattered down, and near the bottom were overtaken by Dillon and Pellett, panting. In the basement they took a narrow side hall and came to a back door, closed, with a man standing there. Dillon handed the man something, and the door opened and they passed through. The large paved court where parking was reserved for officials' and employees' cars was almost deserted and they hurried across it to a maroon sedan which Delia recognized as Dillon's.

He told her, "Pile in!"

Delia balked, shaking her head. "I'm not going home."

They stared at her.

"I mean not now. Not first. First I'm going to see Doctor Toale."

"Holy smoke!" said Uncle Quin. "Listen to her!"

"You're not going to walk, are you?" Ty demanded. "Pile in anyway!"

They all climbed in, Ty taking the wheel. The engine roared and the car leaped forward, circled careening, and scooted for the gap leading to the street. Delia caught a glimpse of many faces as they swept by. She demanded of Clara's ear, "But why a mob? Not after me!"

"Sure they are." Clara squeezed her arm. "They want to give you three cheers and carry you home on their shoulders. The radio said you were being questioned as a witness and would soon be released. What's this about going to see Doctor Toale?"

"I'm going, that's all."

Clara opened her mouth to reply, but the car careened again, turning a corner, and she grabbed for the strap; and then, apparently, thought better of it. Three minutes later the car rolled to a stop at the curb, under a tree on River Avenue, and Ty Dillon, behind the wheel, twisted himself around to face the back seat.

"Now," he said, with a challenge in his tone. "The place for you is home. I thought you said you had been doing some thinking the past two days?"

"I have, Ty." Delia didn't quicken to the challenge. "Of course the place for me is home. But first I'm going to see Doctor Toale."

Pellett demanded, "What for?"

"Not for anything foolish, Uncle Quin. I know you all think I'm a fool. I've been locked up in a jail, and you think as soon as I get out I want to do something mysterious and dramatic, but I don't, I swear I don't. What I'm going to do is quite simple and straightforward. You can drive me home and I'll take my car—where is my car? I left it on Halley Street."

"It's home in the garage," said Clara. "Frank Phelan had it brought around yesterday."

"Then if you'll drive me home I'll take it—"

"Nothing doing," Ty declared shortly. "If nothing else, with that open car you'll collect a crowd wherever you go. Damn it, you're a sensation! The whole town thinks you shot Jackson and you've been turned loose through Sammis's influence. I'm telling you, you ought to go home and lock the door. What do you want to see Toale for?"

Delia shook her head. "I've changed, Ty." She frowned into his eyes. "Really I have. But before I go into that house again that was Dad's house, where my mother died, I'm going to do something and I know what it is, and it's all right."

He looked at her. "Okay." He twisted under the wheel. "We'll drive you there and we'll wait out front."

The comfortable and attractive parsonage occupied by the Reverend Rufus Toale, widower, was at the rear of the church, on Maltbie Street. The table on which he ate his modest evening meal, when he had no guest, was in the bay window of the sitting room, which he preferred to the dining room at that time of day because it was cooler, and because from his chair there he could see the tinted enlarged photograph of his deceased wife hanging on the wall. He was gnawing fragments from a lamb chop bone when his house-keeper entered to announce that Miss Delia Brand wished to see him.

"Who, Mrs. Bonner? Are you sure?"

"I am, sir."

"Praise God! Seat her in the library." He slowly and methodically wiped his fingers on his napkin, his lips moving in silent prayer, took a drink of water, arose and buttoned his coat, and went to the library, a smaller room across the hall.

Delia was standing up with her eyes fixed on the door, awaiting his entrance.

He stopped three paces short of her. "Sit down, my child."

She shook her head, swallowed, and said nothing.

She swallowed again and said, "I just came to tell you something."

"But you can tell me sitting. Guests and friends who talk, children of God—"

"I'm not a guest or a friend, Doctor Toale. I'm not a child of God either—not your God—"

"My poor child, you are overwrought with this ordeal—"

She blurted, "You told Sheriff Tuttle today that it was you I wanted to kill."

"So I did. I had tried to see you—"

"You were right." She stood with her back straight, her arms straight at her sides. "I did want to kill you. I even thought I was going to kill you. I decided to. But I've been seeing into parts of me that I never saw into before and I don't think I would ever have done it. I think I was hysterical. I think I was a false alarm and a four-flusher. Anyway, that is all past and everything that is gone is past. I want to tell you that I know you killed my mother, I don't know how or why, but I know you did, and that's all I want to say. And I don't care whether you are punished or not, because when I was lying there on a cot I was looking at Mrs. Welch and thinking about it—and something she said to me—about evil and wickedness and mercy. I couldn't ask for mercy for you, even if there was anybody to ask, but I'm not going to be a faker and a four-flusher any more and try to pretend that I—that I—"

She faltered. Her lips were working but not saying anything, and she couldn't stop them.

The Reverend Rufus Toale stepped forward with a hand outstretched. "My poor child! God bless you—"

"Don't you dare to touch me!" she gasped, and turned and fled from the house.

He stood in the hall five minutes, his lips moving

silently, looking at the front door she had left open. Then he went and closed the door, returned to the table in the bay window of the sitting room, glanced up at the tinted picture of his wife and, glancing down, saw that the other lamb chop was cold and greasy.

Chapter 11

County Attorney Ed Baker was laying down the law to two of the three men who were seated in his office with him. "You can either keep your mouth shut, Chambers, or get out. I didn't send for Hurley in order to badger him, but to get information from him. You keep out of it unless you get an invitation. Understand?"

The Sheriff of Silverside County allowed grudgingly, "I guess I do."

"Okay—and you, Hurley, if you find it painful to have any contact with Sheriff Chambers—"

"It makes me puke just to look at him."

"Then keep your head this way and you won't see him. I'm letting him stay because it will save time if I want to ask him something. As I told you, the first thing I want to know is exactly what happened Tuesday evening. I know you've told it before, but it's a different setup now. It's not as simple as I thought it was. Now go ahead and don't leave anything out."

Squint Hurley looked out of place, and he looked as if he felt out of place, sitting on a chair in an office. He looked too big for one thing, and those physical characteristics which made him a homogenous part of the landscape on a sagebrush flat or the rocky chaos of the dry sun-baked hills rendered him, in these ordered surroundings, almost grotesque. He muttered, "I ain't talking to Ken Chambers. That pile of dried-up guts. That's understood. If he starts asking me anything—"

"He won't. You're talking to me."

"All right. I'm not a good talker, because out in the hills I get talking to myself. I've been doing that for forty years and it's not the same thing. It's a different kind of talk." He raised a horny old hand, with one finger gone, to chase a fly from his ear. "But you want me to say what happened Tuesday night. The first thing happened Tuesday night, I was the biggest goddamn jackass I've been since 1898 when I went to Cuba. I had two hundred and ninety-one dollars, enough to last in the hills to the other end of luck. Slim Fraser says come along to a joint and take a whirl, and I went. First time in thirty-two years. I think it's because I'm just as strong as I ever was but my will power's getting wore out. Anyhow I went, and he took me to that place The Haven—"

"What time was that?"

"That was around eight o'clock. The sun was on a good slant. I played the wheel a while with four-bit chips, mostly nineteens because it was in 1919 that I come on that streak over on the Cheeford range—"

"How long did you stay there?"

"I stayed there too long. I anted right down to my seams. I was only playing little ones, but after two hours, a little more than two hours I guess, I was as dry as last year's skeleton. I didn't come to even then, the fever was up, and I asked Slim for some but he was low too and wouldn't do it, and it came in my head that there was only one man in this town I could prospect and that was Dan Jackson. I knew where he lived and I thought I would walk out there, but when I got on the sidewalk it came in my head that his office was right there and it wouldn't hurt to see if maybe he was around. The door wasn't locked and I went in and up the steps and saw there was a light there and the door was standing open. I went in. I guess I was walking easy because I don't often walk on boards and I don't like the noise my feet make on boards. Anyhow I saw that girl with the popgun in her hand with her back to me, walking over to him hanging over the side of the chair."

"Had you heard a shot as you were going up?"

"No."

"Was there a smell in the room as if the gun had just been fired?"

"There was a little smell. I wouldn't say like the gun had just been fired. I don't know much about things in rooms, smells or anything. I've told you all this before."

"I know you have, but I want it again and more of it."

Baker proceeded to get it. The warmth of the gun, the way Delia was holding it when first seen, the position of the bag on the desk, what Delia had said and how she had acted and looked, the exact position of Jackson's body—those details and many others were thoroughly and monotonously explored.

Finally Baker said, "All right, Hurley, that seems to cover that. Now to go back a little, you say you got to The Haven at eight o'clock?"

"I recollect I said around eight o'clock."

"Were you in The Haven all the time until you left to see Jackson and get money from him?"

"Yes I was. The fever was up."

"Would Slim Fraser or anyone say you were there all the time?"

"I guess he might. I guess the man at the wheel might, he ought to."

"Do you know exactly what time it was when you left?"

"No, I don't. I didn't have any timepiece, and anyhow I didn't care, and anyhow you can tell if you want to because you know when I made that phone call and I left The Haven about four or five minutes before that."

"Sure." Baker eyed the old prospector, not with hostility. "I tell you frankly, Hurley, I don't think you shot Jackson, but everything has to be considered. The doctor got there at 10:35, twenty minutes after you called the station. He said Jackson hadn't been dead more than an hour, and he died as soon as the bullet hit him. So if you can establish that you left The Haven only five minutes before you made the phone call, you're out of it entirely and—"

"Like hell!" It was Ken Chambers exploding. "He could have sneaked—"

Hurley's massive form started to lift from the chair. Baker snapped with ferocity, "Can it! One more yap and out you go!"

"But he could have—"

"I said can it! I know what he could have done as well as you do and probably better." Baker finished his glare before turning back to his witness. "For one thing, Hurley, if I thought it likely that you shot Jackson, I'd have to find out how you got hold of that gun, because it's been proven that it was that gun that fired the bullet. I'm being frank with you because I want you to be frank with me. Now, for instance, what gave you the idea that you could get money from Jackson?"

"It came in my head."

"What put it there?"

"What put it there was that he already gave me some."

"When?"

"That morning. That same day."

"How much?"

"He gave me three hundred dollars."

"What for?"

"For what would anybody suppose? For a stake. He grubbed me."

Ken Chambers got up from his chair, went and stood directly in front of the county attorney, and scowled down at him. "I'm not talking to him," he said, "I'm talking to you. Do you want me to whisper in your ear, goddamn it? What he says couldn't be true, and I know it couldn't be. For the past year and a half, since that pie-eyed jury turned him loose, he never got a cent from Dan Jackson. Jackson wouldn't have anything to do with him. I tell you I know every move he's made—"

"Go back and sit down. Much obliged." Baker lifted his brows at the prospector. "Well? Do you want me to repeat—"

"I heard him." Hurley's squint, as he returned Baker's gaze, became so pronounced that his eyes were all but buried. "And now I guess I'll tell you something. I'll tell you and Ken Chambers will hear it, and that would make a coyote laugh. That's right that Jackson wouldn't stake me after I got out of jail over in Silverside County. I always suspected Ken Chambers set him against me and I still do. I damn near ate my boots. Finally Bert Doyle down at Sheridan gave me a stake, but I didn't have any luck and when that was used up it looked bad. I tried around, but when it seemed like I would have to sell my tools or go on relief, and I didn't like one idea any better than the other, I worked up a plan. I got a lift to Cody, and Tuesday morning I went to the office and said to him, look here—"

"To who, Jackson?"

"Yes. I said, two years ago I was down in the Silverside Hills on Charlie Brand's stake and I got word to meet him at the canyon cabin on a certain day, and I got held up by a bad leg and got there a good many hours late, and when I got there he was laying on the cabin floor dead with a bullet through his heart. Now, I said, Ken Chambers, the sheriff down there, hates me because I testified against him once on a claim—"

"That's a damn lie! I never carried—"

"Shut up, Chambers. Go on, Hurley."

"I said, he hates me and he carries a grudge, and as far as that goes it wouldn't surprise me any if it was him that shot Charlie Brand himself. Anyway, I would as soon've shot my own eye out as shoot Charlie Brand, and I've only got a rifle and never a popgun which is what he was shot with, and anyway whoever shot him took thirty-two thousand dollars from him and where is it? But, I said, in spite of that Ken Chambers arrested me the first thing and kept me in the coop, and him and that knock-kneed wart of a lawyer tried to convict me. And to make it short, I said, one result of the way they acted was that I hung onto a piece of paper that I found under Charlie Brand's body that day when I turned him over, and I never said anything about it and this is the first time I've mentioned it. And I mention it to you now because Charlie Brand was your partner and I know you'd like to know who killed him, and it might help if you had that piece of paper because it has writing on it, so I—"

"You dirty rat! Or else you dirty liar! I don't believe—"

Baker said sharply, "Haul him back, Bill! No, hustle him out! Go on, out with him!"

From the standpoint of the majesty of the law it was a deplorable sight, one sheriff giving another sheriff the bum's rush; or, rather, starting to, for Chambers jerked away from Tuttle's grasp and stood panting with indignation. He growled, "You can't expect—"

"On out, Chambers. I mean it."

"But did you hear—?"

"I say beat it! Didn't I tell you to keep your trap shut? On out!"

Bill Tuttle made a move. Chambers backed up a step with an inarticulate growl, wheeled, and tramped to the door, which he pulled to with a shattering bang as he disappeared. Tuttle went back to his chair and sat down. Squint Hurley said in an uncommunicative mumble, "By all hell, some day I'll take my rifle and put a peephole in his belly." Then he glanced as in startled surprise from Tuttle to Baker and said in apologetic explanation, "Excuse me, I was talking to myself."

"All right, Hurley. You were telling Jackson about a piece of paper with writing on it which you found under Charlie Brand's body. Why had you kept it for two years without mentioning it to anyone?"

"Because I saw it wouldn't do any good. Was I going to show it to Ken Chambers and let him take it away from me when he had me in jail and keeping me there was all he wanted?"

"Didn't he search you?"

"I had it put away."

"Where? Under a rock somewhere? Why?"

"I said I had it put away." Hurley's squint buried

his eyes. "Listen. Don't waste time trying to jump me. I'm telling you exactly how it was because for one thing I'm glad of a chance to and for another thing I've got to have a friend somewhere. I've got to get away from all these crowds that keep bumping into you and all these damn buildings and this damn grass they keep watering all the time. I'm going to die if I don't get back where I belong. I know you won't let me go till this thing's finished because you said so, and anyhow maybe you know someone that might stake me, or maybe you might. I had that piece of paper in my boot lining. I didn't show it to Ken Chambers or that lawyer that was working with him because they would only of tore it up. After I was let loose I thought I might show it to Jackson who was Charlie's partner, but he wouldn't even talk to me. I thought I might even show it to Lem Sammis, but he had me kicked out. Ken Chambers was back of all that. So I just kept it, until finally it got to the place where I would have to sell my tools, and then I decided to try Jackson again, and that's what I did Tuesday morning."

"Did you show the paper to Jackson?"

"That's what I went there for. I showed it to him and gave it to him. I told him all about it and about Ken Chambers having that old grudge and how I felt about Charlie, and I said for instance where in the holes of hell have I cached the thirty-two thousand dollars? Am I saving it till they bury me and I go there? So I gave him the paper and he believed me and he staked me. Three hundred dollars. I was going down on the Cheeford range again, and then like a goddamn jackass I let Slim Fraser—"

"It was the money Jackson gave you that you lost at The Haven?"

"Yes it was."

"Was anybody there when he gave it to you?"

"There was that girl, Charlie Brand's girl, in the other room. The door was shut, but he called her in and gave her a receipt I signed."

Bill Tuttle put in, "Could she have heard your talk with Jackson?"

"I don't think so, not through the door, and her running that printing machine that I could hear."

"Printing—?"

"Typewriter," said Baker. "Now, Hurley, that piece of paper. Was it a single sheet of paper?"

The old prospector made no reply.

"Well, was it?"

Still no reply.

"What the hell's the matter with you?"

"Nothing really the matter." Hurley looked at Tuttle and back at the county attorney. "You see, I'm not so young maybe, but I'm as strong as I ever was and I'm an old hand and my eyes is good. You didn't exactly reply to what I said about you might know someone who would stake me or maybe you might do it yourself."

"I'm not in the grubstaking business. What has that got to do with that paper?"

Hurley only squinted at him.

Baker glowered at the squint. "Are you trying to extort a promise that I'll see that you get staked?"

"I wouldn't try any extorting, no, sir. But a man naturally considers this and that. It came in my head that Jackson was killed pretty soon after I gave him that paper, and maybe there was a hitch-up, and maybe the news about the paper would help you about who killed Jackson, and maybe you'd be glad enough to get it so that you'd be willing to risk a little—not that there's any risk to speak of, because I know that Cheeford range and I know a certain tumble back—"

"Can it!" Baker leaned forward for emphasis. "Listen to me. You removed evidence from the scene of a crime and concealed it. How would you like to be turned over to your friend Chambers and let him work on that? As for your getting staked, that's your problem. The county will see that you don't starve as long as you're held in Cody. I won't lock you up, at least not now. Provided. I want to know about that paper."

"I won't live much longer if I'm locked up again. I couldn't breathe."

"Then don't get locked up. Was it a single sheet of paper?"

"It was a piece about as big as my hand, folded up so it was maybe three inches square."

"What color was it?"

"White."

"Was the writing on it in ink or pencil?"

"It was black ink."

"What did the writing say?"

"I don't know."

"Do you mean to say you kept it two years and never read it?"

"Well, naturally I looked at it, but I never read it because I can't read."

Baker stared. "Hurley, you're lying."

"No, I ain't. Would I lie to you when you'd lock me up if I did? I can read reading but I can't read writing."

Baker turned to the sheriff. "What about it, Bill? Do you believe it?"

"Search me."

"Go downstairs and use your phone. Get Clara Brand and ask about Hurley's visit to Jackson's office Tuesday morning. All about it. Whether she could hear what they said and about the three hundred dollars, was it entered on the books as a grubstake, and does she know if Hurley can read and write, and did she see any paper that Hurley gave Jackson—wait a minute! I don't like all that on the phone. Just ask her—Let's see, Mrs. Cowles is due at nine. Ask her if she can come here for a talk at ten o'clock. On your way out ask one of the boys to get hold of Quinby Pellett and have him here at eight—and hey! Ask another one, Ray if he's out there, to get me a couple of hamburgers and a pot of coffee."

The sheriff lumbered out. Baker swiveled, leaned back and gazed at Hurley. "So you can't read, huh?"

"Not writing I can't."

"Can you write?"

"I can print pretty good. I never got onto writing."

"Can you write your name?"

"I can sign it. I don't guess you could call it writing it exactly. A man showed me how once."

"You know, Hurley, if you're lying, I can investigate and find it out. But that doesn't help me any right now."

"I don't hardly think it ever would help you much."

Baker sat scowling, rubbing his lip. In a little he resumed. "How much writing was there on the paper? Was it on both sides?"

"Only one side. There wasn't much, maybe five, six words."

"Goddamn it, what did it say?"

Hurley shook his head.

"What did it look like? What was the first letter?"

"I couldn't say the first letter. Maybe I could have told one or two letters if I'd worked at it, but I just knew I couldn't read it, so I didn't use up any time on it. But about what it looked like, I could tell you one thing, it wasn't Charlie Brand that wrote it. Because I've seen him write things, like a receipt for me to sign maybe, and it didn't look like that at all. He wrote sort of a hard trot, sort of up and down, but this was more like . . . like . . ."

"Like what?"

"Well, I would say big and round and heavy. Like what the hell, ink don't cost much. I signed my name once with Charlie Brand's fountain pen and it wrote thin."

"You say you found this paper under his body?"

Hurley nodded. "It was there on the floor under him. When I turned him over there it was. I got a habit of keeping little things I don't want to lose in my boot lining and I tucked it away. Then I lugged him out and tied him across his horse that was outside, and led the horse into Sugarbowl. The first yelp out of Ken Chambers, just to show you, first thing when he got there, he ast didn't I know a dead body shouldn't be moved, and I said sure, what I should've done was come on to Sugarbowl alone and leave him there for the rats and coyotes to play with and then he would've been a pretty looking thing. Next thing I knew—"

"All right, save it. Where was the paper when you saw it last, Tuesday morning?"

"I gave it to Jackson."

"What did he do with it?"

"He stowed it away in a wallet he had in his pocket."

"The same wallet he got the three hundred dollars out of?"

"No, he got the money out of the safe. This was a sort of a brown leather wallet."

"Did he put it back in his pocket after he put the paper in it?"

"Yes, he did."

The county attorney had reached for his phone and now he spoke into it. After a little wait he spoke again and then waited some more. Finally he said, "Mac? This is Ed Baker. They tell me Frank's gone home to supper, and I don't want to disturb him. Maybe you can tell me, did anyone go through Jackson's pockets Tuesday night? You did yourself? Good! Did you find a brown leather wallet? Did you examine its contents? Was there a piece of paper—no, wait a minute, it was a piece of white paper . . ."

Five minutes later he shoved the phone back and stood up. Looking down at Squint Hurley, he said shortly, "It wasn't there."

Hurley made a noise with his tongue. "By all hell, I saw him put it there. Somebody must've took it. Or maybe he shifted it to another pocket—"

"It wasn't on him. It wasn't anywhere. I like your first suggestion better. Somebody must've took it. By God, Hurley, if you're stringing me I'll stake you to something that will make you wish—"

"I ain't stringing you. What I told you is exactly what happened."

"It better had be." Baker strode to the door leading to the anteroom, opened it, looked out, and called, "Come on in here, Clint, and bring Luke!"

Two men entered. When the door was closed behind them Baker said, "This case has been messed up till it stinks and it's only partly my fault. Where the hell are my hamburgers?"

"Ray ought to be back any minute."

"All right. Luke, take a fingerprint kit and go to Jackson's office. You'll find Mac Losey there with a couple of men. Go over the whole place, and while you're doing it find a piece of white paper as big as your hand that has been folded double. It has writing in black ink on one side, five or six words in a round heavy hand. If you find—"

"What does the writing say?"

"I don't know. If you find it don't let Mac have it. Find it and bring it to me and you'll wear diamonds. Clint, go to the Jackson house on Blacktail Avenue and see Mrs. Jackson. The stuff that was found in Jackson's pockets was given to her, and among it was a brown leather wallet. Get it. Not the contents necessarily, just the wallet, but the contents too if you can. Use diplomacy or anything you've got. Then go over it for prints and do it good. It's probably hopeless now, but we'll try it anyway. All right, step on it."

The two men asked a couple of questions and departed.

Baker turned. "You can go out and get something to eat, Hurley, and come back around ten-thirty. I may want you again after I see Clara Brand." Something in the old prospector's face or attitude made him add, "How much money have you got?"

"None of your damn business," Hurley growled.

Baker pulled a roll from his pocket and peeled off a bill. "Here, take it. Go ahead and take it! Call it a loan, I'll be glad to get it back. Come back around ten-thirty."

"I don't know as I can stay awake till ten-thirty. You won't need me anyhow, on account of anything Charlie Brand's girl will tell you. If you do, you know where my bunk is."

"Okay. But don't you try any tricks."

"I don't know any," said Squint Hurley as he headed for the door.

Chapter 12

It was nearly nine o'clock that Thursday evening when Quinby Pellett entered the room where the county attorney sat, with the sheriff and the chief of police also present. He had arrived at eight, as requested when the telephone had found him at the Brand home on Vulcan Street, but had been compelled to wait by superior urgencies. The undersized prognathous man who had put in an appearance around seven-thirty, entering Baker's room by the private door to avoid the anteroom, was the governor of the state; and upon his departure by the same route, some twenty minutes later, Baker had let fly with both barrels. He had sent for every good man available on the sheriff's staff as well as his own, with Tuttle acquiescing, and had scattered them on a variety of trails and errands. In the midst of that activity there had been another entry by the private door, leading to a difficult, not to say stormy, quarter of an hour with Ollie Nevins, the largest mine operator in the West. If Nevins had happened to arrive before the governor the story might have been different, but Baker had already made his decision.

When Pellett was ushered in a little before nine

o'clock, Tuttle and Phelan were having what appeared to be a private altercation, since they were muttering it in low tones, and Baker, with his elbows planted on the desk, was resting his forehead in his palms. He raised his head, pressed his finger tips to his eyes, blinked a couple of times and barked, "Sit down, Pellett. What was on that piece of paper that Jackson showed you Tuesday afternoon?"

Pellett's stooped shoulders lifted a little. "Godamighty," he said plaintively, "you starting off like that?"

"I want to know what was on that paper!"

"Well . . . I'd like to know myself."

"Didn't he show it to you?"

Pellett compressed his lips; and then let his shoulders drop, apparently, deciding to be patient. "I told Bill Tuttle all about it yesterday. Didn't he tell you?"

"He told me you had just been knocked out by somebody when you were talking with Jackson and you couldn't remember much. But he showed it to you, didn't he? What did it look like?"

"It looked like a piece of white paper, not a big piece. I was still in a daze and couldn't hardly sit up. But I remember one thing all right, and that ought to be enough for you. He told me that he got it from Squint Hurley that morning. It was Hurley that—"

"I know. Much obliged. Did you take the paper in your hand?"

"I don't think I did. I'm sure I didn't. I was using my hands to hold my head up. He saw I was no good and he took me down and drove me home. That was after I realized the bag was gone—my niece's handbag that I had."

"Was there writing on the paper?"

"I didn't see any, but I didn't really look. But there

must have been, because he had told me on the phone that what was on it didn't mean anything to him and that was one reason he wanted me to come and look at it, to see if it meant anything to me."

"Didn't he tell you on the phone what was on it?"

Pellett regarded him a moment, then said quietly, "It strikes me you're acting pretty damn foolish. Even making all allowances. If you just want to find out what was on that paper, all you have to do is ask Squint Hurley; he gave it to Jackson. But I notice you seem to be wanting to ride me, and another thing I notice is that you don't seem to have the paper or you wouldn't have to ask Hurley or me either. Is the paper gone?"

"I don't know. I haven't got it. Have you?"

"That's more like it." Pellett nodded approvingly. "I like a straight question. I haven't got it. If there was any good reason for me to lie to you about it I guess I would all right, but there isn't. I didn't see what the writing was and Dan didn't tell me on the phone. There in his office I didn't see the writing, except maybe so hazy that I don't remember it, and he didn't hand me the paper and I didn't take it away, which is what I suppose you had in mind. Is it gone?"

"It hasn't been found." Baker was frowning at him. "Why did he want to show it to you? Why did he want to consult you about it?"

"I suppose because he knew I'd be interested and I might be able to help. He knew that the detectives my sister had hired for over a year had reported to me as much as to her. He knew that I never had believed Squint Hurley had killed Charlie."

"Why hadn't you?"

"Well, besides the evidence about the bullet, I knew Squint and the kind of man he was. I had been getting specimens from him for years—coyotes and pronghorns and other things. I knew him."

"Can he read?"

"What? Read? Certainly he can read."

"How do you know he can?"

"I've seen him. I've been with him in the hills, getting hides and showing him how to handle them. I've given him old magazines and things—"

"Can he read writing?"

"Writing I couldn't say." Pellett screwed up his lips, considering. "I don't know that I ever saw him read writing. But I should—Oh, I see! That's it! He can't tell you what was on that paper because he couldn't read it? Godamighty!"

"So he says. So you never thought Hurley killed Brand?"

"No, I didn't. And I don't."

"Have you any idea who did kill him?"

"No. My sister spent a fortune on high-priced detectives from San Francisco, and they never really started a trail."

"Have you any idea who killed Jackson?"

"Yes. I have."

"You have?"

"Wait a minute." Pellett shook his head. "Not the identity of him. But I said it to Bill Tuttle yesterday, and now that you say that paper can't be found, I say it double. It might have been only coincidence that Dan was killed only a few hours after he got that paper from Squint Hurley, but if the paper's gone it must have been taken from him and that couldn't be coincidence. It's not just guessing, it's a cinch. It was one and the same man that killed Charlie and Dan both. And what hauls me up, it was the same man that cracked me on the skull when I went upstairs there

Tuesday afternoon. That's when he got the bag with the gun in it. I've wished to God fifty times I'd let that bum walk off with that bag. Then at least Delia—my niece wouldn't have been mixed in it." Pellett's lips tightened, and his shoulders sagged more than ordinarily.

Baker eyed him and said, "There are objections to that theory."

"I know it. I've thought about it. Why did he want to use that particular gun so bad that he knocked me out in order to get it? And how did he know I had it— did he see me taking it from the bum that stole it? Or say he wasn't after the gun at all, but after he knocked me downstairs he saw the bag and felt what was in it and that gave him the idea of using that gun—in that case, why was he laying for me? What did he want to ambush me for? He couldn't have mistaken me for Jackson, even up there in the dark, because he must have known Dan was there in his office. Another thing, if he wanted that paper so bad he killed Dan to get it, why hadn't he got it by killing Hurley, or not necessarily killing him even, long before? Sure, I know there's objections, but when there's no objections to a theory it stops being a theory. That's your job, to clear them up."

Baker grunted. "I was going to ask you about that blow you got on the head. You have no idea who did it, huh?"

"If I did—" Pellett's lips tightened again. He said shortly, "I haven't."

"You didn't hear anything or catch a glimpse of anyone?"

"All I caught was a piece of that ore right here." Pellett touched the bandage on the side of his head.

"Anyway Dan and the doctor said it was a piece of ore."

"And you think it was the murderer of both Brand and Jackson who did it."

"I do. Also I think you might be a lot further along than you are now if you hadn't lost two whole days taking it for granted—with my niece locked in a cell charged with murder—"

"Under the circumstances anyone would have taken it for granted. Her bag on the desk, her gun in her hand—"

"You learned about the bag being stolen yesterday noon, nearly thirty-six hours ago."

"We learned it from you. Her uncle. Without corroboration." The county attorney gestured. "But I admit it was unfortunate and God knows I admit we've lost time. I'm much obliged for your theory and we'll work on it along with others. Regarding one of the others, I'd like to ask you a question. I'd rather ask you than anybody else, and I expect you'd rather have me. It was generally known around here that before she married Dan Jackson Amy Sammis was—well, she had a good opinion of Charlie Brand. That was common knowledge. But Charlie married your sister. I was just a kid in school then. Now around three years ago there was talk. You must have heard it. It concerned Charlie Brand and Amy Jackson—God knows no one could have blamed Amy, the deal she was getting from Dan. What about it? What was there to it?"

"I don't know," Pellett muttered.

Baker appealed to him: "Charlie's dead. Your sister's dead. Amy's life is ruined anyhow. They can't be hurt any more, Pellett. If anyone can answer that question, you can. I don't mean the talk, I mean the facts."

"No." Pellett shook his head. "I don't know any facts. If I did know any I'd bury them. If there were any, there's no place you can get them, thank God. My sister is dead but her memory is not and her children are not. No. No!"

"You want this murder solved, don't you?"

"That wouldn't solve it."

"You don't know whether it would or not. Your own theory may be right and it may be wrong. I have no intention and no desire—"

There was a knock on the door which led to the anteroom. Baker said come in. It opened and a man entered and closed it behind him.

"Well?"

"Mrs. Cowles says her appointment was for nine o'clock and it's half past and she's leaving in one minute."

Pellett arose. Baker said, "I want to talk with you some more."

"Not about . . ."

"All right. About various things. About your theory. Can you be here at eight in the morning?"

"I'll be here." As he went out, Pellett's stooping shoulders were a load on his spine.

"Bring her along," Baker told the man.

Frank Phelan said, "Quin Pellett's right. As sure as God made little apples."

Bill Tuttle said, "You'd better get transferred to Silverside County. It was a woman that killed Jackson and I've got—"

Ed Baker said, "Can it."

Wynne Cowles was dressed up. In her suite at the Fowler she had a wardrobe which would have been adequate for any of the capitals of gaiety on either side of the Atlantic and, since her own opinion of her appearance was the only one she cared much about, she attended to it in Cody much as she would have done in Juan-les-Pins or White Sulphur. She looked as out of place in that courthouse office as had Squint Hurley, but not at all as if she felt out of place. As she dropped into the chair indicated by Baker, she let her shimmering yellow wrap fall from her shoulders and drape itself on the chair's back; and the three men, sitting down again, evidently found it necessary to study her. At night her pupils were elliptical only in a bright light or when contracted by an impulse from within. They were so now. She directed them at Ed Baker and told him energetically, "You got me here by a trick."

"On the contrary, Mrs. Cowles, I—"

"Yes you did, though perhaps you didn't know it. I agreed to come only because I thought I might get a shot in for the Brand girl, and as soon as I get to town I learn that you've set her free and she's all cleared up. I came anyway because I had said I would." She glanced at a circlet of emeralds on her wrist. "We start dancing over at Randall's at ten o'clock, so if I'm suspected of shooting Dan Jackson you only have a little over twenty minutes to make me confess." She turned abruptly to Bill Tuttle: "Yes, I have very nice arms and I'm glad you admire them."

Baker said with creditable aplomb, "I'll be as brief as I can, Mrs. Cowles, and we'll postpone your confession till tomorrow. All I know is that you were having an argument with Jackson in his office when Delia Brand got there Tuesday afternoon around four o'clock. Is that right?"

She shrugged the admired shoulders. "Call it an argument. I went there to make a face at him."

"Did he threaten to run you out of the state?"

She smiled. "I believe he actually did."

"Did he yell at you to keep your hands off of him?"

She frowned; her face was always doing something. "That doesn't sound likely. I don't try pawing and clawing very often. Of course you got this from Delia Brand, and she looks as if she might have some imagination—Oh! That must be it. He was telling me to keep my hands off of the grubstaking business and especially he didn't want me—but I guess that's confidential."

"Is that what the argument was about, the grubstaking business?"

"Yes." She twisted her lips into a little grimace. "Are you thinking of the dear dead past, Mr. Baker? I'll tell you about that. When I was in Cody two years ago I heard about grubstaking and it sounded fascinating—having men working for you, partners, dozens and scores of them, out in these old hills, looking for gold and silver in the rocks—and other things. I decided to take a hand in it, I like to take a hand in things, and I was told that Charlie Brand knew more about it than all the others put together, so I went after him. Without shame, you know? We all try whatever keys we have on a door we want to get through. But my keys didn't fit with him. He was worse than contrary, he was absolutely deaf and blind. I was about to give him up when the news came that he had been found murdered. That shocked me naturally, but I was still fascinated by the idea of grubstaking and it seemed that Charlie Brand's partner would be the best place to get the necessary information. I like to do things, but I like to know what I'm doing and do them right. So Dan Jackson and I became quite friendly. It worked out very well, until he learned that I had opened a little office and hired Paul Emery and had started grubstaking on my own. Naturally I wanted the best prospectors available and the information I had got from him was quite valuable. Also that old orangutan that thinks he owns from the Rockies to the Sierras, Lem Sammis—he was foaming at the mouth. I said it's a free country and went ahead. Then I left and Paul Emery was supposed to keep it going, but he's not much good. When I came back a couple of weeks ago I looked into it and decided it was still worth trying. I was in Jackson's office Tuesday afternoon having a talk with Clara Brand when Dan came in, and he promptly hit the ceiling. Clara left to keep an appointment and I stayed to quiet Dan down, because I would always rather have a friend than an enemy provided the cost is the same, but I didn't get very far because we were interrupted by Delia Brand coming in. It wasn't any fun anyway, so I left." Wynne Cowles lifted a hand to catch, over her shoulder, a corner of her yellow wrap. "There. All right?"

"Sure it's all right." Baker was looking, apparently, at the dazzle of the emeralds. "If you don't mind—when you left Jackson's office, did you see anything in the upstairs hall?"

"See anything?" She frowned.

"Did you see anybody?"

"In the hall? No."

"Or on the stairs or the lower hall?"

"No."

"As soon as you left the office, did you go right down the stairs and out to the street?"

"Naturally, I did."

"You didn't, for instance, go to that old bin against the wall to get a souvenir?"

She stared. "I haven't the faintest idea what you're talking about. I didn't know there was a bin. That hall is so dark you have to feel for the stairs with your foot."

"You didn't know there was a bin there containing pieces of ore?"

"Good heavens, no. Is it worth prospecting?"

Bill Tuttle cackled. Baker shot him a glance of disapproval and went on, "I asked if you saw anyone in the hall because shortly after you left a man went up those stairs and when he got to the top he was hit on the head with a piece of that ore and knocked unconscious."

She smiled. "I didn't do it. Honest. Who got hit?"

"A man named Quinby Pellett. The Brand girls' uncle. Do you know him?"

"No, I never—Oh, yes I do, too! Pellett the taxidermist?"

"That's him."

"Yes, I've met him. He looks as if he'd just eaten something sour and his hair needs washing. Since he knows how to handle animals' hair so beautifully, you'd think he'd take better care of his own. Was he badly hurt?"

"Not much. He's all right." Baker glanced at the clock on the wall; he, too, felt that he would just as soon have a friend as an enemy, especially since his scene with Ollie Nevins. "Just another question or two, Mrs. Cowles, please. Was your argument with Jackson exclusively about the grubstaking business?"

"Yes. The time's up, you know."

"I know it is. You said that Jackson was telling you to keep your hands off of the grubstaking business, and especially he didn't want you—and then you stopped and said that was confidential."

She nodded. "That was also about the grubstaking business and it concerned a third person."

"Who?"

"No." She smiled. "It couldn't possibly help you any."

"All right, I'll take your word for it, for the present anyhow." Baker returned the smile. "Now you know I'm investigating a murder. The last two questions are out of stock and you probably know what they are before I ask them. Where were you Tuesday evening between nine and ten o'clock?"

She made a face at him. "The answer's out of stock too. I was at the scene of the crime."

He opened his eyes at her. "You were at Jackson's office Tuesday evening?"

"No, not at his office, but at that address. Under the same roof. I was at The Haven and I won a thousand dollars."

"Anyone with you?"

"Several people. We went over from the Fowler around . . . oh, a little after nine, and it was close to midnight when we left. If you want, I'll send you a list of the names." She got up, and Phelan and the sheriff bumped into each other on their way to manipulate the wrap for her. "No, thanks. I—thank you so much. I'm sorry, Mr. Baker, but you kept me waiting half an hour, you know." She fastened the wrap at her throat, in readiness for the chill evening outside. "You said two last questions. Is there another?"

"The other out of stock," said Baker, standing. "Have you any idea whatever of who killed Jackson, or why?"

"And the other answer also out of stock." She smiled at him. "Not the slightest, and if I did have I wouldn't tell you. Good night."

Tuttle, beaten to the wrap, had made a flanking movement to the door and now opened it. She passed through with a nod of thanks and he closed it. Then he returned to his chair and sat down, heaved a sigh, and told his companions in a tone of deep conviction:

"If that woman wanted to she would kill a man and eat the giblets for breakfast."

Frank Phelan shook his head emphatically. "Surface tough," he pronounced. "You just don't understand the type, Bill. Look how she treats the boys out at Broken Circle. When Larry Rutherford broke his leg—"

"Shut up, please," from Baker, stopped them. He was busy at the phone. In a moment the door opened, a man entered, and Baker said, "Send Miss Brand in."

"She's not here."

"She hasn't shown up?"

"No, sir. At ten o'clock I phoned to see if she had left, and her sister said she had been gone twenty minutes. Now it's ten after, but she's not here."

Baker frowned. "Hell, it would take her only five minutes. Maybe she stopped on the way. Is Clint back yet? Send him in."

The talk with Clint was brief. Amy Jackson had refused not only to give him the wallet, but even to show it to him. She seemed, he said, to be either peeved or scared, or maybe both. Baker sent for others from the anteroom, got reports, and gave orders. The microscope stated that the cartridges in the gun, including the one that had been fired, were of a different make from those Delia Brand had purchased at MacGregor's. A man with a swollen jaw reported that an attempted finesse to get a sample fingerprint of Lem Sammis had ended disastrously. Luke arrived with the information that no one could tell whether the missing paper was in Jackson's office or not, because Judge Hamilton refused to give a court order to open the safe and Judge Merriam could not be located; they had got a magnificent crop of fingerprints and would appreciate a suggestion what to do with them.

At a quarter to eleven Baker went to the anteroom and scowled around. "Miss Brand not here yet?"

"Not a hide or hair of her."

"It's been over an hour since she left home." The county attorney heaved a weary sigh. "Phone the house again and let me talk to whoever's there."

Chapter 13

The Brand girls, their Uncle Quin, and Tyler Dillon ate ham and cheese sandwiches, raspberries and cookies, and coffee, at the breakfast nook in the Brand kitchen. The recital to Delia of the details of the discovery of the cartridges, by Clara and Ty, and of the saga of the stolen bag, by Pellett, was punctuated by frequent interruptions. Reporters were repulsed at the threshold by Ty Dillon. Friends and acquaintances calling with congratulations on their tongues and hungry curiosity in their eyes were told by one or the other of the men, also at the threshold, that Clara and Delia were exhausted and required seclusion and rest. Inquiries on the telephone got the same polite answer, except the call from the county attorney's office requesting the presence of Pellett at eight o'clock and Clara at ten. There was some discussion as to whether Clara should decline the invitation, but she insisted that she would prefer to go and get it over with.

A little before eight Pellett departed. The trio had another round of coffee, and when the cups were empty Clara dragged herself up and began to collect the dishes.

Ty arose, took them from her, and declared, "You

girls are both dead on your feet. Del, you go up and go to bed, and Clara, you go in front and lie down for an hour. I'll clean this up and I'll call you in time to go down to the courthouse if you're still set on it."

He got opposition from both of them. The upshot was that Clara capitulated and was sent off to the couch in the front room, and Delia and Ty together tackled the dishes. For some minutes the only sounds in the kitchen were the clatter of cups and saucers and plates in the sink, the faucet being turned on and off, the opening and closing of cupboard doors. Delia, her shoulders sagging almost as much as her uncle's, washed the things mechanically, anything but *con brio;* Ty moved briskly about, bringing them, wiping them, putting them away. Suddenly he burst forth: "Wiper, a wiper, a dandy dish wiper, I'll mowa da lawn and washa da diper!"

Delia glanced at him and made a feeble effort to produce a smile. He abandoned rhyme and offered further information in prose: "A lawn is clipped greensward surrounding a happy and prosperous home. Diper is a poetic term for diaper, the last word in chic for babies. Babies are what make a home happy and keep it from being prosperous. A home is the abode of a man and woman who are, let us hope, married to each other. What makes this testimony relevant, competent and material is the fact that you and I are going to marry each other."

"My lord, Ty. Please don't. Not now."

He picked up a plate and started the towel around it. "I won't, Del," he assured her. "I mean I won't press it to a conclusion now. As soon as we get the dishes done I'm going to leave you to the seclusion that I've told a hundred people is what you need. But there's one statement that I've got to get off my chest before I leave."

He put the plate away and got another. "You told Harvey Anson today that you wouldn't have him for a lawyer because he had thought you shot Jackson, and not only that, he thought you shot him for intimate personal reasons. You should know, and you have a right to know, that you're going to have for a husband a man who thought the same things—now wait a minute. I'm going on wiping dishes because I want to keep this casual and even flippant. I'm not going to submit a brief on it. I'll only say that under the circumstances as given any man alive who wasn't a brainless boob would have thought the same thing. You know the circumstances as well as I do. I thought you had shot Jackson, and since I couldn't suppose you were flighty enough to kill a man because he had fired your sister from her job, and there was no other apparent motive, the rest was inevitable. What I thought has no importance or significance, not any more. What is important, to me anyhow, is how it made me feel."

"Please, Ty. You don't have to submit a brief. I suppose under the circumstances—"

"Excuse me. It'll soon be over. The dishes, too. I was damn close to a maniac. I wanted to go and pull the jail down with my hands to get you out. I would have done anything, absolutely anything, to get you out. I was in a state that I wouldn't have thought possible. Driving here yesterday morning, coming to see Clara, I asked myself why? In view of Jackson, you know? Chastity and purity? I only realized then what the situation was and must have been before, though I hadn't known it. I had told you I loved you and wanted you to marry me, but that was milk and water stuff. To go on living meant to have you—hell, I don't know how to say it, and anyway, I said I would stay casual. Only I'm yours. For keeps. Statement of relevant fact." He picked up the last plate. "Of course that's only the introduction, but I had to get it off my chest after what you said to Anson today. When the time comes I'll go on from there. Shall I hang this towel back on the rack or what?"

She nodded. "Put it there to dry." She was cleaning the sink.

He propped himself against the table and watched her. As she was wringing out the dishrag he asked, "I don't suppose you've come to any conclusion about me? The last two days? Did you think about me at all?"

She didn't reply till after she had washed her hands and dried them. Then she looked up at him and said, "I thought about everything in the world. About the past and present and future, and my father and mother, and death and life and the things people have done, and things people have said, what they have said to me and where the truth was, and how hard it is to tell whether you're doing what you really want to do. I thought of being locked up forever, and of losing my life, of being executed for murder, and of being set free and what I would do. It wasn't all profound and it wasn't all even thinking. I dramatized that, the being set free. You were in it. You put your arms around me and kissed me and I cried. I mean when I dramatized I cried—I didn't actually cry once. Then when the sheriff took me into that room and they were letting me go I told you to kiss me on the cheek and you didn't do it."

He growled, "The room was full of people."

"It isn't now."

"What—" He gulped. "What are you trying to tell me?"

"Nothing. Only you've accused me of faking scenes so often, you might help me act one of them out."

"If I kiss you, you'll know it."

"Remember you put your arms around me, too."

He did so. Whether in quality the kiss she got was up to the one she had imagined in her cell she alone could tell, but in duration there was surely no question about it. It lasted long enough to wipe a dozen plates if there had been more to wipe. Finally she stirred and he released her.

"Now you go home," she said.

He took a breath, and another. "I'm not going home."

"Yes, you are—"

"I mean I'm going somewhere else. I'm going to see old man Escott." He made a movement. "Could I—?"

"No, Ty. Please. One was all I dramatized."

"I'll phone you in the morning and ask if I can come to see you. Remember you've fired your lawyer."

"I don't need a lawyer any more."

"You need *this* lawyer. Good night, Del."

"Good night, Ty."

They went on tiptoe through the hall because a glance into the front room had shown them Clara on the couch with her eyes closed and breathing deeply. After he had gone Delia went in there quietly and turned out one of the lamps, the one close to the couch. Then she sat on the edge of a chair and gazed at her sleeping sister. It looked wonderful, that deep peaceful sleep. When she herself had slept again like that, and her head was clear and her nerves calmed a little, was she going to be angry at Ty for having thought that of her? She considered it unlikely and that was queer. The things he had said—they were a jumble in her head now—would she be able to remember all of them

tomorrow and the way he had looked? What he had
said about chastity and purity, now, she would never
have believed—

She lifted her head. Damn. Someone on the porch.
Apparently, from the sound, several someones. The
doorbell clanged and Clara stirred, opened her eyes,
and struggled up. "That darned doorbell," Delia said
savagely. "I'll see who it is."

"I guess I must have gone to sleep." Clara was upright. "For heaven's sake don't let them in."

But that, Delia found, was too large an order.
Switching on the porch light, she saw through the
glass that the bell ringer was one from whom no Cody
threshold was barred if he displayed a desire to cross
it. So she opened the door, and Mr. and Mrs. Lemuel
Sammis entered.

Delia got another kiss immediately, this time on the
cheek—really more of a puff than a kiss, for climbing
only the five steps to the porch had been an overdraft
on Evelina's air-conditioning system.

"You look awful, girlie! But here you are! In again,
out again! I remember when that fellow, Marbie or
Marble I think his name was, when he was in the pen
for two years for cheating the Indians, as if anyone
could cheat an Indian, he came out as fat as a pig—
Hello, Clara. What did I tell you? Didn't I say Lem
would have her out of there before night? I admit that
was yesterday, but here she is!"

"Shut up, Eva," her husband snapped. "I had nothing to do with it. Escott's partner and Quin Pellett got
her out. I was afraid you girls might be in bed. Probably you ought to be. We came over from Amy's . . ."

In the front room Delia turned on the lamp by the
couch again and they found seats.

"We won't stay long," said Sammis brusquely. "I

was coming over from Amy's to ask you a couple of things, and Eva had to come along to give Dellie a smack." He reached to pat his wife on the knee with the most predatory hand between Utah and the Sierras. "First you, Clara, what do you want to do about the office?"

"Why . . ." Clara was a little flustered. "I was fired from the office."

"No, you weren't. Didn't Dellie tell you? I had it in mind some time ago to give up grubstaking, but I'd hate to see that old office closed like the one in front. A thing I said to Dellie, I'd like to put you in charge and run the thing if I could think of something else to do with Dan. Well, somebody thought of something and did it. You're a smart girl, but you're a girl and it's not like it was twenty years ago. With mining what it is, do you think there's any chance you could make it pay?"

"Why, I think—" Clara was not at ease. "I think so."

"Say at ninety a week and a third share?"

"I think I could." Clara suddenly straightened, her chin up, with decision. "But I may as well tell you and get it over with. I've about accepted an offer from Wynne Cowles to go into partnership with her."

An ejaculation came from Delia. Sammis glowered.

"You mean that woman with cat eyes? The one that's been backing Paul Emery?"

"Yes. She made me an offer about two weeks ago, but I turned it down. Then I got fired. I had an appointment to see her Tuesday afternoon, but she came to the office for me because she's the kind who does what she pleases, and Jackson saw her there and they started quarreling. I went away and left them. Later I met her and told her I would go in with her. She'll ante up to two hundred thousand, and I'll draw seven thousand a year and get half of the net."

"You will." Sammis's eyes were narrowed. "And you'll take my men."

"I suppose I will, as their stakes peter out." Clara stretched a hand in appeal. "What was I to do? I was fired, wasn't I?"

"You should have come to Lem, girlie." Evelina was emphatic. "Everybody should. Everybody does. Come to Lem."

"I'd been to him enough already. Anyway, I was really glad to get away from Dan Jackson and I wasn't sorry he had fired me." Clara turned. "I didn't tell you, Del, because I didn't want anyone to know until it was settled. But if I'd told you, you wouldn't have gone there Tuesday night with that note, and—I'm sorry. I should have told you." She shifted to Sammis. "I was sorry to be doing anything you wouldn't like, too, but I couldn't help it. And the way it is now, since you wanted to get out of the grubstaking business anyway, I'm sure Mrs. Cowles will make a deal to take it over—"

"I don't like her." Sammis grunted. "It would be a hell of a note, two women taking over Sammis & Brand. We'll see. What do you think of it, Eva? Tell me later. I'm tired. You're right, Eva, I'm tired." Evelina returned the pat on the knee she had previously received.

Sammis sighed. "We'll see. We'll talk it over. I wanted to ask you, Dellie, did you tell Baker that you saw me in Amy's car Tuesday night there at her house?"

It was Delia's turn to be flustered, at the unexpectedness of it. She opened her eyes at him. "Why, no. I couldn't very well tell him that, because I didn't see you."

"You didn't?"

"No."

"You didn't see me and you didn't tell him you did?"

"That's right. He asked if I saw you in the car and I told him no, and I said you couldn't have been there anyway because you were out at the ranch."

"Well, you were wrong. I wasn't at the ranch. I was there in Amy's car."

Delia stared. "But when I left—I supposed—"

"It don't pay to suppose, Dellie. When you left the ranch I was starting to eat supper, that's true. But it was ten o'clock when we drove in at Amy's. I want to ask you girls a question. Let's say Amy went to Dan's office and shot him because he was a polecat and she couldn't stand it any more. She didn't, but let's say she did. Where would you girls—"

"But she couldn't! Where would she get the gun—"

"I said she didn't do it, didn't I? But say she did. Where would you girls stand? You know what Dan Jackson was. Would you want to see her arrested and tried and convicted?"

They gazed at him. Delia said, "I wouldn't."

"Neither would I," Clara agreed.

"I don't know about this, Lem—"

"Shut up, Eva. I'm not telling anything Baker don't already know. All right, you girls say you wouldn't, and I believe you. I believe you because I know you and you're Charlie Brand's daughters. Now here's something Baker does know. Two people have told him that about 9:45 Tuesday evening they saw Amy coming out of the door from the stairs leading to Dan's office, and they're right. Dan had told her he was going to the office, and she suspected he wasn't and had gone there

to see, and had climbed the stairs and found the office
dark and quiet, and came away again without going in.
That's the way it happened. Where I came into it don't
matter—anyway, she had phoned me and I met her."

Sammis set his jaw sidewise, then, after a moment,
relaxed it. "Ed Baker wants to question her. He wants
to make trouble. He can never in God's world explain
how she got that gun and that handbag, but he might
even arrest her and try her. He wants to make the
Sammis name stink all over Wyoming. He wants to
fasten a motive on Amy by dragging it all out about
Dan and his dealings with women. That's why I asked
you girls that question—especially you, Clara. Dan
was pretty careful and cagey, and he didn't leave any
trails to speak of—I know, because I was trying to find
one and he knew I was. Twenty times I've wanted to
ask you about telephone calls and messages and letters
there in the office, but I couldn't bring myself to it,
turning Charlie Brand's daughter into a spy on a
woman chaser. But Ed Baker won't be squeamish. He
knows you're the best source of information he can get
and maybe the only one. He's expecting you at his office at ten o'clock. That right?"

Clara nodded. "He is, but—"

"But you don't know how I knew it. I guess I've got
one or two friends left up at that courthouse. By the
time this is over I'll have more than Baker has or I
won't have any. Maybe you remember I made him stop
questioning you yesterday morning. Even then, when
he thought Dellie here had done it, he was starting to
get his nose dirty. Now he's had a talk with the governor and he's already sunk a pick, and I can't stop him
that way. So I'm making a few motions. It's important
about you, Clara. You must have seen and heard a lot
in that office without trying to. I want to ask you, don't

talk to Baker. Don't even see him. I'm asking you for me and for Amy. Will you do it?"

Clara said, "All right."

"Don't go to see him. If he comes here don't let him in, and if he gets in don't talk to him. If he arrests you, phone Harvey Anson right away."

"But good heavens—what can he arrest me for?"

"As a material witness. That don't mean anything. The judge will fix a low bail and Anson will have you out in five minutes. Will you do it?"

"Yes."

Sammis nodded. "I thought you would. You're good girls. But you want to realize what you're signing for. If this happens, if he arrests you and you're released on bail, the county and the whole state are going to buzz. About you. That's what people are like. But you already know that, even at your age, the way they've been buzzing about your dead mother and that preacher Toale. They ought to have their necks wrung, the whole damn caboodle! What won't they say about Amy or you or anyone if they'll say that Lucy Brand sneaked down to that cabin with a gun and murdered her husband? I don't—what's the matter?"

Delia was on her feet, staring, her mouth hanging open. Clara was gazing at him, also speechless.

He repeated, "What's the matter?"

"What you said," Clara gasped. "That they say—"

"That your mother killed your father? Sure they do. Now I'm sorry I mentioned it, I might have known no one would say it to you. But they say it, all right. That she killed him—you might as well have it all if you've got some—she killed him because she thought he was carrying on with Amy, which is a lie too, and she took the money off him, and her hiring the detectives was a bluff, and that preacher Toale found it out somehow, and he worked on her and remorse worked on her until she killed herself. They even say—"

"Shut up, Lem," Evelina commanded him.

Delia, still staring, was in her chair again, gripping the arms of it. Clara said in a low incredulous tone, "But that—that's horrible."

Evelina stood up. "When you're a fool you're a good one," she told her husband disgustedly. "What the hell good would it do to say that even if they had already heard it?" She waddled to Clara and patted her on the shoulder. "Forget it, girlie. There's more coyotes in the hills than anything else. Come on, Lem. We've got to get back to Amy. It's nearly ten o'clock."

"I'm not going back to Amy. I've got to see—"

"Well, I am, and you've got to take me. Come on before you make a bigger fool of yourself."

Lem halted in front of Clara to ask, "Can I count on you?"

"Yes. You can count on me."

"Good. I'm sorry if I—holy smoke, I—"

"All right. That's all right. I'll let you out."

Delia didn't know if she responded to the good nights. She was aware of them in the hall, and of the door opening and closing, and then was aware that her sister was back in the room, standing in front of her.

She looked up. "Well?"

Clara didn't say anything.

"When Rufus Toale came to see you—these last two weeks—did he say that?"

"No." Clara turned abruptly and went back to the front hall. In a moment Delia followed. Clara was pulling on a wrap she had taken from the rack.

"Where are you going?"

"I'm going to see Toale."

"I'm going, too."

"No, Sis. No, you're not." Clara had the wrap on. "I'm the older. I insist, I beg—you know very well you're excitable. Please, Sis. I'm just going to find out." She opened the door. "Please, Del?"

"All right."

Delia went onto the porch, and called to the form of her sister receding in the dark, "Hurry back!" She stood there until she saw the car turn from the driveway into the street, and then re entered the house. After she got into the front room she remembered that she hadn't closed the front door, but that was of such vast unimportance that she didn't go back to shut it. Instead she flung herself onto the couch, face down, and, not having cried in her jail cell, did so now.

The crying ended after a while; her shoulders stopped shaking and shudders no longer ran over her; but she stayed with her face buried in the cushion. She had thought that she had things pretty well figured out there in her cell, and now here was this. The town where her father had lived and worked, where she and her sister had been born and gone to school and had danced at parties and had given parties at their house —the people of that town were saying that her mother had murdered her father. That finished everything; that was enough—but here she was again, not thinking. She must think about it, and first she must decide in what way it could be thought about. . . .

When the phone rang she answered it to stop its ringing—and it might be Clara or Ty. But it was someone at the county attorney's office, asking why Clara wasn't there. She didn't know what to say, whether to say that Clara would not go, so she merely told him that she had left the house at twenty minutes to ten. After she had hung up she looked at her watch: ten after. It took only four or five minutes to drive to the parsonage and Clara might be back soon. She threw herself onto the couch again.

She had promised Ty she would go to bed and try to sleep, and one of the things she had decided in jail was that she would keep all promises, but she wouldn't go upstairs until Clara returned. There would be no sense in that. Anyway, she had to think. One thing to think about was what to do. She and Clara would go away, would leave Wyoming. There was nothing—there was Ty. What about that? What kind of a feeling was it that he had for her, and what kind did she have for him? Had he heard what people were saying about her mother? If he had, shouldn't he have told her? Wouldn't a man in love with a girl tell her a thing like that? . . .

Was that a car in the driveway, or was it next door? Clara? No, it hadn't gone on to the garage. Probably next door. Wouldn't a man in love with a girl? . . .

The footsteps—now on the steps, now on the porch—were certainly not Clara's, they were much too heavy. She wouldn't answer the door no matter how long they rang; she should have turned out the lights. But she had left the door open! The steps were in the hall! She jerked herself up, swinging her feet to the floor, and saw the Reverend Rufus Toale entering the room, his face white, wearing no smirk and displaying no blandness.

Chapter 14

Rufus Toale kept on coming, advancing with a heavy dragging tread. At the big chair in front of the couch, lately occupied by Lem Sammis, he stopped, resting his hand on its back; then he edged around it and lowered himself with ridiculous carefulness onto its seat. Delia started to rise, but her knees wouldn't take it. She sat and stared.

When he spoke he didn't begin with "Praise God," and his voice was as preposterous as his manner of movement had been and his white face still was. Instead of being deep and sonorous and musical, it was little better than a hoarse squeak as he said one word: "Clara?"

Delia shook her head without willing it.

"She's not here?"

She shook her head again.

Rufus Toale put the palm of his right hand, the fingers outspread, against his breastbone, and pressed it there. "I mustn't breathe much," he declared with no improvement in his voice. "I feel it bleed inside when I breathe. I've been wounded. Shot. I plugged it with my handkerchief to keep the blood in. If I'm dying . . . your sister?"

Delia shook her head. "She's not here." His zealot's eyes, out of his white face, bored into hers. "Can I trust you with God's errand? Do you believe in the vengeance of man?"

"Who—" Delia stopped with her mouth working. "Who shot you?"

He ignored it. "Do you believe in the vengeance of man, my child? I think I'm dying. Answer me."

That was one of the things Delia had figured out in jail, and apparently she had got it fixed in her mind, for she said clearly, "I don't believe in vengeance. But if you're wounded—I must—"

"No!" His voice and his eyes held her to the couch. "This comes first, then whatever comes. You must know it all—if I can—" He controlled a grimace, then inhaled a long slow breath, with a catch in the middle of it. "I thought some day to tell you this, you and your sister, as we kneeled to God—as I did your mother. Now without the preparation of prayer—oh, I entreat you, take the guidance of God! The facts are brief, but follow His guidance!"

"The facts—"

"About your father. God rest his soul. He was not a devout man, but he was a good and friendly man. When he left on that fatal trip two years ago he had with him much worldly money and a little of God's money. I gave it to him. It was my own money, but it was for my church. It was God's money. I gave him ten twenty-dollar bills, and in the corner of each one I wrote R.T. for Rufus Toale. He was to select a worthy man to receive them, and whatever treasure that man found in the rocks was to return to my church for the glory of God who made the hills and all the treasure in them. I gave that money, God's money, to your father.

He had it. He was killed and it was taken from him, with the other money he had."

Rufus Toale stopped, to take another long careful breath, with his hand still pressed against his chest, where it had stayed without movement. His lips twitched and he went on, "That money was taken from your father by the one who killed him. I said nothing about it. I furnish no fuel to the fires of man's vengeance. But I am human. I didn't often see twenty dollar bills, for God's money is smaller sums, but when I did see one I looked at it. And the day came when, to my horror, I found that I had in my possession one of those bills I had given your father. The R.T. was in the corner just as I had put it there twenty-one months before. I knew where I had got it. Under the circumstances there could be little—little doubt—"

He stopped again to breathe. "I think—" He gasped, trying not to; the fight he was making showed on his face; he reinforced his right hand by spreading his left one over it to hold it tight. "I think—I must finish. The blood inside—chokes me. The bill was taken from me—there where I was shot—as I lay pretending I was dead—to escape death."

He gasped and a spasm went over his face. Delia, paralyzed with horror, could make no movement. He swayed in the chair and braced his elbow against the arm.

"Praise God!" he whispered fiercely. "I must leave you—with His errand! I must finish! The guilty must confess and submit—but not to man, to Him! You must go to—God! Help me!" His elbow slipped from the chair's arm and he started to crumple. "Praise God!" he croaked, gasping, and collapsed, hanging on the arm of the chair almost precisely as Dan Jackson had done, arms dangling to the floor.

Delia, staring, said, "No." She repeated it. "No!" Without moving her eyes from him, she got to her feet and backed away. "No," she said again, and stopped. She could scream. She, who had thought everything out so carefully and definitely, could scream. Someone would hear her. "No," she said. A doctor. Yes, of course a doctor; but Clara? Clara—

The telephone rang. She took a deep shivering breath, then, with no hesitation and with firm steps, went to the little table, put the receiver to her ear and said, "Hello?"

"Is this the Brand residence?"

"Yes. This is Delia Brand."

"Is your sister there? Clara Brand?"

"No, she isn't here."

"Well, hold the wire. The county attorney wants—"

"Wait a minute." Delia's voice was clear and steady. "Hello? Send a doctor here at once. There's a man here that's been shot and he may be dying. Send a—"

"What! You say shot? Who—"

Delia hung up. Her fingers trembled as she got the phone directory and flipped the pages to the T's, but she found the number without fumbling, took up the receiver again, and dialed. As she waited her back was to the couch and the chair.

"Is this the parsonage?"

"Yes, ma'am. This is the housekeeper."

"This is Delia Brand. Is my sister Clara there?"

"No, ma'am, she's left."

"How long ago?"

"Oh, maybe five or ten minutes. I let her in the church because she said she'd rather wait there, and she came back and said she wouldn't wait any more and she left."

"Thank you very much."

Delia hung up again. For the next call she didn't need to consult the book, for she knew the number of Ty Dillon's little apartment on Beech Street. In a moment she removed the receiver once more and dialed. There was no answer to the ringing. When she heard a car in the driveway, continuing to the garage, she kept the receiver to her ear; at the sound of steps on the porch, she lowered it; as Clara appeared in the door she dropped it on the rack.

"He wasn't there," Clara said. "Why didn't you go to bed? I waited an hour, but Mrs. Bonner didn't know —" She stopped, transfixed, her eyes aimed past Delia's shoulder at the middle of the room. "Del! Good God, what is it?" She ran across, stooped, peered, straightened up, faced her sister. "Del! For God's sake, Del—"

"No!" Delia said fiercely, bitterly. "He came here— he came in and sat down and said he had been shot and he was dying—and I thought you had—I thought you —and now you thought I—we are thinking each other—"

She burst into laughter. She stood laughing crazily, swaying, her shoulders shaking and rocking back and forth. Clara sprang for her, seized her shoulders, and pressed her forcibly into a chair. "Sis, for God's sake stop—Sis! Stop it! I didn't think anything! Sis, Del darling, you mustn't, you mustn't—"

Ed Baker's voice sounded from the door. "They're both here."

Clara froze. Delia was giggling.

Baker went on, entering, "Over there, doc, in the chair. If he's dead don't move him till I get a look. Bring the boys in, Frank. There's enough here for everybody."

Chapter 15

The average daily circulation of the *Times-Star* for the year was 9,400. Wednesday and Thursday the pressrun had been 12,000 and 14,200, respectively. Friday it was 17,600, an all-time high.

Rarely did the Fowler Hotel have newspaper reporters, much less photographers, registered as its guests. Even when a public figure was within the county, the world learned of their daily doings only through the services of local journalists. But by Friday noon the register could boast eleven such entries, from Spokane, Denver, the coast, and points between.

Governor Matthews of Wyoming was a democratic man. Ordinarily no qualification was necessary in order to achieve entrance into his office at the capitol at Cheyenne except two legs to walk in with. But on Friday he didn't even go there himself. He was in a room with a locked door at the Pyramid Club in Cody and the only people who knew it were there with him.

The church of which the Reverend Rufus Toale was pastor had always been open on weekdays, for those who might wish to enter to pray, but seldom might more than one or two suppliants have been discovered there. Friday they straggled in and out all day, pointing out to each other inside, with whispers, the place where Clara Brand had sat the evening before, just prior to murdering the pastor. At the same time other people were slowing up their cars as they drove past 139 Vulcan Street, pointing out the windows of the front room in which Delia Brand had shot and killed Rufus Toale, forty-eight hours almost to the minute since she had shot and killed Dan Jackson, which was surely a record. The contradiction was merely one aspect of the raging controversy which had divided Park County into two hostile camps.

In his office on the top floor of the new Sammis Building on Mountain Street, Lem Sammis, with his jaw permanently sidewise, sat gazing across his desk at a man, ten years his junior, whose dark intent eyes displayed neither friendliness nor good humor but yet were not antagonistic. The man was saying:

"No, Lem, I'm not selling any soft soap. You may cut my throat some day or I may cut yours. But we're together against these rats. Baker turns it off before this day's over or he's done, and we'll get Carlson. The mining business made this state, and by God, the mining business will run it. Maybe your daughter killed Jackson or maybe you did it yourself. I don't give a damn. I hope to put the screws on you some day, but not like this, and not with that bunch helping me. Matthews has crawled into a hole, but I'll find him and I'll deal with him."

Lem Sammis said coldly, "I'm asking no favors, Ollie."

"Favors hell. You know and I know how it stands. We can deal with each other after we've dealt with this. I'll get hold of Matthews."

"When you find him tell him from me—"

"I'm not telling anybody anything from you. I'm telling 'em myself."

"Go to hell."

"After you, Lem."

Ollie Nevins departed. Sammis sat awhile without moving, then reached for his phone and spoke into it. In a moment the door opened and Chief of Police Frank Phelan entered, glanced apprehensively at the old face with the rigid sidewise jaw, crossed to a chair, and sat.

"Well, Frank? They froze you out?"

Phelan nodded gloomily. "They did. They wanted to use my men on a warrant to search Dan's house and I balked."

"Who gave 'em the warrant—Merriam?"

"Yes."

"They going to use it?"

"Yes. A pair of them goddam county tramps."

Sammis's jaw went another quarter of an inch sidewise. "Searching Amy's house. Lem Sammis's daughter. Huh? Tell me what happened before you left."

Phelan cleared his throat and started. That was around noon.

It was still happening, at the courthouse. In the county attorney's office Baker was at his desk, a stenographer with a notebook was across from him, Sheriff Tuttle stood by a window with his hands in his pockets, and Clara Brand was seated in a chair which directly faced Baker's. She looked resolute and tense, but played out, with her eyes swollen and bloodshot, and her hands, in her lap, kept clasping and unclasping. She was saying:

"I don't care what you've found out or haven't found out. I told you everything last night and I told you the truth."

Baker himself looked the worse for wear. His eyes were bloodshot, too, and he had the general appearance of a man indulging in a hangover. He gazed at her and demanded, "Then you stick to your story as you told it last night?"

"I do."

"And you expect me to believe it? Do you remember what you said? You said that when the housekeeper told you she didn't know where Toale was or when he would be back, you told her you would wait and you would like to wait in the church, and she got the key and let you in at the rear. So far all right, Mrs. Bonner says the same thing. You told her that no matter what time Toale returned you would be in the church and she was to ask him to join you there. You groped your way down the aisle to the pew your mother always occupied, and you sat there an hour without moving. Then suddenly you decided to leave, to go home, and you went and told Mrs. Bonner and then got in your car and drove home. That was your story."

"It still is."

"But it's not as plausible as it sounded last night. As I've told you, you are not charged with the murder of Rufus Toale. You are not at present charged with anything. But at least one detail of your story is next to incredible. Last night we had no notion of where Toale had been when he was shot. This morning we learned that it must have been there alongside the church, between the drive and the rear entrance. We found where he had fallen into the edge of a flower bed. His hat was there and there was blood on the grass. Undoubtedly, returning, he had either taken his car to his garage or left it there on the drive and, before entering the parsonage, had gone toward the church for the nightly visit which was his invariable custom. That's where he was shot. The rear door of the church was standing open. You were seated in that pew, in silence and darkness. Will you tell me again that you heard no shot fired?"

"Certainly I will. I've told you why. If the shot was fired there."

"It was. You said you were buried in your thoughts. You were oblivious. Frankly, I don't believe it. So oblivious you didn't hear a shot fired as near as that? It must have been from a point between the flower bed and the church, if Toale was headed for the church, as he must have been, for the bullet entered the middle of his chest, pierced the lung and lodged in the spine. No matter how deep you were in thought—"

"I tell you I didn't hear it." Clara clasped her hands again. "Or maybe I heard it but I didn't know it. I've told you I had just learned what people were saying about my mother. I've told you that's what I went there to ask him about. I didn't hear any shot, and that's all I'll ever say about it. It's all I can say."

"You heard no shot, no call for help? Nothing?"

"Nothing."

"And you were in that pew continuously from the time Mrs. Bonner let you in until you went and told her you were going home?"

"I was."

"And—we'll put this on the record again today— you didn't shoot Toale yourself?"

"I did not."

"You didn't hear his car on the drive and conceal yourself in the shrubbery and, as he approached with the lights of the car behind him, shoot him?"

"I did not."

"It was Lem Sammis who told you what people were saying about your mother, wasn't it?"

No answer.

"Wasn't it Lem Sammis who told you that?"

"That's none of your business. I've already told you that I won't say who told me."

"Didn't Lem Sammis, with his wife, call at your home last evening?"

"That's none of your business either."

"Well, he did, and it was soon after he left that you went to see Toale." Baker leaned forward and narrowed his eyes at her. "Look here, Clara. Will you listen to what I say?"

"I'll listen."

"All right. I want you to believe, because it's the truth, that I'm not trying to build up anything against you. Things like your telling me Wednesday morning that you had gone to see Atterson Brothers Tuesday afternoon, and my learning that you hadn't been there, and your saying now that you went to the Fowler Hotel and waited there for Mrs. Cowles—I'm not holding that against you. I don't even hold it against you that you refuse to tell me any of the things that happened, that must have happened, in Jackson's office the past year or two. I don't hold it against you because I understand it. You're being loyal to Lem Sammis, the old friend and partner of your father. How would you feel if you knew that Sammis had tried to frame both you and your sister on charges of murder?"

Clara stared.

"I ask you, how would you feel?"

"It's a silly question," she said shortly.

"Maybe and maybe not." Baker was earnest, urgent. "I'm not accusing him of it, because I'm not ready to. But here are some facts. It's a cinch that someone framed your sister for Jackson's murder—her gun, her handbag there on the desk. But whoever did it must have known that Delia would be going there that evening. Who did know it? Even you didn't; you've said so. There was only one person who knew it, and that was Sammis; he himself had written the note for her to take to Jackson. What do you think of that?"

"I don't think—" Clara stopped. In a moment, "It's absurd," she snapped.

"You don't mean absurd, you mean it's hard for you to believe. Lots of things are hard to believe, and Lem Sammis has done a few of them. You know as well as I do how much tenderness he has for anyone he has decided to crush. Those are the facts about Delia. Now you. It must have been Sammis who told you what people were saying about your mother. Wasn't it?"

No answer.

Baker spread his palms. "It must have been. Why did he decide to tell you that, and the part that scandal gives Toale in your mother's suicide? Did you go at once to see Toale? You did. Was he murdered? He was. Under circumstances that threw suspicion on you? Yes."

Clara shook her head. "It's simply fantastic."

"It's not fantastic at all. There's a logical connection right straight through. Sammis thinks that I suspect he or his daughter shot Jackson because of his affairs with other women. I don't. At least I'm inclined not to since last night. I more strongly suspect that Jackson was killed because he had recently got hold of evidence that might lead to the solution of the murder of your father two years ago."

"My father—"

"Yes. That comes from Quinby Pellett, your uncle, and a man named Squint Hurley. And now Toale. You know what he told your sister while he was dying. With a hole in his lung and that bullet in his spine, he got himself back to his car and drove to your house and walked in there to tell it—and then all he told was about the marked bill and its being taken from him after he was shot. If he had it on him it was taken, all right. That marked bill, again, was evidence that might solve the murder of your father. So Toale was killed for the same reason that Jackson was. And he was killed by someone who either murdered your father or had a hand in it. And that someone was Lem Sammis. Well?"

"I don't believe it. It's crazy."

"It's far from crazy." Baker leaned at her again. "You're thinking, of course, that Sammis was your father's partner and best friend. But you must have heard some of the talk around that time about your father and Amy Jackson—or maybe you didn't, since you're Brand's daughter. Anyway there was talk and certainly Sammis heard it, and you know what he thinks of his daughter. It's the one spot in him that's probably tender clear to the bottom. So it's far from crazy."

Clara shook her head.

"You don't believe it?"

"No."

"You don't even think it's possible?"

"No."

"All right, you don't. You're shocked. You're incredulous. You're probably wondering, or you will, why I've told you all this, since it's ten to one that you'll pass it on to Sammis as soon as you get a chance. I've risked that and told you about it because I've got to get a lot of information from someone who has been close to Jackson and Sammis and I'm expecting it from you. I want you to think about it. I'm going to put you in the next room, alone, and I ask you to think it over for an hour, two hours, as long as you want to. Remember the facts I've told you. Remember all the little things, and big ones too, you've heard and seen back over the years. Consider it all. I don't think you want to be loyal to Lem Sammis or help him cover up if there's any amount of possibility that he killed your father or was responsible for it, and Tuesday night and last night he was willing to direct suspicion at you and your sister in order to divert it from himself. Will you go in that room and think it over?"

Clara was gazing at him with fresh trouble in her bloodshot eyes. But she said firmly, "I don't think I need to."

"I'm going to put you in there. Will you think it over? Then I want to have another talk with you."

"Do I have to? Stay in there?"

"For a while, yes."

"Well . . . I would know better what to think if I could have a talk with Mr. Sammis first."

"No doubt," said Baker drily. "I'm sorry. Nothing doing."

"Then if I could telephone my sister. Or Mr. Dillon."

"You can do that afterward." Baker abruptly stood up. "It's comfortable in there. Come on. It's far more comfortable than the quarters you'd have if you had been charged with murder, as it was intended you should be."

Chapter 16

By two o'clock Friday afternoon, the hour at which Clara Brand was shut in a room alone to think it over, the commotion at the Brand house on Vulcan Street had almost completely subsided. Cars, slowing down for their occupants to stare, frequently passed in the street and a uniformed policeman was hanging around the sidewalk in front to discourage collections of pedestrians, but that was all. Intent heavy-footed men were no longer peeking under shrubs to find where a revolver, hurled through a window by Delia Brand after shooting Rufus Toale, might have landed; that activity had been stopped some five hours earlier, when the ludicrous straw hat and the bloodstains had been discovered at the edge of the flower bed in the churchyard, as had been a similar exhaustive search inside the house itself. The same discovery had freed Delia from any further badgering, which had gone on intermittently all night; at least twenty times she had had to repeat her conversation with Toale after his staggering in, or rather, his monologue; and thrice she had re-enacted the scene for them, with her on the couch as she had been and Sheriff Tuttle in the chair doing Toale.

Now, at two o'clock, there was no one in the house with her except Ty Dillon, not even the *reliquiae* of the pastor who had fought his way there on God's errand and had been choked to death by his own blood before he could complete it. Upstairs in Delia's bedroom, she was lying down and Ty was slowly pacing the floor. Each time he turned at the end of his beat he halted and gazed at her, as she lay there on her back with her eyes closed and her fists clenched at her sides, but he said nothing. They had talked it all out. They were agreed: that they believed Clara's story and she had no knowledge of the shooting of Toale; that whatever had motivated Lem Sammis's request to Clara to withhold information from the county attorney, she should disregard it and tell everything she knew about everything; that if she were arrested Phil Escott should be her counsel; that anything like peace of mind and a tolerable existence for the Brand girls, in Wyoming or anywhere else, was impossible until the murders of Dan Jackson and Rufus Toale were cleared up; that the murder of their own father two years ago should be included, in view of the stigma which gossip had attached to their mother's name; that they should not run away from it but should stick in Cody and see it through; and that if they, Ty and Delia, were to do anything about it, they hadn't the slightest idea where to begin. Quinby Pellett, who had been there and talked with them for two hours, had likewise agreed to all those points, including the last one; he had no more cards up his sleeve, he confessed in cold and impotent rage, like his knowledge of the theft of Delia's handbag; and he had gone off with vague mutterings about what he would do and what he would see to. That was the hopeless and dreary situation at two o'clock when Ty, halting for the hundredth time to gaze at Delia and to wish to God she would relax or take the drug the doctor had left her, heard the doorbell ring.

He opened the door to leave the bedroom as silently as possible, but Delia opened her eyes. "Who is it?"

"I don't know. I bribed that cop to keep everybody out. I'll see."

"Maybe it's Clara—no, she has a key."

"I'll see."

Downstairs, when he opened the door, he found two men standing there: the cop, and towering beside him one with a weathered face and nearly white hair, his eyes scarcely more than slits. The cop broke in on Ty:

"Yeah, I know, but the only way to stop him would have been to plug him one. He's like a burro in everything but size. Maybe you don't know who he is? It's Squint Hurley. The one that was tried for the murder of Charlie Brand and got acquitted."

Ty regarded the old prospector. "What do you want, Hurley?"

"I want to see Charlie Brand's girl on a business matter."

"Which one?"

"The older one, I guess she is. The one that was working down at Jackson's office."

"That's Clara. She's not here. She's down at the courthouse."

"When'll she be back?"

"I don't know. Possibly not till tonight."

Hurley grunted. "I'll wait here on the steps," he said and turned, tramped the width of the porch, and sat on the top step.

"If you need help moving him"—the cop grinned— "phone the station for a squad." He detoured around Hurley and strode down the path toward the sidewalk, where a group of schoolgirls had halted and seemed about to enter for an attack on the house.

Ty demanded of the denim shirt that covered the broad back, "What do you want to see Miss Brand about?"

"Who are you?" Hurley asked without turning.

"I'm Tyler Dillon, Clara Brand's lawyer. Also Delia Brand's lawyer."

Hurley grunted. "Wherever you go in this damn town you run into a lawyer." He twisted his head around. "Delia? That's the one I found in Jackson's office the other night with the gun in her hand. Maybe I might see her instead of her sister. Is she here?"

"What do you want to see her about?"

"Business."

"What kind of business?"

"Important business. It ought to be important to Charlie Brand's girl if she's got any curiosity about who killed her dad."

"Explain it to me and I'll tell her about it."

Hurley shook his head. "I guess not. I guess I'll just wait here till the older one comes."

Ty stood, frowning, through a long silence. Finally he asked, "You say it is something about the death of her father?"

"It sure is."

"Wasn't it you that discovered Brand's body in that cabin?"

"It sure was."

"Wait here, will you?"

"That's what I'm doing."

Ty went in and back upstairs to the bedroom. Delia had swung her feet around and was sitting on the edge of the bed with her shoulders drooping. "Who is it, Ty? Anyone?"

He told her, and then advised her: "If I were you, Del, I'd go down and see what he has to say. You might as well be doing that as lying there clenching your fists . . ."

She consented to go, but with no eagerness, saying that if Squint Hurley knew anything he would have told it long ago. She brushed vaguely at her hair without making much impression on it, pulled her shoes from under the bed and put them on, and followed Ty downstairs. Not caring to enter the front room after what had happened there the evening before, she went to the dining room and was seated at the table, plucking at an edge of the embroidered cover, when Ty, having gone to the porch for the visitor, ushered him in. They sat. Hurley, on the imitation Sheraton chair, looked even more incongruous than he had in the courthouse office, but Delia didn't notice it. Looking at him, she was trying to control the quivering of her nerves as she remembered the scene when that man who had been accused of killing her father had last entered a room and found her there.

She mastered the quivering and said, "Mr. Dillon says you want to see me about something."

Hurley nodded. "You or your sister." Keeping his squint directed at her, he aimed a thumb at Ty. "We don't need him. I don't do much talking anyhow and I do it better with just one."

"That's all right. He's my—my lawyer."

Hurley grunted. "You're starting in awful young to have lawyers. I don't know, maybe I ought to wait for your sister. It's a matter of business. I've got to get back into the hills and I want a stake. I know a place in the Cheeford range—"

"Mr. Dillon said you told him it was about my father."

"Sure it is. But I'd like to mention about the stake first. You're Charlie Brand's girl and I'd trust you same as I would your dad. I'd go ahead and tell you and trust you for the ante, but what makes it hard to talk is this lawyer sitting here. I go on and tell you and then he begins to talk and when he gets through neither one of us has got anything."

Ty said, "I'll go out if you want me to. But if you tell Miss Brand something, and she wants to grubstake you, I not only won't talk against it, I'll help her put up the stake. It's true I'm her lawyer, but also I'm . . . we're going to be married."

"Oh." The prospector slowly shook his head. "That don't make it any better. I expect you'll find it makes it worse. But I'm no good as a trader—if I was, I wouldn't be reduced to asking a woman for a stake at my age. Anyhow, I ought to tell it for Charlie Brand's sake, and by all hell, I won't tell it to that coyote up at the courthouse. I told him too much already."

"You mean Baker? The county attorney?"

"That's him. He had me in there yesterday and I mentioned maybe he would stake me, and from the way he took it you might think I was a desert rat. I had already told him that that day when I got to the cabin and found Charlie Brand there dead, when I turned him over there was a piece of paper under him with writing on it, and I stuck it in my boot lining the way I do, and when I put Charlie on his horse and took him out to Sugarbowl and Ken Chambers came and began to slobber his bile, I didn't mention the paper because I knew it wouldn't do any good and I thought I'd better hang onto it. I never did mention it. I would have to Lem Sammis later, but he treated me like a desert rat, too. So I never mentioned it to anyone till Tuesday morning this week when I showed it to Dan

Jackson and give it to him and he put it in his wallet, and he staked me. Three hundred dollars. I paid a couple of debts, and that night like a jackass I went to The Haven with Slim Fraser and dropped it all on the wheel. So since Jackson had been glad to get that paper I thought he might put up another stake and I went upstairs to see him. That was when I found you there with that gun in your hand."

He shifted his squint to Ty and declared, "You ain't much of a lawyer or you'd be asking questions."

"Go on and tell it."

"I already told it. That's all. That's what I told that Baker yesterday. Except that Baker told me that the piece of paper wasn't in Jackson's wallet when they went over him, so whoever killed him must've took it, so since they didn't even take his money from him it must've been the piece of paper they killed him for. So whoever killed Charlie Brand two years ago killed Dan Jackson Tuesday night. That's plain reasoning. Then of course Baker wanted to know what was on the paper and I told him I couldn't tell him because I could read reading but I couldn't read writing. So I told him it was a piece of white paper about the size of my hand, and it had been folded up, and the writing on it was five or six words, and that was all I could tell him—"

"You couldn't tell him what was written on it?"

"No, sir, I couldn't."

"And the paper's gone?"

"It sure is. Took out of his wallet by whoever shot him."

"And you say you found it under Charlie Brand's body?"

"Yep. When I turned him over."

"And now nobody knows what was written on the paper?"

"That's the way it looks."

"And this is what you came to tell Miss Brand?"

"That's it exactly. To tell her all that, and then tell her what was written on the paper if she thinks she might like to know."

They both stared. "But you said you couldn't read it."

"No I didn't. I said I told that Baker I couldn't read it. After he acted the way he did about the grub-stake—"

"Oh." Ty was squinting back at him. "I get you. You want a stake. If Miss Brand will stake you, you'll tell her what was on the paper."

"That's about it."

"What if there never was any such paper? What if you made all this up?"

Hurley grunted. "That would be too bad. It sure would. But I didn't make it up. I lugged that paper around with me for two years."

"What if Miss Brand refuses to stake you? What are you going to do then?"

"That's just the hell of it." Hurley looked disgusted. "I'll have to tell her what was on the paper anyway. She's Charlie Brand's girl and she has a right to know. But I'm telling you that place I know down on the Cheeford range—"

"I'll stake him, Ty," Delia blurted. "I have enough saved up so—"

"I'll stake him myself." Ty pulled papers and envelopes from his pocket, dumped them on the table, and found a checkfold among them. From another pocket he took a fountain pen and laid it on the checkfold. "All right, Hurley. Tell us what was on the paper, and I'll give you a check now, or if you prefer cash—"

"I don't want it now. I don't want it till they're

letting me leave this town." The old prospector's lips twitched with an eagerness he could not conceal, and the tips of his fingers, one missing, were rubbing the table cover. "You mean you'll stake me? Up to three hundred dollars?"

"Yes."

"Half and half?"

"Whatever is usual."

"All right." His lips twitched again. "You don't sound much like a lawyer. All right. What was on that paper was 'Mountain cat ready for prey four hundred and fifty WD.'"

Delia exclaimed, "Mountain cat!"

Ty said urgently, "Wait a minute! Was it written in pencil or ink?"

"Ink. Black ink."

"Was it—would you know if it was in Charlie Brand's handwriting?"

"It wasn't. I knew Charlie's writing. This was big and round and heavy."

"Was the whole thing written right along on one line?"

"No. 'Mountain cat' was on one line and below that was 'ready for prey' and below that was the 'four hundred and fifty' and below that was 'WD.'"

"Was the four hundred and fifty written out or in figures?"

"In figures. Just a four and a five and a zero, no decimals or anything. Then the 'WD' was in capital letters, at the bottom."

Delia exclaimed, "Ty! I tell you the 'mountain cat' stood for Wynne Cowles! I tell you it did! She was after Dad just then, trying to find out about his business—he used to joke about it at home—"

"It might have," Ty conceded, "or it might not.

Wynne Cowles is certainly always ready for prey. But the 'WD' sounds like a signature, initials. WD?"

"I don't know. But the 'mountain cat' is Wynne Cowles."

"Possibly. Do you know anyone whose initials are WD, Hurley?"

"Nope. I've had that in my head for two years."

"You're sure it wasn't Brand's own writing?"

"As sure as sand eats water."

"You say the paper was under him? How, under him?"

"Just under him. I turned him over to get a hold to carry him out to the horse and the paper was there, folded up."

"It might have been there before he ever got there."

"Damn lawyer," Hurley said impatiently. "Who put it there? I had been in and out of that cabin for two months and no one else."

"It might have been just a paper he had with him and it fell out of his wallet when the murderer was going through him for the money."

"Charlie Brand never carried a wallet. When he had a bulk of money like that he kept it belted to him, and papers, receipts and things, in a little leather case he could put in a saddlebag. It was there with the saddle on a post outdoors—hadn't been opened." Hurley's eyes were buried by his squint. "If you want to know how that paper got there I'll tell you."

"You mean you know?"

"I mean I'll tell you. I ain't a lawyer, but I can figure out how a thing worked. I've had two years to figure this. The fellow that killed him left the road about two miles north of Sugarbowl, across the hills on the hoof—"

"Why two miles north?"

"Because that's the only place along that road you can hide a car where it won't be seen, where them cliffs are."

"Why on the hoof? Why not on a horse?"

The prospector looked disgusted. "And exactly where the hell would he get a horse and no one know it?"

"All right. Go ahead."

Delia put in, "That's right about the money belt and the leather case. He always took them on a trip."

"Sure he did. Who says he didn't? So this fellow hoofs it across the hills and gets to the cabin before Charlie does—"

"Why before?"

"Because Charlie was riding Bert Oakley's palomino he had got at Sugarbowl, and he had tied him to a post just outside the cabin door. That horse has got a habit when he's tied, if anybody comes anywhere near except the man that's riding him, he snorts fit to rip a gut. Charlie would have heard him and gone to the door, and he probably would have got his gun out with all that money on him. But his gun was still in the holster, and where he fell and died he was all of ten, twelve feet away from the door. So the fellow was already there, hid in the cabin."

"Go ahead."

"Well, Charlie comes in and the fellow shoots him. It only takes one shot, as close as that. What he wants is the money and he goes after it in a hurry because he don't know I'm going to be five or six hours late on account of my leg. That belt is good and bulky, and he takes off his coat or jacket so he can strap the belt up high on him and when he puts the coat back on it will be covered when he's hoofing it back. Them hills is plenty lonesome, but it always might be someone sees him. He thinks I might be coming any minute and he's nervous and he works fast, trying to get the belt off, and he don't notice that when he jerks his coat off a piece of paper drops out of a pocket. When he turns Charlie over, working at the belt, he flops him on top of the piece of paper and never sees it."

Delia was chewing at her lip. Ty was frowning, intent. He demanded, "Why did he hoof it back? Why didn't he take Brand's horse?"

"I wish to God he had. Even Ken Chambers couldn't have locked me up if that palomino had been untied and gone and found two miles north of Sugarbowl. That fellow was smart enough to let the horse alone. Speaking of which." Hurley squinted at Delia and back at Ty. "Ken Chambers is in Cody now. For all I know he was there Tuesday night when Jackson was killed. Whoever killed Jackson took that piece of paper from him. All I'm doing is telling you what was on that paper, but if I was you and I was really smart I'd get so curious about Ken Chambers I'd split my britches."

"Do you think Ken Chambers killed Brand?"

"I ain't saying I think. I say I'd be curious."

"Have you any reason to suspect him? Any evidence?"

"Just common sense. I know him, that's all."

"Could he have done it? Where was he that day?"

"I don't know. That's part of what I meant I'd be curious about." Ty shook his head, scowling, and was silent.

Delia said, "It couldn't have been Chambers if the 'mountain cat' on the paper meant Wynne Cowles. I'm sure it did, Ty. How could there have been any connection between her and Chambers?"

"I don't know, Del." Ty let her have the scowl. "That damn paper that no one has even seen except Hurley here, and now it's gone." He shifted the scowl again. "Was it good paper or cheap paper?"

"Well—it was white paper."

"Nothing else on it at all, nothing printed."

"Not a derned thing."

"Was it cheap and easy to tear like newspaper, or was it good tough nice white paper?"

"I didn't tear it. It was just white paper."

"You carried it in your boot lining for two years. Did it begin to come apart where it was folded?"

"No, it hung together all right. Of course it didn't improve any as it went along. It got kinda seedy."

"About as big as your hand?"

"About that. Maybe a little bigger."

"What was the writing—wait a minute." From the assortment on the table which he had taken from his pocket with the checkfold, Ty took an envelope, and on the back of it, with his fountain pen, wrote "mountain cat." He handed it to Hurley. "Was the writing anything like that?"

The prospector squinted at it. "Not a bit. Bigger and more ink."

"Forget the ink. That depends on the kind of pen you use. Just the kind of writing. Here, Del, you write it. Mountain cat."

She wrote it on another envelope. Hurley took it and shook his head at it. "That's even worse."

"Well, here. Give him the pen, Del. Write it down yourself, as near as you can the way it looked."

"Not me." Hurley didn't take the pen. "Except my name, I ain't wrote more than a hundred words in forty years."

"Try it."

"No, sir. I could do it better with a pick on a chunk of rock."

"But I just want to get an idea what the writing was like. Turn over that envelope and look on the other side. Was it anything—oh, it's typewritten. Look at that other one. Anything like that?"

Hurley looked at the inscription on the envelope. "A little more, but not much. This is stubby."

"Try this one." Ty tossed another envelope across.

Hurley picked it up. As he regarded it, his lips slowly parted and his squint widened until he nearly had eyes. He lifted them from the envelope and gazed at Ty. "By—all—hell," he said incredulously. "That's it!"

"What's it?"

"That's the same writing! That's it!"

Delia reached across and snatched the envelope. She saw, written on paper of good quality: *Tyler Dillon, Esq., 214 Mountain Street, Cody, Wyoming.*

And in the upper left-hand corner, neatly printed: *Broken Circle Ranch—Cody, Wyoming.*

She dropped the envelope on the table and Ty picked it up. She said, only half a question, "Wynne Cowles."

He nodded, glared at the envelope, and then at Hurley. "You mean the writing on the piece of paper was like this?"

"I mean it was that." Hurley looked as if someone had pulled a coyote out of a hat. "That word 'mountain.' I couldn't mistake that word 'mountain' as often as I've looked at it."

"It looks exactly the same?"

"It is the same."

"I'll be damned." Ty stared at the envelope. He

looked at Delia. "That's luck. I got this yesterday at the office, she was sending me a paper connected with her divorce suit, and ordinarily I'd just have tossed the envelope—"

"Oh! It was a paper connected with her divorce suit?"

"Certainly. What did you think—Hey! I'm dumb and so are you! It was there anyway—that WD! Two years ago her name wasn't Wynne Cowles, it was Wynne Durocher! She not only wrote it, she signed it!"

"I was right, Ty. Mountain cat."

"Yeah, you were right."

"And that paper she wrote was found under Dad's body. So she was—she knows something about it."

"Not necessarily. You've got to go at it logically." Ty screwed up his lips. "With what Hurley says about the writing, plus the WD at the bottom, we can regard it as settled that she wrote it. Okay. Then either she dropped it in the cabin herself and she did the murder, or it was dropped there by someone else and she knows who she gave it to. That's easy. Ask her when she wrote that paper and what she did with it. But it's not so easy if she dropped it in the cabin herself. In that case, since the paper is gone, there's no evidence or proof of anything and it would be foolish to put her on her guard by asking her about it. So maybe that's not the thing to do. Look here, Del. This is no time to hide anything, no matter what it is. Do you know of any motive Wynne Cowles might have had for killing your father?"

"No." Delia looked straight at him. "And I wouldn't hide anything, Ty. Not now. It's not a question of vengeance, it's stopping this . . . all this horrible . . . and Clara down there alone . . ." She swallowed hard.

"And I don't think Wynne Cowles killed Dad. She had no reason to. She wouldn't do that anyway, I mean take that money from him. I don't like her, but that isn't a thing she would do. We must ask her why she wrote that on paper and who she gave it to. Somebody must."

"It would be a big mistake if she had a hand in it. Maybe she didn't do it herself but she was behind it."

"I don't think so."

Ty gazed at Hurley. "Did you ever get a stake from Wynne Cowles?"

"Never heard of her."

"The woman that bought the Broken Circle ranch."

"Oh. Heard of her but never saw her."

"Or did you ever get a stake from Paul Emery?"

"Hell no. That little squirt."

Ty sat and frowned. "Well," he said finally, "I can go and ask her. It seems pretty damned naïve. Of course there's another alternative we might want to consider, we can turn it all over to the county attorney. He has resources—"

Hurley growled. "You mean that Baker? And let him lock me up because I told him I can't read? I swear to God if I get locked up again—"

Ty waved it aside. "It's no good anyway. Baker's so deep in the politics of it he couldn't see straight even if he wanted to, and there's no assurance he wants to. We can't trust any of them. The sheriff is only Baker's office boy. Frank Phelan is Lem Sammis's man and this may touch Sammis." He gathered the papers from the table, including the envelope addressed by Wynne Cowles, crammed them into his pocket, abruptly shoved his chair back, and got up. "All right. I'll go and see her."

Delia arose. "I'll go along."

"No, Del. Please. She's more apt to spill it to one than to two. I ought to go alone. And you ought to be here if Clara comes home. Another thing. What are you going to do, Hurley?"

"Me?" The prospector grunted. "Go to my room and sit. I'd rather do that than tramp these derned sidewalks."

"Do you realize you're a target?"

"Target for what?"

"For a bullet. Jackson was in possession of evidence against the murderer of Brand, and he was killed and it was taken: Rufus Toale—oh, you don't know about that. But Toale was killed for the same reason. You are now the only living person who can offer a scrap of evidence against Brand's murderer. You saw that paper and what was written on it. Chances are the murderer knows it. Who knows that you told the county attorney you can't read?"

"Search me."

"Well. I'm just saying that maybe you'd like to go on living."

Hurley grunted again. "I've been pretty successful at it for close on seventy years."

"I think you ought to stay here. Inside this house. There's a spare bed upstairs."

"Me?" Hurley's squint widened. "In this kind of an outfit?" He pushed his chair back and stood up. "No, I guess I'll do better if I mosey along to my room."

"My car's outside. I'll drive you."

"Nope." He was positive. "Rather walk."

"Suit yourself. Burro is right." Ty turned to Delia. "I'll be back as soon as I can. It takes forty minutes to get out there, if I don't find her in town. I'll come straight here."

"Do." She touched his arm. "Ty? Please . . ."

"I know, Del. I'll do my very best."

He kissed her. A blush of embarrassment showed on Squint Hurley's cheek, faint but perceptible on his weathered old skin, as he hastily turned his face away.

Chapter 17

Lem Sammis opened the door of the two-storied frame building and entered. Five paces inside he stopped and stood peering around at the confusing array of animals and birds—deer, grouse, eagles, chipmunks, jack rabbits, the elk, the bear, the cougar. But nothing alive was there, so he tramped to the rear behind the partition and found what he was looking for. "I sent for you three times," he growled.

Quinby Pellett, seated at the workbench, looked up. His graying hair looked dustier than ever, and the hump of his stooped shoulders was almost a semicircle. "I don't give a damn," he declared calmly, "if you sent a thousand."

Sammis approached him, glaring. "Look here, Quin. You've always been independent. That's all right. But if we're working the same claim, and in this case we are, there's no help in this kind of an attitude. Baker's got your niece shut up in the courthouse right now. He won't hang any murder on me or mine or you or yours, but it looks like he can raise a big stink before I can stop him. He's digging into your sister's life and maybe her death, too. And my daughter. And Charlie and Dan. He's got Clara there now. He had you for two hours this morning. I want to know what you told him."

"I told him nothing."

"You were there two hours."

"I told him nothing."

"Frank Phelan was there part of the time. I've had a talk with Frank."

Pellett put down his scraping knife. "If Frank said I told Baker anything about your family or my family that neither you nor I would want him to know, or want anyone else to know, he lied. The reason I didn't come to see you was because I don't want to talk about it even to you. There's too much talk already."

"There's too much shooting, too, Quin."

"I know damn well there is."

"You're not telling Baker about Amy and Dan or anything?"

"No."

"You're not going to?"

"No."

"That's straight?"

"That's straight." Sammis stood gazing at him for ten seconds, then turned and went.

Chief of Police Frank Phelan hissed in rage, leaving his desk to advance threateningly on the trio of city detectives in plain clothes. "Suffering snakes! Is it a button in a boulder I asked you to find? No! I want you to find the Governor of the State of Wyoming! God-damn it, shall I draw a picture of him for you? I don't care where he's hid or who hid him! Find him! Lem Sammis wants him and Ollie Nevins wants him! Shall I print it out for you, you half-witted apes? Get out of here before I boil you down for boot grease!" They clattered out.

County Attorney Ed Baker blurted truculently, "What do you want?"

Ken Chambers, Sheriff of Silverside County, stood his ground in front of Baker's desk. He drawled, "I came to tell you something about Squint Hurley."

"What about him?"

"I've been keeping an eye on him. He's just been making a call at the Brand house on Vulcan Street."

"What if he has?"

"I thought you ought to know. He was there over an hour. He only got back to his room a little while ago."

"What makes you think I ought to know?"

"Jesus." Chambers lifted his shoulders and drooped them again. "What did they elect you for, to keep you out of mischief? If you've got no curiosity about what Squint might be after at the Brands—"

"Who did he see there?"

"I didn't go in with him."

Baker made a noise of exasperation, got his phone and spoke in it. The door opened to admit a husky but tired-looking young man. Baker asked him if he knew where Squint Hurley was rooming and he said he didn't.

"I'll show him," Chambers offered.

"Much obliged. Go with Chambers, Jack, and get Squint Hurley and bring him here."

"Is there a warrant?"

"Good gracious." Baker was wearily sarcastic. "I forgot. Stop at the printers and get an engraved invitation."

"Okay. Excuse me for breathing."

When they had disappeared into the anteroom, Baker went to another door, on the opposite side, and passed through into a smaller room. It had a skylight and a ventilator was whirring, but there were no outside windows. Limp in a chair, with her eyes closed, was Clara Brand. At Baker's entrance she opened her eyes and blinked.

He stood in front of her. "Come to any decision yet?"

"I want to go home, Mr. Baker."

"I said you could go at dinnertime. That's no great hardship. You want these murders solved, don't you?"

"Of course I do. They have to be."

"You realize that can't be without someone getting hurt."

"I suppose not."

"You know not. Do you want to shield a murderer?"

"No."

"Then help me, Clara. Get it over with."

She shook her head.

"You won't?"

"I don't know, I—I believe I went to sleep. I'll stay awake now."

"Do you want a sandwich or something?"

"No, thanks."

Under an awning on the tiled veranda at Broken Circle Ranch, Wynne Cowles, in yellow silk lounging pajamas, reclined on a portable chaise longue with chromium frame and pneumatic tires. Handy was a little table with cigarettes, matches, books, accessories. At the sound of approaching footsteps she let her magazine drop and pivoted her head, her pupils contracting as she faced the blazing sunlight beyond the awning's edge.

"Hail, traveler!" she cried. "At the very minimum, an excuse for a highball, which is exactly what I needed." She frowned as she extended a hand in greeting. "But what a face! You're absolutely haggard! I've promised to be at Saratoga in August. You sounded on the phone as if it was something important, but you look like a cataclysm. Turn that chair around. Scotch or rye, and charged or plain?" She rang a bell.

"Rye with bubbles." Ty Dillon sat down. "I must be an awful exaggerator if I look like a cataclysm."

"Then it isn't one?"

"Lord, no. Just something I want to ask you. A little information to help a struggling young lawyer."

"I'm flattered." A Chinese appeared and she instructed him about the drinks and sent him off. "But if you don't mind, I'd like some information myself first. What about Clara Brand? Did she shoot that person?"

"No."

"Is she going to be arrested?"

"I don't think so."

"That's good." Wynne Cowles removed the magazine from her breasts and put it on the table. "Darn her anyway. She's as independent as a hog on ice. I phoned her three times this morning, and twice she refused to come to the phone, and the third time she said she didn't-need-any-help-of-any-kind-thank-you."

"Naturally." Ty attempted a grin. "I'm her lawyer."

"Don't try to achieve flippancy, it just makes you look sick. I know you're gone on the young sister. Sunk you are. That's why I don't waste effort on you. She's a nice kid. When you phoned I thought possibly you wanted finances for the defense. I'd be glad to."

Ty shook his head. "Not now, thanks, but I'll bear it

in mind. All I need at the moment is a little information about something that happened two years ago."

"That's a long time for a memory like mine. Is it going to require a feat of memory?"

"Not much of one. One day you took a sheet of white paper and wrote on it 'mountain cat ready for prey.' 'Mountain cat' was on the first line and 'ready for prey' on the second. Beneath that you wrote the figures, 450. At the bottom you signed it with your initials, WD. You wrote it in black ink. Your name was Wynne Durocher then."

"So it was. O Time in thy flight. . . . Here we are." She pushed at books to make room on the table for the Chinese to put the tray down, stirred the tinkling ice, handed a glass to him, and took hers. "So I wrote 'mountain cat' on a piece of paper. It was two years ago that I was given that lovely name, Mountain Cat. By the way, I owe your girl friend a bottle of wine. If you'll take it to her she'll probably accept it. She thinks I'm hooked on a life contract with the devil."

Ty sipped his highball. "You remember writing that?"

"Now do I?" Her brow wrinkled. "So many things are apt to interfere with my memory, and one of the worst is curiosity. I'm as curious as a mountain cat. If I did write that on a piece of paper two years ago, how the dickens do you happen to know it? And if you do happen to know it, why is it worth driving out here thirty miles to ask me about it?"

Ty waved a hand. "I'm a lawyer, I know everything. As for asking you about it, that may be only an excuse to have a highball with my most attractive client."

"Baloney. I've seen your eyes on Delia Brand. How's the drink, all right? Too thin?"

"No, thanks, it's fine. You know you're attractive."

"I certainly do." She smiled. "I also know whether you're candid or not. About my writing things on white paper with black ink. What a grasp of details! I'll tell you what—refresh my memory by showing me the paper."

"I'd like to, but I can't."

"Why, haven't you got it?"

"No."

"Who has?"

"I don't know."

"Where did you see it?"

"I've never seen it."

"Oh." She looked disappointed. "From the way you described it, I was sure you had been keeping it under your pillow." She drank, and licked her lips with a quick red tongue. "I call that a good highball."

"So do I." He put his glass down. "Look here, Mrs. Cowles. You're playing with me, you're having fun, and ordinarily I wouldn't object to that, but this is important. You do remember writing that, don't you?"

She shook her head. "Not yet. Quit shoving. As soon as I remember it and tell you about it, you're going to gallop off to court or prison or somewhere, and I need you for another drink." She rang the bell. "I'm scared to death of lawyers. I always think they're trying to trap me."

"Yes, I can see you tremble."

"Of course you can—More ice, John—Anyhow, you can't blame me if I'm curious. You say you've never seen this paper, you don't know where it is or who has it, and yet you describe it as if you had seen me write it. After all . . ." She shrugged.

"It was described to me by someone who saw it."

"Who?"

"A prospector named Squint Hurley."

"Where did he see it?"

Ty tried not to scowl. "He saw it lots of times. He carried it around with him for two years."

"Where did he get it?"

"He found it."

"Where?"

Ty surveyed her a moment without further attempt to hide the scowl, then said abruptly, "All right. You'll either help us or you won't. He found it under the dead body of Charlie Brand in the cabin where he was murdered."

"Oh." Her lashes flickered. "Indeed. A paper I wrote found under a dead body. You don't suppose I did the murder and have forgotten about that, too?"

"No. If I had I wouldn't have come to ask you about it."

"But you did come to ask me, trying to keep it casual, without telling me what I would be letting myself in for." Her pupils were contracted, though she was not facing the sunlight, and her voice had an edge. "I was under the impression that I'm a client of your firm? That I've paid you a satisfactory retainer?"

"You wouldn't be letting yourself in—"

"No? Really, Mr. Dillon. It sounds as if the least I could expect would be the witness chair in a murder case, which would be—shall I say inconvenient?"

"But I'm only asking—confidentially—"

"Oh, no. You're cheating. If I admitted I had written such a paper, and its being found under the body of a murdered man made my testimony vital as to whom I had given it to, would you still keep it confidential?"

"In that case I'd ask you—"

"Of course. You'd ask me to testify, and I'd refuse, and I'd get a subpoena to appear written on white paper with black ink. Here's the ice. Have another highball." She poured and mixed. "It'll brighten you up. You've only partly satisfied my curiosity. For instance, how did the prospector know the writing on the paper was mine?"

"He didn't."

"Then who else saw the paper?"

"No one that I know of."

Her brows lifted. "Did you do it with mirrors?"

"I showed Hurley an envelope you addressed to me and he said the writing was identical. The word 'mountain.'"

"Ah! Then you already suspected me by intuition? Whose? Not yours?"

"It was an accident. I happened to have that envelope in my pocket with others." Ty hadn't picked up his second highball. "You are wrong, Mrs. Cowles, if you think there was the slightest intention of causing you any trouble—"

"Oh, I don't! No trouble at all. Just the key witness in a notorious murder case." She shivered delicately. "This prospector must be quite a handwriting expert. I'd love to see the paper. What happened to it?"

"Hurley gave it to Dan Jackson Tuesday morning. That night Jackson was killed and the paper taken from him."

Wynne Cowles's glass had been started toward her mouth, but was halted midway on its course. Then it went on to its contact with her warm firm lips, and she drank. She put it on the table. "Well!" she said. "Not just one murder. Two murders. Thank you so much!"

"You're welcome." Ty leaned forward to her. "I'm a first class boob. I've messed this all up. I had brains enough to know you wouldn't want to be mixed up in a murder trial, no one does, but I should have gone on from there and considered what kind of an appeal would be effective with you. I should have told you the whole thing to begin with and then put it to you: we need your help. The Brand girls need it. You say Delia is a nice kid. That's putting it mildly. I heard you at the courthouse, day before yesterday, offering Clara your assistance up to any amount. I know you meant money, but money isn't what they need. Your information, who you gave that paper to, is absolutely vital. It's the only trail we have—"

"You're assuming as a fact that I wrote such a paper."

"Well, you did. Didn't you?"

"No."

"You didn't write that on a piece of paper and put your initials on it, WD?"

"No."

He looked straight at her eyes and said, "I don't believe it." She shrugged. He said, "What you mean is that you did write it, but the paper can't be produced as evidence, so you propose to avoid inconvenience and notoriety by denying it. If you mean that, why don't you say so and I'll know where I stand? We're here alone."

She shrugged again. "I'll say that if you'd like it better. Delia has been released from jail, hasn't she?"

"Yes."

"Is there any danger of her being arrested again?"

"No. I think not."

"And you told me Clara isn't going to be arrested. They are already having their inconvenience and notoriety, but that can't be helped. So I'll say this: if I had written such a paper, and if I thought it would convict a murderer for me to admit it and get summoned to a courtroom and testify on the stand about it, I wouldn't do it. Does that let you know where you stand?"

"It does," said Ty bitterly. "It lets me know where you stand, too."

"I know." She grimaced, and picked up her drink. "I'm a cockatrice, a mugger, a harpy—hell, I'm a mountain cat. I don't mind. I don't like murderers, but I'm not crazy about hangmen either. Maybe I'm an anarchist. You have not touched your drink."

"I don't want it. Listen, Mrs. Cowles. Tell me in confidence and I swear you can trust me—"

"You're in love. I'd be a fool to trust you. No."

"Damn it, you offered to help Clara—"

"I'll help her. How much?"

He kept it up ten minutes longer, but it was futile. All he got was a few scratches from the mountain cat's claws. He lost his temper, and he left without it.

He drove back to Cody in thirty-five minutes, narrowly missing a collision with a flock of sheep in Engel's Gulch. It was a quarter to five when he turned into the Brand driveway on Vulcan Street. Delia opened the door for him. His face answered her question before she asked it, and she proved her right to some rarer appellation than "nice kid" by not asking it.

"Did you lie down?" Ty demanded.

She shook her head. "I just fooled around. Wishing I had gone with you."

"It's just as well you didn't. Mountain cat? She's a hyena. Come and sit down and I'll tell you about it."

When he had finished, leaving nothing out, he sat and stared at her miserably, glum, licked. Her lips were moving, nervously jerking, and she put her teeth on the lower one to stop it.

"I did it wrong," he said. "I'm a fish. I'm a goddamn worm. Two words from her was all I needed, and I muffed the chance. If I'd had an ounce of brains I'd have figured it out better. Like this: either she had a hand in the murder of your father or she didn't. If she did, she already knew about that paper and it didn't matter what kind of an approach I made, nothing would drag an admission from her. But if she had nothing to do with the murder, which we had agreed to suppose, then the approach made all the difference, because she couldn't have known why I was asking about that paper. I could have cooked up a plausible tale that wouldn't have alarmed her, and she would have told me. Now she's on guard, and there's not a chance. It was our one measly lead and I've thrown it away."

"You did your best, Ty."

"If that's my best, my worst would be a world's record."

"You think she does remember writing it and what she did with it?"

"I know she does. A million to one."

"Do you still think she had nothing—that she didn't—?"

"The murder? I don't know. But ten to one she had nothing to do with it. Why would she? Can you conceive of any reason?"

"No." Delia slowly shook her head. "No. We should have been smarter. We weren't clever enough."

"I know. You can't possibly feel as much contempt for me as I feel for myself."

"I don't feel contempt for you, Ty."

"You should." They sat and said nothing.

Finally he heaved a deep sigh that shook his frame. "Well," he said grimly, "now for the next mistake. I'd like to make this a grand one. What good would it do to take it to the county attorney? Even if he's on the level and wanted to put the screws on Wynne Cowles, how could he? There's no evidence except Squint Hurley's word that there ever was such a paper, and even less that she wrote it. Do you believe Hurley told the truth?"

"Yes."

"So do I." Ty abruptly got up. "I'm sunk. I'm grabbing for straws and there aren't any. The only gleam of hope I see is to go and put it up to Phil Escott. I wish to God I had done that instead of beating it to Broken Circle Ranch with my chin stuck out. Have you heard anything from Clara?"

"I phoned about an hour ago. They wouldn't let me talk to her, but they said she would be home for dinner at seven o'clock."

"She has no car there. Shall I go after her?"

"They said they'd bring her."

"I'll put that up to Escott, too. They can't keep on hounding her. Will you let a high-grade moron kiss you?"

She put up her face. He kissed her, not as one who deserved it, pulled away and strode to the door, where he turned. "God, Del. I'm sorry."

"It's as much my fault as yours, Ty. Phone me after you've talked to Escott."

After she heard the front door close behind him she buried her face in her hands, her elbows on her knees, and stayed that way a long time. She wasn't crying; she didn't feel like crying. There was no energy or purpose left in her; her nerves and brain and muscles all were flabby with fatigue. There was no coherence in anything; nothing in the world, within or without, had any significance. She was, in fact, about to surrender to a state of unconsciousness which could only by euphemism have been called by so sweet a name as sleep, when suddenly something happened in her brain which made her lift her head. There was, after all, something significant, something which she told herself she must remember to do that very day. What could it be? She frowned. What was it? Oh, yes, of course. Butter. There was no butter in the house, and she had neglected to order it with the other things on the phone.

Her brain struggled desperately with the question of butter, and finally solved it with the heroic decision to go to the Vulcan Market two blocks away and get some. She got to her feet and her knees held her up. Good. She went to the drawer in the dining room where she usually put her handbag, but it wasn't there. It wasn't in the kitchen. Upstairs then. No. The county attorney had it. That recollection threatened to floor her mind again with a thousand urgencies more pressing than butter, but she had decided to get some butter. They carried no account at the Vulcan Market, and she needed cash. She needed cash anyway, and there was no telling when she would get her handbag back.

She trudged to the stairs and ascended, helping herself with her hand on the rail, and went to her bedroom. She closed the door behind her because that was her habit whenever she entered there with the intention of opening that drawer. From the dark corner of a shelf in the closet, between the folds of a scarf, she got the key, and with it unlocked the top drawer of the bureau which stood between the windows.

Butter nearly got abandoned again, for that drawer was all she had of treasure. The silver spurs her father had given her, the clippings from the *Times-Star* praising her performances in high school plays, the soda fountain straw through which she and Ty Dillon had both sipped root beer one day a year ago (Ty would have given something, any time those twelve months, to have known it was there), many letters, and especially the letters her mother had written her on various occasions. . . .

She resolutely fought the memories back and reached to a box at the rear of the drawer for a brown paper envelope, opened the flap and inserted her fingers, and extracted a twenty-dollar bill. The mere sight of it was enough, momentarily, to cause one memory to crowd out all the others—the story Rufus Toale had told her as he died, only the night before. Involuntarily she looked at the bill in her hand, and even turned it over and looked at the other side. Then she gaped. Her mouth dropped open and her eyes bulged in an idiot stare. In the upper right hand corner of the bill, small and faint but unmistakably there, were two letters in fine script: R.T. It was God's money.

Chapter 18

She stood and stared at the bill for twenty heart-
beats, then the hand holding it dropped to her
side and she stood and stared at nothing. Her
nerves and muscles and brain, no longer flabby from
fatigue, were galvanized with horror.

She went to the window and thrust aside the curtain and looked at the bill in the direct sunlight. Nothing could be made of the inscription but R.T. It was
R.T. and nothing else. And that was the only twenty in
the envelope; the others were all tens and fives. Or
were they? She flew to the drawer, standing open, and
got the envelope and removed the contents, and fingered the bills one by one. Yes. All tens and fives. Then
that was the only twenty, and she knew definitely, irrevocably, where it had come from. She had known
anyway, since she had taken it from the top, the last
one she had put there, six weeks ago, when she had
received it as a birthday present. She returned the
twenty to the envelope and took out a ten, replaced the
envelope in the box and closed the drawer and locked
it, put the key back on the closet shelf, and sat down in
a chair.

This was grotesque and not to be believed.

She could go and say, "The twenty-dollar bill you gave me on my birthday is one of those taken from Dad when he was murdered. Where did you get it?" As Ty had gone to Wynne Cowles to ask about the paper. With no result. What if she got the same? No.

She could phone Ty and ask him to come, and show it to him and tell him. Then he would . . . No. Two days ago she had herself been thought guilty of murder by people who loved her. No. She must first, somehow, find out herself. She could think. She must think.

Her father two years ago. Two hours to drive to Sugarbowl. Two hours across the hills to the Ghost Canyon cabin, if you hurried, if you had a desperate purpose. Four hours to return. Possible? She forced her brain to recall everything from that day. Yes, possible.

Dan Jackson Tuesday night. Possible? So far as she knew, quite possible. And besides, there was the fact, what she herself had seen . . . good God. Rufus Toale's God, whose errand he had brought to her. She gulped. More than possible. She stiffened her jaw again.

Rufus Toale last night. No fact there which she herself had seen, but no disproof, no veto. Then it was all possible. She could say, she could ask. . . . No, she couldn't do that either. There must be no bungling about this, and no one could be confided in, and no one could be trusted to help figure out a way. But there must be a way. There had to be. She had to find out, and she had to find out quick. There could be no eating or sleeping or facing anyone until she did find out. But she mustn't make a mistake. She mustn't make a wild stab and be left where she was now, as they had done with Wynne Cowles—

Wynne Cowles! She considered it, her face twisted in an agony of concentration.

Yes, she decided. She could try that, because if it didn't work she would have given nothing away and she could try something else. But it would work. She would make it work. On her way there she would decide how to do it, and it would work. She looked at her watch: twenty to six. She sprang to her feet. Clara might come any minute. . . .

She ran downstairs and scribbled a note: *Clara, I'm off on an errand, will be back around eight or nine. This is for Ty too if he brings you home or phones. Del.* She left the note under a cup on the kitchen range, ran out to the garage for the car and made the gravel fly as it scooted down the drive for the street.

During that forty-minute drive there were two distinct areas of activity in her brain, one managing the driving and the other considering plans of attack on Wynne Cowles.

She had never turned in at Broken Circle Ranch before, though she had often passed it. There was no one around as she left the car at the edge of a graveled space adjoining the tennis court and made for the house, toward the veranda with its bright-green awning. She started off briskly, but after ten paces her steps lagged, for she had not actually made up her mind what she was going to say; and her gaze wandered to take in the ensemble of the picturesque retreat this rich cosmopolite had fashioned here in the Wyoming hills, as if from that she might get a hint. Not that she had any conscious expectation of finding one; so that when she did find one in fact, astonishment stopped her in her tracks. She stood with her head tilted back, staring up to where, on the forked limb of the tree near the veranda, a cougar, startlingly lifelike, crouched in readiness to leap.

A voice said, "Excuse me please. You want something?"

She jerked around and saw the Chinese who had emerged from the house. "Yes. I want to see Mrs. Cowles."

"Name please, lady?"

"Delia Brand."

His face twitched. "I tell her. You come in the house?"

"No, thanks. I'll wait here."

Her knees were trembling. She pulled a wicker chair away from the table under the tree and sat down. She wanted to look up again, to see how it looked from directly beneath, but resisted the impulse. Then she wanted to move, not to have it just above her, but she resisted that impulse, too. She was sure now, miserably sure. She might get up and go away and not see Wynne Cowles at all—but no. She would have that satisfaction and that confirmation before she left. Left for where? What could she possibly—

"Hello, hello!" Footsteps clicking on the tile, approaching. "John wasn't sure about the name and I thought maybe it was Clara. How is she? Where is she?" Wynne Cowles stood smiling down at her.

"She's all right."

"Is she home?"

"Not yet. She will be at seven o'clock."

Wynne Cowles made a noise of depreciation. "You poor kids. It's hellish. Won't you come inside or on the veranda?"

"This is all right. I want to ask you something."

"Sure you do." She kicked a chair around and sat.

"I'll bet I know, that bottle of wine. I told your cavalier to take it to you, but he went off mad."

"You can't blame him much, can you? Since you told him a damn lie?"

"Oh, now." Wynne Cowles looked reproachful. "Tut tut, my dear. When you say that, smile."

"I don't feel like smiling." Delia met, steadily, the intentness of those strange eyes. "I haven't smiled any too much for two years. I suppose that's what I'm fighting for now, a chance to smile again some time. You would understand that, you're a clever woman. I don't like you and I wouldn't be like you if I could, but I know you're clever. I've been a melodramatic little fool. I thought about you while I was in jail, while I was thinking about everybody and everything, and I saw that there are good things about you as well as bad. Of course I didn't know then that I would soon have to make you do something you didn't want to do, but it was what I thought then, what I found out by thinking, that made me capable of doing it."

"Good for you!" Wynne Cowles smiled. "Intelligence always wins. What are you going to make me do?"

"I'm going to make you tell the truth about that paper you lied to Ty about."

"Fine! That'll be fun. Go ahead."

"I am." Delia's gaze was unwavering. "Just to show you—you probably thought we supposed the 'mountain cat' on that paper meant you. Of course it didn't."

"No? What did it refer to?"

"Look up into the tree." Delia's tone sharpened. "No, straight up! That's it. Mountain cat ready for prey. It is called cougar or puma or catamount or mountain lion or mountain cat. You like mountain cat, so that's what you called it on that paper. Didn't you?"

Wynne Cowles shrugged. "My dear girl, use your intelligence. I'm willing to grant you have some. What's the use of discussing a paper that no longer exists, if it ever did?"

"I came here to discuss it. We're going to discuss it. I have to know. On the way out here I thought of ways to make you tell about it. One way I thought of, since you lied to Ty just to save yourself notoriety, I thought I could easily tell a lie myself that would give you notoriety anyway that you couldn't prevent. I could tell the police that Tuesday afternoon, when Jackson and I heard a noise in the hall and went to investigate I saw you there hiding behind that bin. Jackson saw you too, and you begged us to let you go and we did. Now my conscience makes me tell about it."

"My *dear*!" Wynne Cowles's eyes had widened. "Didn't I admit you're intelligent? But they wouldn't believe you."

"Oh, yes. I assure you they would. They'd believe me enough to make it very unpleasant."

"Amazing. Do you mean you're threatening to do that?"

"I mean you're not going to stick to your lie about that paper. I'll do anything I have to do to get the truth from you. I have got to know who you gave it to and I'm going to know."

Wynne Cowles, with movements uncommonly deliberate for her, leaned forward to reach the carved bishido box on the table, got a cigarette and lit it, sat back and sent a puff of smoke ascending toward the cougar in the tree.

"You already know, don't you?" she murmured.

Delia gulped. "You admit you wrote that on that paper?"

"I admit it here to you, yes."

"You gave it to—you gave it to my—" Delia gulped again.

"Yes. As you have guessed, it was an order for that. A sort of a memorandum. Apparently I didn't put a dollar sign in front of the 450. Carelessness." Wynne Cowles leaned at her and said brusquely, "Look here. Haven't you had enough? What the devil good is it? What good is any talk about that paper? The paper has certainly been destroyed. He killed Jackson Tuesday night and took the paper and destroyed it. Even if he were arrested and tried, what kind of evidence would it be? That prospector would say he found it and I would say I wrote it and tell what I did with it. What would that amount to? The fact that a man was given a piece of paper is no proof that he killed a man who was found lying on top of it, especially when you can't even produce the paper. I tell you it's no good. I think you *are* intelligent. If you are you ought to realize—now wait—now—don't—Delia!"

So rarely had he heard his employer's voice pitched high and loud in urgency that the Chinese came trotting onto the veranda in a flurry of concern, all the more since the lady caller was one who shot people; but at the edge of the tile he halted, seeing that no assistance was required. The lady caller was moving swiftly across the graveled space beyond the lawn, headed for her car; and the lady employer, quite unhurt, was standing under a tree watching and no longer raising her voice. John, ashamed of his intrusive agitation, shuffled to the table and arranged magazines, pretending that his sally had been in the interest of neatness, but out of the corner of his eye he observed that the lady caller had hurried to her car not to produce a weapon but merely to climb into it and drive away.

Wynne Cowles stood and looked around as if she might see something she could hit somebody with. "Damn," she said, in a civilized tone, but not without feeling, and entered the house. "The damned incredible outrageous idiocy of the general manager of the universe," she said, and went to a corner of the living room where stood an inlaid cabinet and stand, and got out the telephone directory. Having found the number, she got the phone and dialed.

No answer. She waited. Still no answer.

Then possibly he was still at the office. She looked up another number and tried that, but with the same result. No one answered. In exasperation she fluttered the pages of the directory and found still a third number. From that one, at least, she got a voice which told her, yes, that was Mr. Escott's residence. She asked to speak to Mr. Escott, and he was put on. No, he said, with the decent courtesy due a $5,000 client, he didn't know where Mr. Dillon could be found at the moment. Mr. Dillon had been there speaking with him, but had left only a few minutes ago. It was possible that Mrs. Cowles might find him, then or a little later, at the Brand home on Vulcan Street, if she cared to try. . . .

So she looked that number up and tried it too, but again there was no answer. She gave it up in disgust. Anyway, it would be another thirty minutes before Delia would get to Cody, and she could try again later.

Chapter 19

The idea of the mountain cat popped into Delia's head as she sat in the car, stopped at the roadside a mile or so beyond Frenchy's Corners. She had stopped there because she didn't want to enter Cody until she had resolved what to do. At the moment the idea came she had about decided that the only possible thing was to run away. She could go home and get the money from the drawer, all but that twenty-dollar bill, facing through it somehow with Clara if she was there, and leave at the first opportunity. She would go in the car, heading for California, perhaps taking a train from Ashton for the coast . . . at least, somehow, somewhere, losing herself.

The vengeance of man. God's errand. She could be the instrument of neither. Not now. What others might or might not do about it, that was either God's business or man's, but not hers.

What kept her from instant execution of her plan of flight was the germ of doubt that still existed. If she had possessed certainty it would have been at once incommunicable and unbearable, and to flee with the unsharable secret would have been the only recourse of desperation; but she was not certain. She was horribly sure, but she was not sure.

It was there at the roadside near Frenchy's Corners, where she had stopped for a decision, that she thought of the mountain cat and remembered the scene three days earlier when her coyote's howl had interrupted the inspection of a furry belly on which no hair was slipping.

That would prove everything. She might, if she had that proof, even be able to tell Clara and Ty, and share the secret and not have to carry it all alone. . . .

She started the engine, swung into the road, and in five minutes was in Cody. It was exactly half past seven. He wouldn't be there. The usual dinner hour in Cody was around six o'clock, but it was his custom to work at his bench until seven and then go to the Pay Streak lunchroom three blocks away. Even if by mischance he were there he would be upstairs, and she needed only three minutes. And as a sudden impulse to repeat a childish trick had been responsible for the scene three days earlier, so now the memory of another childish trick from the days of Del the tomboy was the inspiration of her strategy.

She parked the car around the corner and walked to the two-storied frame building, with the plate-glass window, elevated above the sidewalk level, displaying the brown bear licking a cub. Without making undue noise, she climbed the four steps and tried the door. It was locked. She nodded to herself, and stood there a moment, aware that her heart was beating too fast and that her hand had been far from steady as she had turned the doorknob. But coolness was not especially required; the chief thing was speed, to get it done. She descended the steps, went to the corner of the building and passed along its side to the rear.

In the rear was clutter and chaos. Amid a stack of discarded mounting frames of rusty wire, weeds grew up to a man's belt. Bales encased in burlap were stacked under the rickety steps. Packing boxes of all sizes and conditions were scattered around, and weeds were everywhere. Delia took it in with a swift glance, and saw that one of the packing boxes, a long narrow one, needed to be shifted only a few feet to serve her purpose. She grabbed a corner of it and tugged, got it moved, and upended it, propping it against the wall of the building. Then she scrambled up. It teetered and nearly fell, but she lunged to seize the window sill above her, got it balanced again, and pulled herself upright so that the window sill was at the height of her breasts. She saw that the window was open and the screen was apparently unfastened, and was trying to get purchase with her finger nails under the frame of the screen, when she nearly toppled off at the sound of a sharp call from somewhere behind her: "Hey there!"

She twisted her head and saw a man in a back yard among tomato vines. She waved a hand, clinging to the window sill with the other, and called, "Okay! The human fly! Free seats in the grandstand!"

"You'll fall and break your neck!"

"Oh, no! You just watch!"

She stood a moment, her brain whirling. But why stop for that? Why stop for anything? She got her nails under the frame again, broke one prying it up, squeezed the tips of her fingers in the slit, exerted all her strength, and the screen went up with a bang. The rest was easy. Taking a firm grip with both hands inside, she leaped up and dived through, hung there an instant, wriggled on, and flopped onto the floor. She scrambled to her feet, waved from the window to reassure the horticulturist, and closed the screen. Her heart was a hammer on the wall of her chest. Four steps took her to the workbench, where a miscellany of tools were arrayed in slotted cleats. She had long ago been permitted to play with many of those tools, though never the sharp knives; now a knife with a long sharp blade was what she took. With it in her hand she went to the door at the end of the partition and passed through it into the large front room. She had thought, anticipating this moment, that now she would go to the foot of the stairs and call his name, to make sure he wasn't above in his living quarters, but the momentum of her urgency abandoned that precaution. Without even a glance at the stairs, she went swiftly to the mountain cat on the platform in the center of the room, the cougar with his paw resting on the carcass of a fawn; and, throwing herself on her back underneath its belly, ripped the tough hide with a savage sweep of the knife. But it was well mounted and there was only a slit, so she wriggled her shoulders and slashed crosswise, once, twice, three times. She seized the corners and jerked at the flaps, and the hole gaped open, and objects tumbled out and fell on her face and shoulders, and she squirmed away as if they had been deadly snakes, though a glance showed her that they were money, currency, packets of twenty-dollar bills. Her heart was hammering her chest.

A voice came: *"Del!"*

Her heart stopped. She became rigid, there under the mountain cat on her back. She was aware of steps, a hand touching her, fingers gripping her ankle, and she jerked her leg away, rolled over, rolled from under the mountain cat, causing two of the bundles of bills to fall from the platform, and was on her feet. Quinby Pellett stood there, looking at her, his face pale and contorted, his lips twisted like those of a child trying not to cry. "So," he said.

She nodded her head without knowing it. "So," she said.

"Del." His hand lifted, fluttered, and dropped again. "Godamighty."

She was looking at his middle, where a fold of his untidy shirt was escaping from his belt. She couldn't look at his face. Involuntarily she took a sidewise step, and another one. He moved toward her.

"Where you going?"

There was a noise from her throat, but no word.

"Nowhere," he said; and, apparently satisfied that the command was sufficient, he stooped to pick up the two bundles of bills and lay them on the platform. Seeing the knife there under the cougar, he picked that up too and held it in his hand, not as one arming himself but rather, automatically, as a man who doesn't like to see tools thrown around. He faced her again. "Who sent you here?"

She shook her head. "Nobody." Her voice was a croak in her ears. "I came alone. When I was climbing in a man saw me—"

"I know he did. I heard him, from upstairs. I heard you, too. I was behind the moosehide when you came in here. I wanted to see—but you acted too quick before I could stop you." He glanced at the platform. "I know why you did that. The way you saw me looking at it the other day. You've got a brain like mine, you don't miss things. You remembered how I looked at it that day, didn't you?"

She nodded without knowing it.

He nodded back. "Sure you did. I know how your brain works. I was afraid it might. Since Toale came to me yesterday and showed me the bill he had that I gave him Easter time, and I was afraid the one I gave you for your birthday was the same kind, and if you looked at it you would know because Toale had told you. I was afraid your brain would work that way, but I didn't move the money because I knew if you had that bill I knew you would find out some day and I didn't want to wait for it. I didn't want it to be like it was with your mother, when I knew she knew, but I didn't know how and I didn't know how much—"

Delia gasped, "Mother knew?"

"Sure she did. Toale told her." A spasm went over Quinby Pellett's face and left it distorted. "He didn't believe in the vengeance of man. He wanted to drive vengeance from her heart, and he wanted her to persuade me to repent to God. What he did was drive her to suicide. She wouldn't—she couldn't tell me about it. He told me yesterday, and showed me that bill, because he knew I had killed Jackson, too."

Delia wanted to tell him to stop talking. She felt her knees giving. The edge of the platform was there and she sank, sitting on it. "Oh, don't!" she pleaded.

"Don't what, don't talk?" Pellett demanded with sudden ferocity. He gestured with the knife. "Godamighty, Del, I've got to talk, to you. It's you I've got to talk to. Because it was an awful thing I did, but I didn't mean to. Of course I didn't have it worked out to use your gun until after I took it away from that fellow that stole it from your car. Then I saw how good it would be to do that. I put the handbag with the gun in it under the seat of my car before I went in there and went up the stairs and got a piece of ore from the bin and hit myself with it. Later I found there were no cartridges, but my own gun's a .38 and I had some. That night I thought it would be good to leave the gun there and the handbag on the desk, because I supposed

naturally you'd be with Clara and maybe other people
and your alibi would keep you out of it, and it would be
good for me because everybody would know that I
never in God's world would frame you. Then you went
right there to the office and Hurley found you there.
That was terrible. That made me feel worse than anything. Except . . ." The spasm distorted his face
again. "Except your mother," he said.

Delia couldn't look at him. Her eyes gazed straight,
at their own level as she sat, at the long-bladed knife in
his hand.

"Except for your mother," he said harshly, "I've
never repented, Del. I want to be honest with you. I've
never repented about your father. You'll hate me now.
I hated him. He was full of life and full of success. Then
that talk started about him and Amy Jackson. I didn't
know then how much was behind it and I don't know
now and I don't give a damn. When I asked your
mother she wouldn't discuss it. A man has no right to
live so there can be such talk. My own sister wouldn't
discuss it with me. I put it to him, to his face, and he
laughed at me. He always did laugh at me. I was his
brother-in-law, and he'd let me have a little money now
and then because I couldn't make a go of this taxidermy business, but what he really thought, he regarded me as a bum. You know he did."

He gestured at her. "Another thing you've got to
understand, Del. About the money. I wanted that
money and I got it, but I didn't want it for myself. The
day would come, I knew it would, when your mother
would have hers used up, and then I would help her,
and you and Clara too. Her poor bum of a brother
would help her. I could do that when the time came
without being suspected, because my business was
better and I could pretend it was a lot better than it

was. That was all in my head, about the money, before I ever went there to the cabin to wait for him—"

"Please!" Delia begged. "Please don't—"

He nodded. "I know. Now you hate me. Sure you do. But I had to tell you them two things, that I never would have framed you, never in God's world, and I didn't take that money just for myself. I used to think it would be a fine thing some day, that money, for your mother and you girls and me . . . and then she . . . then she knew and I knew she did but I didn't know how . . . she . . . my own sister that I really did it for . . ."

His words gave out. Delia had none. She was benumbed; her nerves were dead and her blood cold. She would hate him, of course, but hate is life and she was not alive; her only feeling was a dull overpowering revulsion to the sight and sound of him. She would get up and go; but she could not move. Could she lift her eyes to look at his face? Yes; she must first see his face. . . .

But before she could achieve that he spoke again, in a new and different tone: "Now you've fixed it, ripping that cat open. I might have known you would." He was scolding a child. "I should have stopped you when you came in here, but I wanted to see. Godamighty, look at it. It's dangerous. You'd better go upstairs and wait. I don't want you to see where I put it."

Her eyes had reached his face and she was gaping at him.

"What's the matter?" he demanded.

She shook her head.

He gestured impatiently with the hand that held the knife. "Go on upstairs. I'll be up pretty soon. It's dangerous as hell. That stuff scattered around."

She shook her head again.

"Go on now." He sounded petulant. "For one thing

I've got to explain to you some more, and for another
thing if you go home right now you'll be apt to blurt it
out to Clara, and that's one of the things I want to
explain, why you're not to tell Clara. There's no reason
for her to know about it. I've got to explain—I've got
to be sure you realize that I'd rather have cut off my
arm than to seem to be framing you or letting you in
for any trouble. Godamighty, Del, it's bad enough as it
is—"

He whirled like lightning and stood tense.

The sounds of steps on the wooden stoop in front
had been faint, but now the turning of the knob was
louder, and the pounding on the door that followed immediately shattered the silence.

Quinby Pellett glanced at Delia to instruct her in a
low tone of urgent menacing command, "Quiet!"

She nodded, and he seemed satisfied, for he faced
toward the door again and stood rigid. The pounding
was repeated, rattling the old wooden panels, and
through them a shout came: "Del! Del, it's Ty! *Del!*"

It is conceivable that even to that appeal Delia
would have been silent. But Quinby Pellett made a
mistake; he mistrusted the depth and force of her dis-
inclination to become an instrument of the vengeance
of man—she who only three days ago had bought a box
of cartridges to commit murder with—or, more simply,
he was overcome by fear. He started for her and she
saw his face; and it was no longer the face of an uncle
trying to convince his niece of his regret at having un-
wittingly let her in for trouble; it was the face of the
malign and ruthless monster who had murdered Charlie Brand and Dan Jackson and Rufus Toale.

She screamed at the top of her voice, Ty's name,
three times before Pellett could reach her. It is quite
likely that he intended only to cover her mouth, to

keep her silent; but her screams changed everything. She lunged to seize the wrist of the hand that held the knife as she heard the splintering crash made by Ty's shoulder when he hurled himself against the door. Pellett jerked back and she missed. She lunged again, missed again, and sprawled on the floor. She got to her knees, and saw that in fact she was not being assaulted at all: Pellett was five paces away, in the direction of the door, crouched behind the forequarters of the yearling elk. For five seconds she stayed there on her hands and knees, staring like a fool. Then two things happened at once: Ty's fifth attack on the door burst it open, and she realized what Pellett was crouching there for; and she screamed Ty's name again to warn him, but too late. As Ty rushed across, Pellett leaped from his ambush and struck; Ty swerved; Pellett's momentum toppled him to the floor; Delia screamed again; Pellett regained his feet before Ty could reach him, and backed off, brandishing the knife, with Ty following him, now cautious but resolute; Delia rushed to grab Ty's arm, pulling at him; he commanded her roughly, without looking at her, "Let go, get behind something, let go!" He shook her off. "Drop it, Pellett. What's the use? Drop—"

Pellett, from a crouch eight feet away, came through the air at him like a mountain cat. But his muscles were old. With his left hand, Ty parried the knife; with his right, he swung, and Pellett went down, stretched out on the floor, the knife falling from his hand and sliding almost to Delia's feet. Ty picked it up and tossed it to a corner of the room. She shuddered, a convulsion shaking her from head to foot. As he put out a hand for her there was the sound, at the open door, of rushing footsteps.

It seemed adequate for an army, but there were

only three who entered: Chief of Police Frank Phelan, a cop in uniform, and the horticulturist who had shouted to Delia that she would break her neck. They came in on the run, put on the brakes and gawked. Pellett, on the floor, did not move.

"What the hell." Phelan gazed at Delia. "By God, again! You look him over, Pete, and I'll—"

"You'll eat your tongue and choke on it!" Ty Dillon was trembling with fury. "You goddamn fools! There's your murderer! Do you think you can handle him? Do you want him delivered f.o.b. your goddamn jail? You ought to be cocky, by God, you ought to be cocky, leaving a girl to do it for you! She might have been killed! She damn near was killed! He was after her with a knife—"

"No, Ty, no—"

"Shut up! You can shut me up the rest of my life, but this once is my turn! You're a fine bunch of lousy poops! I'm taking her home, and try to stop me, and by God, you let her alone! I'm her lawyer and her husband and you let her alone! When you want it explained to you, come to me!"

With an arm around her, he took her away. It was obvious that anybody who tried to stop him would have been murdered, so no one tried.

The World of
Rex Stout

Now, for the first time ever, enjoy a peek into the life of Nero Wolfe's creator, Rex Stout, courtesy of the Stout Estate. Pulled from Rex Stout's own archives, here are rarely seen, never-before-published memorabilia. Each title in "The Rex Stout Library" will offer an exclusive look into the life of the man who gave Nero Wolfe life.

The Mountain Cat Murders

One of Rex Stout's great passions (besides the events of a certain brownstone on West 35th Street) was his work with the Author's League of America. Following is a newspaper clipping from 1951 which describes Stout being elected to head that organization.

Mystery Writer Elected Head of Authors League

Rex Stout

The Authors League of America elected Rex T. Stout, mystery story writer and lecturer, as its president at a membership meeting yesterday in the Barbizon Plaza Hotel. Mr. Stout, who succeeds Oscar Hammerstein 2d, is the creator of the character Nero Wolfe, super-detective. He lives in Brewster, N. Y.

John Hersey, vice president of the league and author of "A Bell for Adano" and "The Wall," presided at the meeting, which was not open to reporters. After the meeting he said that no other officers had been elected because of a pending amendment to the league's constitution providing for two vice presidents.

John Schulman, an attorney for the Authors League, made a report on information he had gathered here and abroad concerning proposed changes in international copyright laws.

REX STOUT'S NERO WOLFE

A grand master of the form, Rex Stout is one of America's greatest mystery writers. Now, in this ongoing program dedicated to making available the complete set of Nero Wolfe mysteries, these special collector's editions will feature new introductions by today's best writers and never-before-published memorabilia from the life of Rex Stout.

☐ Fer-de-Lance	27819-3	$4.99/$5.99 in Canada
☐ The League of Frightened Men	25933-4	$4.99/$5.99 in Canada
☐ The Rubber Band	25550-9	$4.99/$5.99 In Canada
☐ The Red Box	24919-3	$4.99/$5.99 in Canada
☐ Where There's a Will	29591-8	$4.99/$5.99 in Canada
☐ The Final Deduction	25254-2	$4.99/$5.99 in Canada
☐ The Hand in the Glove	22857-9	$4.99/$5.99 in Canada
☐ Black Orchids	25719-6	$4.99/$5.99 in Canada
☐ The Doorbell Rang	23721-7	$4.99/$5.99 in Canada
☐ If Death Ever Slept	23649-0	$4.99/$5.99 in Canada
☐ Murder by the Book	27733-2	$4.99/$5.99 in Canada
☐ Not Quite Dead Enough	26109-6	$4.99/$5.99 in Canada
☐ Prisoner's Base	24269-5	$4.99/$5.99 in Canada
☐ And Four to Go	24985-1	$4.99/$5.99 in Canada
☐ Might As Well Be Dead	24729-8	$4.99/$5.99 in Canada
☐ A Family Affair	24122-2	$4.99/$5.99 in Canada
☐ Please Pass the Guilt	23854-X	$4.99/$5.99 in Canada
☐ Triple Jeopardy	23591-5	$4.99/$5.99 in Canada
☐ The Mother Hunt	27437-9	$4.99/$5.99 in Canada
☐ The Father Hunt	24728-X	$4.99/$5.99 in Canada
☐ Trouble in Triplicate	24247-4	$4.99/$5.99 in Canada
☐ Homicide Trinity	23446-3	$4.99/$5.99 in Canada